THE RUFUS SPY

THE RUFUS SPY

An Aelf Fen Mystery

Alys Clare

Severn House Large Print
London & New York

This first large print edition published 2018
in Great Britain and the USA by
SEVERN HOUSE PUBLISHERS LTD of
Eardley House, 4 Uxbridge Street, London W8 7SY.
First world regular print edition published 2017 by
Severn House Publishers Ltd.

British Library Cataloguing in Publication Data
A CIP catalogue record for this title is available from the British Library.

ISBN-13: 9780727829085

Severn House Publishers support the Forest Stewardship Council™
[FSC™], the leading international forest certification organisation. All
our titles that are printed on FSC certified paper carry the FSC logo.

MIX
Paper from
responsible sources
FSC
www.fsc.org   FSC® C013056

Typeset by Palimpsest Book Production Ltd.,
Falkirk, Stirlingshire, Scotland.
Printed and bound in Great Britain by
T J International, Padstow, Cornwall.

In respectful and affectionate memory of my grandfather, Andrew Raynor Barton

One

It was a chilly, rainy, misty October morning, and I was leaving Cambridge to pay a visit home to Aelf Fen.

That was what I told myself as I stuffed a few possessions in my satchel and picked up my shawl and cloak. In fact, if I was to be honest with myself, there were a couple of things wrong with that bland, innocuous statement.

I was not certain any more where *home* was, and it might well be that it was no longer the small fenland village where I was born and had spent my childhood.

And if I was going to push honest to a painful degree, then I wasn't *leaving* Cambridge, I was running away. As swiftly as I could.

Before I left the town behind, however, there were two farewells I had to say. The first I'd already done, and it was still hurting so much that I didn't want to think about it. The second, to my teacher, mentor and friend Gurdyman, I hurried to do next.

I made my way to his twisty-turny house, hidden away in the jumble of narrow little lanes behind the market square. I love Gurdyman's house and, until recently, it was where I always lived when I was in Cambridge. When I first became his pupil, he gave up his snug little attic room for my occupation, and it was only later that I

1

understood this hadn't been quite as magnani-
mous a gesture as I'd thought, Gurdyman being
too stout now to climb the ladder that led up to
it. I am very aware that I'm probably the only
person I know to have the luxury of a sleeping
space to myself.

I leapt up the worn stone steps to the big old
wooden door, opened it and went in. There was
no need to search for Gurdyman because I knew
precisely where he'd be. I turned right, went down
some steps, went on and down some more,
emerging into the crypt that is Gurdyman's work-
place, thinking place and sleeping place; he only
leaves it nowadays to fetch food and, very occasionally when I'm not there to run errands for
him, to emerge, blinking, into the outside world.

He was occupied with stirring something in a
small bronze pot set on a tripod above a lit
candle. Whatever was in the pot was giving off
blue smoke and a smell that was half-appealing,
half-appalling. He lit a taper from the candle
flame and set it to a second candle; clearly,
more heat was required. Even though he hadn't
looked up and gave every indication of deep and
exclusive concentration, I knew he was aware
of me.

After a while, his hands still busy and a frown
on his round, smooth-skinned face, he said,
'You'll need to keep your wits about you on the
road out to Aelf Fen.'

I didn't bother to ask how he'd known. I just
said, 'I always do.'

Now he stopped what he was doing and looked
at me. 'Perhaps so,' he said, fixing me with an intent

2

stare from his bright blue eyes, 'but listen to me when I say it's even more important today to be alert.' He was holding the not-quite-extinguished taper in his hand and he waved it at me, creating arcs of glittering sparks.

'Why?' I demanded bluntly. It wasn't very polite, given that he was undoubtedly issuing the warning for my own good, but I was desperate to get away.

He didn't speak for a moment. Then he said quietly, 'A young man has been attacked on the track leading around the base of the fens, close to where the track to Aelf Fen and beyond meets the road into Cambridge. The assailant got away, and it's possible he presents a danger to other travellers.'

'If he's a thief, then I wish him luck with robbing me.' I held out my arms, indicating my lack of possessions. I carried my leather satchel over my shoulder, but it contained little more than the materials I require for my healer's work, certain objects which I always carry and a few spare items of personal linen.

'Don't be flippant.' Gurdyman spoke sternly, and I realized he was desperately serious. 'There is no certainty that the attack was for reasons of theft, Lassair. The man was—' Abruptly he stopped.

'Was what?' I demanded. Gurdyman hesitated, and I had the distinct sense that he was wishing he'd never begun this conversation. 'Go on,' I urged, 'you can't alarm me like that and not explain!' I tried to speak lightly, but in truth I was quite worried.

'He was beaten, very savagely,' Gurdyman said. 'Many blows to the face and head from a cudgel, or something similar, and several of his fingers were broken.'

'As he tried to fend off the attack?' I suggested, trying to make my voice sound interested rather than frightened.

'As if he'd been tortured,' Gurdyman corrected. 'Perhaps to make him reveal to his assailant something that he needed to know.' He paused. 'Either that,' he added sombrely, 'or someone wished him to suffer severe pain.'

Something had occurred to me, and I focused on it to stop myself thinking about an attacker breaking someone's fingers and how much it would hurt. 'You seem to know quite a lot about it,' I said lightly. 'Have you been out to the market place to pick up the latest gossip?'

Gurdyman sighed. 'No, Lassair. I tried to help the poor young man. An officer from Sheriff Picot came looking for you' – I was sure there was a note of accusation in his voice – 'and, in your absence, accepted instead my offer of assistance.'

'Well, you're a far more experienced—' I stopped, warned by something in his expression. 'He died, didn't he?' I whispered. 'That poor young man?'

And Gurdyman nodded. 'He did. They had taken him to a house near the river – he was found by a group of merchants on their way home here – and the wife of the man whose house it was had done her best. To summon a healer's help was a last attempt to save him, but there was nothing I could do.'

4

I didn't know how to respond. I picked up the sense that Gurdyman was waiting for me to make some comment, or perhaps he had more to say. But neither of us spoke. I hitched my satchel higher on my shoulder and said, 'Thank you for the warning. I promise I'll be careful.' He regarded me doubtfully. 'I do have the advantage of knowing the road and the track very well,' I reminded him gently. 'I'll be all right.'

'It isn't only—' he began. But then he shut his mouth very firmly and, with a valedictory wave, turned back to his workbench.

I walked fast through the back alleys, along the road that bisects the town and out across the Great Bridge, turning right immediately after it onto the road out that leads to Ely and the fens. I kept my head down. I didn't want to talk to anybody. I didn't want any well-meaning person to say, *Are you sure you know what you're doing?* or *Wouldn't it be best to turn back?*

I wasn't at all sure that I did know what I was doing, and the temptation to turn back was all but overwhelming. But I closed my mind to my misgivings, ignored my hurting heart and strode on.

The hard pace I kept up as I marched along made me puff and pant. Struggling to keep it up and, at the same time, watch out for tree roots, cracks and sudden dips in the road and other obstacles that could trip the unwary absorbed my attention. That was good: I really wanted to be distracted. But then, slowly, insidiously, determinedly, everything I was trying not to think

5

about came bursting back. Finally giving in to my mind's insistence, reluctantly I allowed myself to think about what had happened over the past month.

Jack Chevestrier, Cambridge law officer, good and decent man, had been wounded almost to the death by the sheriff's nephew, a man named Gaspard Picot. I had nursed Jack, staying by his side day and night, our needs supplied by an apparently endless number of townsmen and women who firmly believed that Cambridge's one honest, honourable lawman shouldn't be allowed to die. Jack's wound was in his chest, to the left of the breastbone: Gaspard Picot's sly, concealed blade had been driven straight at the heart. His aim had been fractionally amiss, and the knife had gone in at a slight angle and penetrated deep into the thick muscles that covered Jack's bones. Through the density of sinew, the blade hadn't been long enough to reach its target. Jack had bled until I'd thought the well must surely run dry, and then, a few days after the bleeding had finally stopped and the wound began to crust over into a thick scab, infection had set in. I knelt by Jack's bed with a pail of cold well water, constantly replenished by my army of assistants, bathing him, trying to hold him down as he wrestled, sweated, shouted and struggled in his delirium. Dear God, he was strong. Once he bunched up his fist and swung it at me – I have no idea who he thought I was – and it was only by the swift intervention of two of his friends grabbing his arm that I was saved.

'He doesn't mean it,' one of the men, Walter, said, eyes on mine beseeching for my understanding. 'It's the fever.'

'He'd not hurt you if he was in his right mind,' the other one, Fat Gerald, added. 'Sweet Jesus, girl, you're the very last person he'd—'

But Walter's swift dig in the ribs stopped the remainder of whatever Fat Gerald had been about to say.

Eventually, between all of us, we saved him. Now, slowly, he was recovering. He was eating well, and recently I'd had a hard job to make him rest, for he was wild with impatience and desperate to get out and about again.

I should still have been with him, feeding him good, nourishing food, making sure he didn't attempt too much. The last thing I should be doing was leaving him and walking as swiftly as I could back to my village.

But I had to.

Jack and I had made love, just once, and it had been the most extraordinary experience of my life.

He trusted me, and he believed my flimsy story of having to get away to Aelf Fen for a while because I was worn out with looking after him and needed to rest; at least, I thought he believed it.

But there was another reason why I had to get away from him.

I was pregnant.

If I stayed, he'd notice. There were signs already: my breasts had swelled and once or twice I'd felt very sick on rising. If he noticed, then without a doubt he would ask me to marry him. Decent, honourable man that he was, there would, for him, be no alternative. Besides, I knew he loved me. I didn't think I was being immodest in thinking that he wanted me to be his wife anyway, pregnant or not.

Did I love him too? Yes, I did; I was in no doubt about that. Did I want to marry him? Did I want to marry *any* man? Those were more complicated questions, and I didn't know the answers. Was it enough that I loved Jack? But what about the person I was, or was working so hard to be? What about the healer who was niece and former pupil of a gifted healer and now apprentice to an extraordinary, quietly powerful man with magic at his fingertips? All Gurdyman's vast, glittering array of knowledge was available to me if I went on working with him and didn't allow distractions such as a husband, a home and a family to get in the way.

How could I possibly combine two such different lives?

And, fundamentally, did I truly want to be the wife of a Cambridge lawman?

I couldn't begin to resolve my dilemma.

So I was running away.

I reached my village as evening fell, when the grudging light of the overcast day was fading fast. When I'm at Aelf Fen, it's long been my habit to live with my aunt Edild rather than in my parents' home, partly because there's more room (I have quite a lot of relatives) and partly because it saves time spent in going to and fro if I live in the place where I work and am being taught. Now, though, before I went to Edild's, I called in at the little house that used to be my home.

I was nervous as I opened the door. My mother has very sharp eyes and I really didn't welcome the idea of her noticing my condition. Fortunately the light was poor – she'd only lit one lamp so far and, unusually, the fire wasn't responding very well to her ministrations – and, in addition, several of her village friends were with her, making quite a crowd. The rest of my family, I guessed, were still out at work.

She got up and gave me an intense but brief embrace, just as she always does. She isn't a particularly demonstrative woman. We exchanged the usual comments – how was this person, how was that, what news from Cambridge? – and the village cronies joined in, eager to hear about life in the town. Not that I told them very much; it really was none of their business, and I didn't want to worry my mother.

One of the oldest of the women – it was the widow Berta, the village washerwoman, and I wondered what she was doing there since nobody likes her very much and my mother doesn't like her at all – leaned forward and grasped my wrist in a fat, sweaty hand. Her eyes were very dark, sunk in the fat of her face, but all the same I could see them shining with malice. 'You'll not have heard about your aunt and that Hrype and the carryings-on,' she said in a sharp voice, 'since to the best of my recollection it's all happened since last you honoured us with a visit.' She eyed

9

me, far too intently for my liking. 'Well, let me tell you, it's—'

'Enough, Berta,' my mother said coolly.

Berta spun round to glare at her. 'Come now, Essa, it's only fair and right to tell the girl before she goes bursting in on them, and I—'

'I said enough,' my mother repeated. She rose to her feet and rather pointedly opened the door. Berta had little choice but to obey the clear invitation to leave, and the other women shuffled out after her. 'You've made an enemy there, Essa, like as not,' the last one whispered with a grin.

My mother gave an indifferent shrug. 'I did that a long time ago.' She and the woman exchanged a glance and a swift embrace, then the door was closed and my mother and I were alone. She poked up the fire, nodding to the recently vacated bench, and with relief, because a small persistent pain was worming itself somewhere down in my lower back, I sat down. I'd walked hard today, and this was the result. With quick, efficient hands my mother put water on to heat and mixed pinches of this herb and that ground root in a mug, adding honey and pouring on the water when it was hot enough and then handing the drink to me.

Our eyes met. 'So Hrype has done what he should have done a long time ago,' I remarked.

My mother nodded.

For some time we sat in silence. I was thinking about my friend Sibert, who grew up believing the man who fathered him was his uncle, his dead father's brother, and who had only discovered relatively recently that Hrype was in fact his father. Hrype was a very difficult man to read and I had no idea of his feelings for Froya, Sibert's mother, although I was pretty certain that he loved my aunt Edild, who is my father's sister. For sure, she loved him, and watching her endure a life when the man she adored lived – demurely and innocently, as far as we all knew – with his sister-in-law had been very hard. Now, though, it seemed Hrype had acted at last.

'What happened?' I asked eventually.

'Edild told your father that Hrype revealed to Froya the truth concerning where his heart really lies, and explained to her that it was his wish to leave the home he'd shared so long with her and Sibert and move in with Edild.'

'And how did Froya take that?' I'd always thought of Froya as a dependent, weak woman who, it seemed, had never really got over the death of her husband; or perhaps it was guilt over the fact that she'd slept with his brother while he lay dying that had turned her into a nervous, anxious shadow of a woman.[1] I couldn't imagine that she would have accepted Hrype's departure without protest.

But to my surprise my mother said, 'All seems perfectly amicable, and Froya apparently told Hrype that she was quite relieved to be told at last since she'd known all along something wasn't right.'

'What about Sibert?' If Froya was nursing a secret heartache at Hrype's revelation, then it

----

[1] See *Mist Over the Water*.

11

would be my friend who would bear the burden of it.

'Sibert is giving nothing away,' my mother replied. 'It's always seemed to me,' she added, poking at the fire again and throwing on more wood, 'that Sibert and Hrype never really got on that well, so maybe the lad's pleased to see the back of him.' She looked up at me and grinned. She is well aware, I'm sure, that I don't much like Hrype either.

'Anyway,' she went on, settling back on her stool with a sigh, 'Edild and Hrype quietly made their vows and are now man and wife. The village is still gossiping and they'll go on doing so, but most folks are too scared of Hrype to do so in his presence. Besides, he's still looking after Froya and she doesn't seem dismayed that he's gone, so people are forced to keep their most malicious comments to themselves.'

I smiled. Yes, everyone was wary of Hrype, and for good reason. He was, I well knew, powerful in his way; not as powerful as Gurdyman, but the force that operated through Hrype was undoubtedly darker. You crossed him at your peril.

I'd been staring into the fire, relaxed, warm down to my toes from the delicious hot drink, and it was only now that I realized my mother was studying me.

'So why are you home?' she demanded. She leaned closer. 'You look a bit pale. Not sickening for something, are you?'

'No, of course not,' I said, putting on an aggrieved tone to mask my horrified reaction at her perspicacity. 'I'm tired, that's all. I've just walked all the way from Cambridge. You don't think I'd come visiting if I thought I was bringing sickness to your house and the village, do you?'

She was still looking at me, and now, with a sniff, she said, 'No, I reckon not.'

The sooner I leave, I thought, the better.

After what I hoped was long enough not to rouse her suspicion, I said, 'Well, I suppose I'd better be off to Edild's.'

'Don't you want to see your father, and your brothers, and Zarina and the little ones?'

I gave her a weak smile. 'Tomorrow,' I promised. 'I really am tired, Mother.'

I stood outside Edild's door, not sure what to do. In the past, when she and I had shared the house, I'd always gone in and out unthinkingly, and it had never occurred to me to knock. Now, though, things were different.

I tapped very gently and called out, 'Edild? Are you there? It's Lassair.'

There was a brief pause – I thought I heard a swift whispered conversation – and then my aunt opened the door. She smiled gently at me and, although it was her usual calm, unflappable expression, I saw immediately that something had changed: in the soft light from the hearth and the two little lamps, her skin glowed like pale honey and a sort of illumination seemed to shine out of her. She didn't need to tell me she was happy, for anyone with eyes to look could see for herself.

'What a nice surprise,' she said, standing aside to let me go in and closing the door. 'We didn't know you were coming, Lassair.'

13

We.

It's one of the telltales of a new couple, isn't it? Before they always said *me* and *I*. Afterwards, suddenly and very emphatically and at every possible occasion, it's *we* and *us*.

Well, my dear aunt was now half of an *us*, and I had better begin to get used to it; even, if I could manage it, start being glad for her.

Her new husband lay relaxed beside the hearth, propped up on a bedroll, a mug of some fragrant, steaming liquid to hand. Wooden platters, scraped clean, were stacked close by, and the appetizing smell of what they'd just had for supper still permeated the air, mingling with the usual scent of herbs that always characterizes Edild's house.

I had seen Hrype in just that pose, in that exact position, times without number. But now he had the right to be there, always, every day, every minute. My sensible self told me not to be so silly, that Hrype was a free soul, a wanderer; a man who needed to go off on his own regularly in order to keep sane; that he could no more alter this lifelong habit than stop breathing; that there would henceforth be almost as many occasions when Edild was alone at home as there had always been.

My sensible self knew the truth, but my emotional self wasn't paying any attention.

'Sorry to turn up without warning,' I said, trying to make my voice friendly and warm. By the swift, amused look that Hrype shot me, I reckoned I'd failed.

Edild put a hand on my arm; a brief, warm

touch. 'It doesn't matter, Lassair. There's food if you're hungry?'

'Yes, please.' My empty stomach was growling. It seemed hours since my meagre midday bread and cheese.

Edild ladled a bowl of vegetable and barley stew from the pot over the hearth, and I sat down opposite Hrype. The first few mouthfuls went down almost without my tasting them, but quite soon I began to feel full, and not long after that, slightly queasy. With an apologetic smile, I handed the bowl back to my aunt.

'I seem to be full,' I said.

She smiled. 'You ate too fast,' she replied. 'How many times have I told you? You must eat slowly when you're really hungry, or else you fill up too quickly.'

I went to get up to help her tidy away the remains of the meal and wash the utensils, but she waved me down again. 'No, you stay where you are,' she said. 'You've had a long walk, and you are surely worn out.' As my mother had done earlier, she peered into my face. 'You're ashen,' she observed. 'Have you a head-ache?' She had remembered, then, how my head always pounds when I get very tired, just as hers does.

'Yes,' I lied. 'And you're right, I am very weary. In fact' – now I did get up – 'I think if you don't mind I'll settle down for the night.'

'But we—'

I didn't let her finish. 'Don't worry, I'm not going to insist that you two extinguish the lamps and sleep as well!' I forced a laugh. 'I know it's not late, and I'm sure you're not ready.' I felt myself blush; they were newlyweds and, although I knew full well they'd been lovers for years, there was something about Edild's bride status that seemed to edge all sorts of wedding-night ribaldry into the place. 'I'll sleep out there.' I nodded towards the chilly little stillroom that Edild built on to the back of the house.

Edild and Hrype exchanged a glance. 'It's cold out there,' Edild said.

'I have my shawl, and a thick cloak.' I held up a fold of it to demonstrate.

'Lovely,' Edild said vaguely. She, I thought, was almost as embarrassed as I was. Only Hrype, still lying relaxed by the hearth and with a faint smile playing around his handsome mouth, seemed at ease.

My aunt apparently noticed this at the same time I did. She nudged him with her toe and said, quite severely, I thought, for a brand-new wife, 'Get up, Hrype, and help Lassair! Her bedroll's over there' – she pointed – 'and there's a newly stuffed straw mattress under the bottom shelf of the stillroom. Go and find the least draughty spot and lay it out for her, if you please.'

Hrype's grin intensified. He got up, paused to kiss his new wife, then went through to the still-room to do as he was told.

It wasn't quite as uncomfortable as I'd expected, but it wasn't far off. Thanks to the new mattress, I was cushioned to an extent from the cold, hard stone floor; at the start of the night, anyway, although I'd swear the chilly dampness began

16

to permeate up towards my body the moment I lay down. My shawl and cloak were enormously comforting, not least because of who had given them to me. My soft, thick lambswool shawl, in beautiful, subtle shades of green, was a gift from my sister Elfritha, and she'd presented it to me when both of us first left home, I to look after my other sister in her first pregnancy and she to join the nuns at Chatteris. 'It's to remind you of home and a sister who loves you,' she'd said as she gave it to me. It did, and it still does. Although I wear it almost every day, it shows few signs of wear. My cloak is also wool; heavy wool, dyed a very dark brown that is almost black, close-woven to keep out the cold, the wind and even the rain, unless it is a downpour, and it is lined with linen and interlined with wadded lambswool. The hood is deep and generous.

It was a gift from Jack. Seeing me go out for much-needed herbal supplies as I tended him at the height of his pain, he had been anxious because there was a storm looming. He didn't get up and go to purchase the cloak himself. He was far too unwell for that. He must have asked one of his men to go on the errand – Walter, probably, who is the most intelligent and worldly, who would know which merchants stocked the best garments. When I got back, soaked to the skin and shivering, the cloak had been spread out on my mattress.

As I lay on the stillroom floor, I drew the shawl and the cloak around me. My sister's love enveloped me over time and distance, and I smiled

17

as I sent mine back to her. Jack's gift warmed me from my neck to my toes, and his love too reached out to me.

But I didn't let myself think about Jack.

I must have slept. I was aware of far too many hours of wakefulness, during which the cold draught under the rear door sought me out, always managing to find the one bit of my body that wasn't as well covered as the rest. When at last the faint illumination of dawn began to permeate the dark little room, I braced myself to turn over and try to snatch some more sleep. As I moved, a sharp pain shot through my lower back, for a few heartbeats so intense that I was frozen into immobility. But then it eased, as sore muscles often do if you keep still, and quite soon I was able to move without discomfort.

I slept.

Later, as the faint sounds of Edild and Hrype in the next room drifted through the wall, I woke knowing I was about to be sick. I hurried out of the back door, stumbled a little way up the path to the higher ground behind the village and threw up.

Two

I would have set out back to Cambridge there and then if I hadn't felt so weak, and if I hadn't told myself very firmly that I'd only just run away from the place. I dreaded facing Edild, for I feared that she would instantly detect that I was pregnant. Besides, the prospect of another night on the stillroom floor wasn't in the least appealing.

But there was no choice but to stay, so I would have to make the best of it.

I went back to the house, pausing to draw a ladle of water from the butt. I washed my face and hands, pinching my cheeks to put some colour in them, and rinsed my mouth out very thoroughly. Edild has a nose like a hound and can detect the smell of vomit at five paces. Back inside, I combed my hair, re-braided it and put on a clean white cap. When I was as ready as I was going to be, I went through into the main room and sat down to share Edild and Hrype's porridge; to my surprise, I was ravenous, and cleared my bowl without any problem.

'Unless there's anything I can do to help you,' I said as my aunt and I cleared the bowls while Hrype tidied away the bedding, 'I thought I'd go and see my family. If I go straight away, I'll catch my father before he sets out, and I'll be able to walk with him.'

'Of course,' Edild agreed. She looked even more glowing this morning than she had last night. I didn't want to dwell on that, so I said a quick farewell and set out.

My family had also just finished eating, and my father and brothers were drawing on their boots as I arrived. My father stood up and, without a word, took me in his arms in a firm, loving hug. It felt so good to be enfolded in his strength and his warmth. I could have stayed like that all day. I heard my two younger brothers, Squeak and little Leir, asking excited questions, demanding to know how long I was staying and if there was news from the town. Their lives are so monotonous, out here in the depths of the fens, and sometimes I forget how thrilled they are when something crops up to break the monotony, even if it's only a visit from their sister.

'We're off to the eels,' my father said, letting me go at last. 'Will you walk with us?'

'That's precisely why I'm here,' I replied. So, hand in hand with him while Squeak and Leir jumped and ran along beside, behind and in front of us like a couple of playful puppies, we set off.

My father is an eel-catcher. A very good one; in a tough world, his hard work and expertise ensure that his family live as well as anyone of our station. October is a relatively quiet time with eels, for as the weather grows cold they delve deep down into the thick, black mud at the bottom of the fenland streams, where they usually remain until temperatures rise again in spring. It takes an eel-catcher who has my father's skill with the sharp-barbed trident that we call a gleeve to grab much in this season.

My father and I talked as we strode along, of inconsequential things, of small daily happenings. Once or twice I caught him looking at me, a faint frown on his face. I was very scared: had he somehow guessed my condition? Also, there was another anxiety, for I knew a secret about his past that I hadn't revealed to him and, loving him as I did, this was very hard. But it wasn't my secret to tell and I had no choice but to keep silent.

But then, as if somehow he'd picked up my thoughts, he said diffidently, 'I'm to meet up with a new acquaintance soon. He's sent me a message via the tinker.'

I didn't really need to ask, but I did anyway. 'Oh, yes?' I said with innocent brightness. 'And who's that?'

He grinned. 'Apparently he's a huge, white-haired old man they call the Silver Dragon, although I know that's not his real name.'

'It's Thorfinn,' I muttered unthinkingly, but fortunately my father didn't hear. He had no idea I'd even met the man and I'd almost given it away!

'Yes, he's an Icelander, or so I'm told, and he used to frequent these parts when he was a young man.' He glanced at me. 'Knew your grandmother Cordeilla, apparently, and he wants to look up her kin.'

I could think of nothing to say except for 'How nice', which was totally inadequate.

I knew Thorfinn's tale, for he and I already

21

knew each other; he'd had me grabbed when I was on my way between my village and Cambridge and taken to his island home.[2] Subsequently he'd told me who he was, and why he'd wanted me to be taken to him. It was, I reflected wryly, something of an understatement to say he'd known my grandmother; they'd briefly been lovers and my father was his son, although he didn't know.

This secret – Thorfinn's and my Granny Cordeilla's – was the one I'd been keeping. If Thorfinn had asked to meet my father, I thought and fervently hoped it meant he was going to reveal the truth at last.

'When is the meeting to be?' I asked.

'Soon,' my father replied. 'Before the winter sets in, anyway.' He smiled to himself. 'The Silver Dragon. What a name, eh?'

I left my father and brothers to their work and wandered back to the village. My back was still sore, so I took it slowly. I didn't really know what I was going to do with myself all day. I went back to Edild's house. Perhaps I'd be able to help her in her healer's work.

She was with someone – a plump young woman whose brilliantly blushing cheeks suggested she'd come to consult my aunt on some very intimate matter – so I waited outside until the visitor had gone. Then, going in, I said, 'Where's Hrype?'

'He's gone to look for Sibert. He wants to talk to him,' Edild replied shortly. She was busy,

<hr />

[2] See *Land of the Silver Dragon*.

rinsing out a bloodstained cloth and hanging it by the fire to dry.

'How is Sibert?' I asked. 'How has he—'

My aunt spun round and glared at me, as clear a way of saying *I don't want to discuss it* as I could imagine, short of speaking the words out loud.

I picked up a little basket of dried rosemary and put it down again. Smoothed a folded blanket. Then my aunt said in an exasperated voice, 'Lassair, *I* have work to do, but not sufficient to occupy us both, so why don't you call on your mother?'

Without a word, I left.

My mother was making honey-apples, and the smell of spices and sweet honey filled the house. I fetched a knife and sat down beside her, and together we peeled, cored and chopped the apples. She's not a very chatty woman, and we worked in companionable silence. When the mixture was in the pan and set aside for cooking, she said abruptly, 'You can sleep here, you know. Edild's house must feel somewhat crowded now.'

'I slept in the stillroom,' I replied shortly.

She laughed. 'Didn't want to be a witness, no doubt.'

I smiled, but it was all far too embarrassing to be funny. I said, 'Thank you, Mother. May I think about it?'

'Of course. I know it's always far too much of a crush here, but at least there aren't any newlyweds.'

* * *

23

We worked together for the remainder of the morning, and she set out bread and some thin slices of ham at midday. Afterwards, we were preparing to go out to see if we could gather any last hazelnuts, in the process of finding baskets and putting on our boots, when we heard raised voices outside. My mother flung open the door and we looked out to see Hrype, half-carrying and half-dragging Sibert towards Edild's house. Sibert was bundled inside Hrype's cloak. Without a word, my mother and I raced out onto the track and ran to catch them up. My mother, strong, broad woman that she is, swiftly took some of the burden from Hrype, and Sibert leaned his head on her shoulder.

I hurried ahead to open the door and Sibert was gently laid down on a bedroll beside the hearth, Edild already crouching over him, pushing back his long pale hair to stare into his eyes. 'Sibert?' she said gently. 'Can you hear me? Can you speak?'

His only response was a moan. *At least*, I thought frantically, *he is alive . . .*

Edild was looking up at Hrype. 'What happened?' she asked with remarkable calm.

'He was attacked,' Hrype replied. 'It took me a long while to find him, for he wasn't where he was supposed to be.' He was staring intently at his son and abruptly he raised his hands and buried his face in them. 'I was only just in time,' he muttered, 'for the assault was brutal, and he desperately needed help. He was so cold.'

Gurdyman's report of the poor young man who had been beaten to death filled my mind. Now there had been another attack, and so similar to the first . . .

But there were more immediate considerations. Edild, superficially calm and only her busy hands betraying her urgency, would surely need an assistant, so I made myself concentrate on what she was doing. 'Where was he hit?' she demanded. She was feeling all around his bruised, bloody forehead.

'On the crown of the head and on the brow, or so it appears,' Hrype said. 'Then he must have grabbed one of Sibert's hands and begun forcing back the forefinger – see? – but something, some sound, perhaps, must have interrupted him, for I do not believe the finger is broken.'

Edild now held Sibert's left hand in hers, gently bending each of the fingers backwards and forwards. Sibert cried out in pain. 'You're right, no bones are broken,' she murmured. She looked at Hrype. 'Perhaps it was your approach that the assailant heard, and, if so, you were just in time, it seems. Lassair' – even though she didn't look up, she knew I was right there – 'fetch hot water and lavender oil, soft cloths and my needle and gut. I will stitch the worst of the cuts while Sibert remains barely conscious. You shall help me.'

I did as she commanded, and we crouched either side of Sibert, working together as we had done so many times before. The cut on his forehead was shallow but it was bleeding copiously, as head wounds always do. Edild stitched it, then handed the needle to me to deal with a smaller but deeper cut on the top of the head. Sibert moaned a few times and once screamed out in

25

agony, writhing and trying to twist out of our reach, but Hrype and my mother held him still. After what seemed a long time, we were done.

'He must be put to bed and made to stay there,' Edild pronounced. 'Somebody who understands the treatment of severe blows to the head should stay with him.' She frowned slightly. 'I could go myself, but . . .'

There was no need for her to finish the sentence. There were difficulties and probably bad feelings on Sibert's part concerning his father's marriage, and to have his new step-mother nurse him – in his abandoned mother's house, too, since there wasn't really room for him at Edild's and he wouldn't have wanted to be treated there anyway – was undoubtedly the last thing he'd want.

'I'll go and look after him,' I said. Edild spun round to look at me. 'You know very well I can do it,' I said calmly. 'Caring for the after-effects of bad head wounds was one of the last things you taught me, when the pig man's lad fell off the hay wagon and knocked himself out. Remember?'

She nodded. I could see that she was thinking, swiftly coming to the conclusion that my suggestion was a good idea in more ways than one.

'I will go to speak to Froya,' Hrype said, 'and explain what has happened.' Edild made a small sound, and, understanding, he added quietly, 'Don't worry, I'll tell her he's not badly hurt. We don't want her worrying, not just now.'

Before any of us could stop him, he hurried away.

26

My mother stared after him. Her expression was carefully neutral, and she made no comment.

'Will you stay, Essa, to help carry Sibert home?' Edild asked. 'Lassair and I could do it, but you are the strongest and it's best that he's not jolted about more than can be helped.'

'Of course,' my mother said.

We did not have long to wait. Quite soon Hrype returned, and I caught a sheepish expression on his face. 'She's making a bed by the hearth,' he said.

'Is she all right?' Edild asked.

'Yes,' he said briefly. He shot her a glance. 'It's as you often tell me,' he added very softly. 'She is indeed tougher than I think.'

He'd forgotten for the moment, I believed, my mother's and my presence.

Froya greeted us at her door and indicated the paillasse, blankets and pillows that she had laid ready beside the hearth. Hrype and my mother gently lowered Sibert, who gave one shout of pain and then lay quiet. Froya waited, silent and contained, while my mother, closely followed by Hrype, backed out again. 'Thank you,' she said politely to them. Then she closed the door.

For a few moments she stood with her back to it, leaning against it as if making sure nobody came in again. Then she looked up and, to my amazement, she was smiling.

I studied her. She was very slim and fragile-looking, with white-blonde hair and very light eyes. Her pale face was heart-shaped, with a

27

delicate chin and a high, broad forehead. I'd always thought she appeared anxious. In that moment, I wondered if I'd ever actually seen her smile before.

She came back towards the hearth, and her injured son. 'I must thank you too, Lassair,' she said. 'I understand that you have offered to stay here and watch Sibert as he recovers, and that was a kind thought.'

'Only if it's all right with you,' I said quickly. 'I didn't mean to imply that you weren't capable of looking after him.'

'I didn't think you were,' she said. 'While I am as accustomed as any woman to caring for the sick and injured, I have few specialized skills, and I shall be very glad of your presence.'

She bent over Sibert, tucking the blanket around his shoulders, and it seemed the matter was settled.

As the day slowly passed and night drew on, I watched Sibert carefully. In the main this was easy, for he slept a lot of the time. I checked his forehead frequently for fever – he was indeed quite hot – and I regularly bathed his stitched wounds with cold water in which I had put lavender oil. I had set out the ingredients for a pain- and fever-reducing drink, wanting to have them ready should he wake up and need it.

Once he stirred, and his urgent mutterings alarmed both Froya and me. 'Not me!' he yelled. 'I wasn't even there, *it's not me you want!*' The last five words were so loud that the echoes rang in the little house. Sibert tried to sit up, fixed

28

his eyes on me and screamed, '*NO!* Stop, oh stop, *I don't know*!'

Froya gave a soft whimper. 'Don't be too concerned,' I said softly, trying to force Sibert back to a recumbent position without causing him pain. 'He's a little feverish, and not aware of what he's saying. The words are not for us.'

She nodded, a quick, curt acknowledgement of her understanding. Then she said, 'Would some of your draught help him now?'

I studied my patient. He was writhing to and fro, muttering again, and I thought he might indeed be sufficiently aware to drink the medicine.

'I'll try,' I said.

Froya brought over the water that we had set to heat and I poured it on the combined herbs. I allowed the mixture to steep for the prescribed time, and by then it was cool enough to give to Sibert. I filtered it and Froya supported him while I held the cup to his lips. He sipped, slowly at first, then greedily, as if he had a huge thirst. He opened his eyes widely for a few moments and said, 'Lassair! Nobody told me you were home!' Turning to Froya, he added, 'Don't get anxious, now, Mother, I'm not badly hurt.' Then, relaxing into his pillows with a deep sigh, he went back to sleep.

Froya knelt by his side, utterly immobile. 'Is he going to be all right?' she whispered.

'I hope so,' I said. Experience has taught me never to promise outcomes about which I cannot be certain. 'He recognized us both, and was sufficiently aware to remember to reassure you. That's a good sign.'

She nodded. Then she got to her feet and said, 'Well, he'll sleep now, for he has drunk your draught to the dregs and I'm sure you know what you're doing. I will prepare food, for you must be as hungry as I am.'

She had surprised me in many ways, this mother of my old friend. As I settled for the night, lying close beside Sibert so that I would hear if he moved or called out, I reflected how little we know other people. I'd been acquainted with Froya all my life; I knew a little about her past, and from those scant details I'd made up my mind that she was a delicate woman, easily distressed, prone to anxiety and to treating even minor problems as huge and distressing perturbations. I'd imagined she would be utterly destroyed if Hrype ceased to share her and Sibert's house and moved in with my aunt. Yet here she was, faced with a seriously injured son and the presence in her house of someone she hardly knew, and she was dealing with it calmly and efficiently. Judging by the soft snores coming from the corner where she lay, the day's events weren't affecting her ability to sleep.

Suddenly I asked myself how *I'd* feel if circumstances had forced me to live with Hrype and all at once those circumstances didn't apply any more and he left. I grinned to myself in the darkness. I'd be delighted.

As I turned over and settled down to sleep, pain stabbed through the sore muscle in my lower back and I suppressed a moan. I altered my position, and it eased a little. To take my mind off it, I thought again about the attack on Sibert. As soon as Hrype had revealed what had happened, it had been only natural to think of that other assault that Gurdyman had told me about. The details sounded disturbingly similar, and I wondered now if Sibert had been in the same area when the assailant fell on him, and why it should be that two young men should be attacked within the space of a few days.

I was just considering what could possibly connect Sibert and the dead young man when my back started to hurt again. I moved again, pushed my rolled-up shawl into the small of my back for support and made myself relax. I'd have willingly taken some of my own sleeping and pain-suppressing herbs, but too deep a sleep would mean I couldn't hear Sibert if he called. Sleep, I ordered myself.

Presently, I began to drift off.

In the depths of the night in Cambridge, a large object floated with the slow downriver current, emerging from beneath the dark shadows of the trees and the vegetation on the bank into the clear area along the quays that lined the river either side of the Great Bridge.

The water moved slowly there. As the current edged the object round a gentle bend, some profound eddy caught it, setting it briefly in motion.

To an onlooker, it might have seemed that an arm waved; asked for help, perhaps.

For the object was a human body. The appeal for help was nothing but an illusion, for the body was quite dead.

31

Time passed, and, yard by slow yard, the body made its way past the moored boats, the majority dark and closed up for the night. It floated on its back, arms and legs splayed out, and gradually the gentle current swept it over to the northern bank. Sometimes its right foot, still wearing a boot although the left one had gone, knocked against the side of a boat. If any sleeper on board heard the small sound, he or she dismissed it as the general background noise of the night.

Now the body drew close to the Great Bridge. Aboard the last boat on the north bank, a woman was awake. She was nursing a baby, and she sat in a pool of light from a single lantern. She was intent on her child, watching the small face as her little son drew the abundant nourishment from her breast, and had no eyes for anything in, or upon, the river.

Had she glanced down, she would have seen a pale face illuminated by her lantern. The face had received a battering, and there had been a great deal of blood. This had all been washed away from the exposed flesh, although the tunic and undershirt were still heavily stained. The hair, long, fair and well cut, floated around the broken head like a halo.

On the right hand, extended towards the nursing woman and her child in silent appeal, three fingers and the thumb were crushed almost beyond recognition.

As the dead man floated beneath the Great Bridge, the trailing edge of some torn item of clothing caught on the ruins of an ancient wooden quay, of which nothing remained but a few rotting wooden piers under the water. For a while, the current tried to pull the body free, and it began to bob about as if eager to assist. But the movement caused another piece of cloth to become caught up, and then the body was still.

It was to remain there, in the dark shadows beneath the bridge, for some time before anybody spotted it, by which time much of the exposed flesh would have been eaten away by the small creatures of the water and the river bank.

It was a sorry end, for a man who had travelled so far.

Three

Jack Chevestrier stood in the doorway of his house, looking up the track. It was where he passed quite a lot of his time. The deserted settlement around him had once been home to the workmen who had built the Norman castle that William the Conqueror commanded into being. There was nobody lurking among the half-ruined dwellings, nobody hurrying towards him up the path. His small flock of geese, kept in their pen beside the house, were calm. He appreciated their eggs, but their main purpose was to be his sentinels.

Part of him believed that Lassair wasn't coming back. He didn't allow that part to have its own way. He had to go on hoping, for he knew in his badly injured, slowly recovering condition he wasn't strong enough to bear the mental anguish of losing her.

She'd nursed him so well and so devotedly, he would tell himself. That must surely indicate that she cared. Ah, but she's a healer, the voice of doubt would reply. She would have done as much for any wounded man. She's seen you on the way to regaining your strength, and now she's had enough and has left.

'I will not give up,' he said softly.

Summoning deep resources of strength, he forced his mind to positive thoughts.

He would return to work as soon as he knew he was capable of staying on his feet all day. He would force his way to advancement, for surely there could not be a better time . . .

The deeply unpopular Sheriff Picot still held power, but his prestige had suffered a blow. Once people had only dared to mutter about him in the privacy and safety of their own homes, where there was no danger of some Picot spy over-hearing; now the fear of retribution had retreated. Sheriff Picot had been forced to face up to how much the town disliked him, and the word was that he was deeply anxious.

The fight that had almost cost Jack his life had taken its victim after all; Gaspard Picot had launched himself on Jack because Jack had been about to implicate him in a crime punishable by death, and in defending himself Jack had killed him.[3] Gaspard was Sheriff Picot's nephew, and the sheriff had instantly cried out for Jack's blood, demanding his arrest, imprisonment and trial for murder.

But the arrest hadn't happened.

Even as the sheriff was trying to organize a band of lawmen to seek Jack out and throw him into the darkest, dankest, deepest dungeon – Jack was lying in a tavern bleeding almost to death at the time – a long queue of townspeople had formed at his door. They'd said afterwards that more than half the town had turned out, but Jack thought that was probably an exaggeration. As Sheriff Picot and his officers demanded what

[3] See *The Night Wanderer*.

business all the men and women thought they had with him, all too soon it became unpleasantly clear.

Every one of the men and women was there to announce that they'd seen what happened and they were willing to swear that Jack Chevestrier had acted in self-defence, that Gaspard Picot had jumped on him and struck the first blow. 'I saw it with my own eyes!' they all claimed, even those who had been on the other side of town and asleep in their beds.

Sheriff Picot, furious, fuming, longing for revenge for his nephew's death – and more crucially, for he hadn't much liked the man, for the way the death had drastically weakened his own position – had been forced to stop and think. And, quite soon, he had reached the conclusion that it would be very unwise to arrest Jack Chevestrier and put him on trial, for the evidence was right before the sheriff's eyes – or, more accurately, his ears, the long and now restless queue becoming increasingly noisy – that the man was far too popular. Threatening retribution to someone who probably had acted in self-defence would do Sheriff Picot no good at all.

The whole business had acted to loosen people's tongues, and the mood in the town, if you were the sheriff or one of his close associates, was dark and becoming ugly. The Picots' star was falling. Was it, Jack wondered, at long last time for something better to take the place of the corrupt Picot administration?

There was no way to be certain, but he was firmly resolved to try.

36

He would throw himself into his work, and save every coin he earned. He would devote time to the tiny lean-to dwelling adjoining his house – it had long been empty and was little more than a shell, although the walls were sound and the roof could readily be made so – and combine it with his own living space, knocking through a new doorway. Within it he would fashion a private room, or perhaps two rooms, for Lassair; a place where she could pursue her own skills, her own work; where she could prepare her potions, her ointments, her remedies; where she could see those who came to her for help. Then when she came back – he would not let himself think *if* – she would see what he had prepared for her and understand that he had no wish to change her; that he treasured her just the way she was and would not stand between her and the work she loved, at which she was so adept.

All of which, he reflected as he turned away from staring down an empty alley and went back inside his house, was perfectly good in theory. In practice, however, he was in pain, weak, uninterested in company, in nourishing food, in drink, in pretty much everything. He wasn't sleeping, his tormenting, doubting thoughts left him no peace and he was more lonely than he had ever been.

Rollo Guiscard, putting up in a mean, dirty and uncomfortable lodging house behind the quayside in Cambridge, was furiously angry with himself. He had made a grave error – or so he believed – and now, he feared, he was forced to run for his life.

It demonstrated to perfection the self-imposed stricture that, until now, he had ruthlessly abided by: don't involve the heart in matters of business.

Well, he'd allowed himself to do just that. Now he was paying the price. His folly had begun a month ago, when he had interrupted his carefully constructed plan to sell the same information twice over to two very powerful men for no greater purpose than to seek out the fenland healer he believed he might love. He had contrived to watch her for a while before making himself known to her, and his observance had repaid him in bitter coin: he'd seen her with another man, a desperately wounded man who might even now be dead. He'd seen the way she looked at the man as he lay bleeding into her lap. Later, when he'd had a chance to speak to her, he'd asked her bluntly if she loved him. 'No. *Yes*. I don't know,' she'd replied. To be fair, she'd told Rollo she loved him as well, but then, when she'd spoken of this other man, whatever thoughts about him that preoccupied her had made her weep.

So he'd left her. Set off on the next stage of his mission. Gone to Normandy, and sought out Duke Robert in Rouen. He had already made a provisional visit there, but then he'd been travel-stained and worn out, his purse all but empty, and in no state to present himself to the Duke of Normandy with any hope of what he had to say being believed, if it were even so much as heard. But he had used his time there well, finding out what he needed to know about the duke and his rule. When he returned, he had gone prepared:

well dressed in costly new tunic, boots and a luxurious fur-lined cloak, freshly shaved, his fair hair well cut and shining with cleanliness. As he had anticipated, he hadn't had to press a surreptitious coin or two into too many palms before he'd been ushered into the duke's presence.

Rollo forbore to tell Duke Robert all that he had previously related to his brother King William of England; his first loyalty was to William, after all, whom he considered far the better man. But he saw no harm in revealing to the duke how matters stood in Outremer; how strife between the infidel and the Christians was intensifying; how rumour and propaganda were stoking the fire of hatred; how Alexius Comnenus, the ruler of Constantinople, was all but sure to demand help from the Christian lords of the West to help him halt the advance of the Turks. This intelligence, Rollo was sure, would soon be known throughout north-west Europe, for how could such an approaching cataclysm be kept secret?

Duke Robert, however, responded just as Rollo had hoped he would, treating the information as if it was Rollo's personal gift to him. And – which Rollo had also hoped – paying him very well.

Duke Robert, Rollo had discovered on finally making his acquaintance, was largely as his people had depicted him. He was short but stout, his ample girth suggesting self-indulgence and an over-fondness of the board and the wine jug. His fleshy face was red and slightly sweaty, and his teeth weren't good. In addition, as Rollo deduced after not many words had passed between them, he wasn't very bright.

But in one crucial aspect, Duke Robert of Normandy had shown wisdom: perhaps in recognition of the fact that his grasp of complex matters of statecraft left quite a lot to be desired, he'd had the good sense to surround himself with cleverer, more astutely minded men than himself.

One of these, or so Rollo believed, had not been as convinced as his lord duke of the authenticity of the unexpected well-dressed wealthy visitor who had turned up so fortuitously, demanded audience with Duke Robert and talked to him for over an hour, emerging with a heavy bag of gold hanging from his belt. This man, whoever he was, had let misgivings harden into suspicion, and detailed a man to follow Rollo and see where he went. So skilful and subtle had been the tail that this close adviser to the duke had set on Rollo – the spy becoming the spied-upon – that, for all his experience in following and detecting when he himself was being followed, Rollo had not begun to detect his – their? – presence until he was almost back in Cambridge.

Now he sat in the darkness of the tiny space that had been let to him as a room, contemplating his own folly. The room was vile. He'd already crushed more than a dozen beetles – the whole building was dank, and didn't appear to have been cleaned for a decade or more – and the sparse, soiled bedding had been jumping with fleas. He'd rolled it up and shoved it in a corner, preferring to sleep on bare boards with his cloak for warmth. The only advantage of his awful lodgings was that nobody would expect to find him there.

I left Rouen as if I already knew my pursuers were after me, Rollo thought. *He, or they, must have assumed my speed was because I feared whoever was close behind me.*

It was ironic, he reflected wryly, that the overwhelming need for haste had been for quite a different reason.

Which brought his depressing, alarming thoughts back full circle to where he had begun: to his stupidity in having permitted his impatience to return to Lassair to overcome his normal caution. Now he was in danger, and he didn't underestimate its gravity. Duke Robert's men would question him, probably, and if he refused to answer, they'd hurt him. Eventually, whatever he did or didn't say, they'd kill him.

He glanced round the dark, stinking space. His eyes lit on the leather bag in the corner: Duke Robert's gold. He smiled grimly. Here he was, wealthy by the standards of all but the richest men in the land, sitting in this hellhole of a room crushing insects.

It was time, he decided, to come up with a plan.

By the middle of the day after Sibert was attacked, it became clear to those of us concerned about him that he wasn't going to die. Or, at least, so we hoped and prayed. He woke from his long, deep, herb-induced sleep, announced that his head hurt like the very devil and asked plaintively

41

if he could have something to eat. While Froya set about preparing food, I slipped out to seek Hrype. He'd said he wanted to be present when Sibert was sufficiently alert to answer some questions, and I reckoned that time had now come.

Hrype had been at my aunt's house. He and I walked back to Froya's house in silence.

We found Sibert sitting propped up on pillows, spooning savoury porridge into his mouth from a wooden bowl, pausing occasionally to dip in a hunk of bread and wolf that down too. As soon as he had finished – I observed that although he looked much better, the effort of sitting up and eating had tired him greatly – Hrype said, 'Sibert, it appears I only just missed a glimpse of the man who attacked you. Even if I had seen him, however, my concern was with you and I doubt that I'd have paid him sufficient attention. Is there anything you can tell us about him?'

Sibert closed his eyes, perhaps as an aid to memory. But after a while he opened them again and said, 'No.'

'You were muttering in your sleep,' I said. 'You seemed to be protesting that it wasn't you the assailant wanted, and that you hadn't been present when – well, when whatever it was they were trying to find out about had occurred.'

He turned to me with a frown. 'Was I?' He began to shake his head, abruptly ceasing the movement when, evidently, it pained him. 'I can't remember. I can't recall talking in the night, nor can I remember answering any questions.'

I met Hrype's eyes. He was scowling, as if Sibert had failed him somehow. Before I could stop myself, I said angrily, 'He can't help it, Hrype! He's taken several heavy blows to the head and it's quite a surprise he can even remember his own name!'

'Sibert,' said Sibert, grinning at me. Then, his smile fading as quickly as it had appeared, he looked at Hrype and said caustically, 'I'm sorry to disappoint you yet again, but I'm not going to remember just because you want me to.'

Several expressions flashed rapidly across Hrype's lean, handsome face. Then – and I reckoned he was having to work quite hard to speak civilly – he said, 'Not to worry, Sibert. Perhaps memory will come back once you've recovered.' He shot a glance at me, then returned his attention to Sibert. 'I only wish to help you,' he said. 'Someone attacked you and it is likely that had it not been for my arrival, you would now be dead.'

With that, he got up, strode out of the house and banged the door behind him.

I hurried out after him. 'Hrype, wait,' I called.

He stopped. He didn't turn round, he just stopped.

'Sibert isn't the first victim of this attacker,' I said. And I told him what Gurdyman had told me.

Or, at least, I started to, but I hadn't said more than half a dozen words before he held up an imperious hand and said, 'I already know.'

'You – how? Have you seen Gurdyman since I left Cambridge?'

'No.' He gave me a superior smile. 'I knew before that, when I visited Gurdyman last week.'

'Then why—' Feeling foolish – Hrype so often makes me feel like that – I stopped. I'd been

43

going to say, *Then why didn't you warn Sibert?* But that was absurd, since how could Hrype or anyone else have predicted that Sibert would be the assailant's next victim?

He watched me, the remains of that annoying smile still playing around his mouth. 'Two young men, roughly the same age, both with longish fair hair' – that was news to me, since Gurdyman hadn't described the first victim's colouring or, indeed, anything else about him except that he was youngish – 'attacked within a few miles of each other.' He paused, staring unblinkingly at me. 'I'm sure you can draw your own conclusions.' Then he turned and strode away.

Draw my own conclusions? Beyond the fact that this attacker seemed to be looking for a specific man – which was so obvious it wasn't really worth stating – I was at a total loss.

I walked slowly back to Froya's house and let myself in. She'd prepared some of the porridge for me, but I shook my head. Anxiety and the lingering pain of the strained muscle in my lower back were combining to make me feel queasy, and I had no appetite. I'd had a headache when I woke up, although it had eased later. I sat down beside the hearth, wrapped my shawl around me and tried to work out what had been so clear to Hrype that I was missing. But, puzzle as I might – and my head was aching again by the time we settled for sleep – I couldn't see what he meant.

I woke to darkness.

The fire had burned low, and nothing remained but a very faint glow. I could hear Sibert's long, deep, steady breathing. I'd given him a second, weaker draught, and I knew he'd sleep soundly for some time. I was just thinking how clever nature is, to give us the gift of profound, healing sleep which is just what we need when we have been sick or injured, when an agonizing pain shot through the very base of my spine.

I gasped. I couldn't help myself.

Then, while I was still reeling from the first onset, it altered its attack. A band of white-hot pain circled round my body from my lower back right into the base of my belly. It seemed to clench me in its fist, and I stifled another cry.

I was wet.

Alarmed, horribly afraid, I put my hand down between my legs and felt the warm rush of my blood.

I heard myself cry out. Then, even as I turned my face into my pillow to suppress it, I whispered aloud, 'Jack.'

There was the flicker of a candle flame. Firm, warm hands were upon me. Froya's long, soft hair brushed across my face and she whispered, 'Hush, now. I am here. I will help you.'

She seemed to know what was happening. Reaching down under my blanket, she took hold of my balled fists; I'd been pressing them hard into my belly, as if that might assuage the pain. 'I know,' she said, in that same calm, gentle tone. 'I know how it hurts, but you must let me help.'

She must have felt the pooling blood. She got up, went to a shelf and returned with a woven basket of soft rags. She bunched up several of

45

them and placed them ready. She poured water from the pot kept suspended over the hearth into a bowl and dipped in another of the cloths. Then she turned back the blanket, folded my under-gown up over my chest and looked down at me. I was watching her face, and saw her expression. She met my eyes, and hers were full of sorrow. 'Oh, my dear,' she said very quietly.

Then she got to work.

Later, when she had finished and we were sipping the hot drinks she had prepared, she said, 'Do you wish me to summon your mother? Or your aunt, perhaps? She's a healer, and perhaps she should—'

'*No!*'

I'd almost spat out the word, and I sensed her slight recoil. 'I'm sorry, Froya, but I haven't told them I was—' I hadn't told anyone, I thought. Not even the lost baby's father. 'Nobody knew.'

Froya nodded. She turned to me, and in that long look I seemed to perceive that she too had been in this exact position. She said, 'Very well, then.'

After a moment, she reached out and took my hand.

That small gesture of solidarity, of sympathy, of kindness, undid me. I began to weep and found I couldn't stop.

When she had made us another drink and I was feeling very slightly better, she said, 'I can see that you do not wish to talk about this, and I shall not try to make you. I promise you that no word of what has happened here tonight will emerge from me.' She shot an amused glance at her deeply sleeping son. 'Nor, naturally, from him, blissfully oblivious as he is.'

'Thank you,' I whispered. Then, for I felt I had to know, I said, 'Why are you being so nice to me?'

She gave a swift chuckle; a sound I didn't think I'd ever heard from her before. 'Why not?' she answered simply. But then, perhaps realizing that the reply wasn't really enough for either of us, she elaborated on it. 'Lassair, I know, because he told me' – she nodded in Sibert's direction – 'that you have been aware of the truth about his paternity for some time. You could have shared such a choice bit of gossip about the stiff-necked, stand-offish Froya, who thinks herself above her peasant neighbours, and the haughty, mystical man who looks down his long and elegant nose at everyone who is not as intelligent as him. But you didn't.' She squeezed my hand. 'You kept my secret, and now I shall keep yours.'

I wanted to thank her but I was weeping again and could not speak.

'You shall stay here, and I shall look after you,' she went on. 'You have every reason to stay with us, for it is you who is caring for my son. When you are ready – when you have decided what you wish to do – then and not until then will it be time for you to go. Now' – her tone was suddenly brisk, and she rose gracefully to her feet – 'let me fetch fresh cloths for you, and then perhaps you can settle down and sleep, right on into the morning if you can.'

47

As soon as she said the word *sleep*, it was all I wanted to do. 'What will you tell Sibert?' I asked drowsily as she worked.

She smiled. 'Merely that you need to rest, having sat up for the majority of two nights caring for him.'

'But I haven't, I've managed at least some sleep, and—'

'Hush,' she said. 'Yes, I know you didn't really sit wakeful for the entire time, but *he* doesn't.'

She had finished. She drew the blanket up to my chin, then bent down and dropped a soft kiss on my forehead. 'Go to sleep,' she murmured.

It sounded like an incantation. It acted like one, too. I was asleep in moments.

Four

In his sordid little room, Rollo had been planning.

He now had the final confirmation that Duke Robert's agents were after him, and that their intent was not to ask him politely what he'd been doing sneaking in to see their lord and selling him information when here he was, back in England, and very likely an agent of the king; there was no logical way that the duke's men could know for certain about his allegiance to King William, but he was in no mood to go by cool logic.

Their intention was not to question him but to kill him.

A body had been found, caught by the tatters of its remaining garments under the Great Bridge. The face had been eaten by rats, and not a lot remained of the clothing except one of the boots, which was of fine quality and had obviously cost a good deal. The body was that of a man roughly Rollo's age. And he'd had shoulder-length, well-cut fair hair.

The rumour-mongers in the market place were bright-eyed with the thrill of spreading the gruesome tale, enhancing its effect by telling each other with avid fascination that the dead man was the second victim, and that the first, too, had been a young and fair-haired man.

Rollo's intelligence and common sense would normally remind him that fair-haired men were far from uncommon in England, and for the two victims to have had the same colouring and hair style was nothing more than coincidence. Once again, however, his capacity for logic was in abeyance and his mind wasn't amenable to reason.

The first conclusion that he reached after his lengthy spell of deep thought was that, having aroused the wrath of Duke Robert – or, at any rate, of one of the men who protected his interests – it was time to ensure the favour of the man to whom he owed first allegiance, King William of England. If the worst happened and somehow William came to hear of Rollo's mission to Rouen, he would have to dress it up as a spying mission for the king. *I needed to ascertain how much your brother knew*, he would say, *and how accurate the information was. We do, after all*, he would add, *want to make sure he is encouraged to go in the right direction.*

That ought to appeal to the king, Rollo thought. William's hope was that when the appeal from Constantinople came and Robert hurried to answer it, his urgent need for cash to fund the excursion to save the East and the Holy Places from the infidel would make him turn to his brother. William would lend him the money, but demand Normandy as surety. When, as seemed more than likely, Robert failed to return, William would win the dukedom without the loss of a single man or horse.

Rollo had agents placed in several towns in England, as well as in outlying, lonely places where nobody went and where it would be safe to hide. Now, he would use his Cambridge contact. Like all the rest, for Rollo had selected them carefully, this one – a woman of middle years or more, widow of a merchant, intelligent, discreet – was good at what she did for him and would, he hoped, be able to provide answers to the questions he planned to ask her.

He always paid his people well. So far, it had always ensured their efficiency and their silence. He prayed that this time, when he needed help so desperately, it would be no different.

'The latest knowledge I have of the king,' said Eleanor de Lacey, 'is that he turns his thoughts to the problem of Malcolm of Scotland.'

'I think,' Rollo replied, 'you'll have to explain.' He gave her a graceful bow. 'I have been away, and news has been hard to come by.'

Eleanor smiled thinly. She was a handsome woman, slim, quite tall, her smooth grey hair tidy under a sparkling white headdress, her gown costly and beautifully cut to flatter. She sat on a padded seat beneath a window overlooking the river, and the house – small but well built, expensively furnished and immaculate – reflected the fine taste of its mistress. 'King Malcolm wishes to arrange the marriage of his daughter Edith, but it seems the girl has shut herself away in an abbey and was veiled when her father burst in on her. King William, I believe, claims it is his right as Malcolm's overlord to arrange this match, and this has enraged King Malcolm. He – Malcolm – has reportedly raced back to Scotland

51

to drum up an army, and William prepares for the expected border raid.'

'So if I wished to seek out the king, I should proceed north?' Rollo demanded.

Eleanor shrugged. 'It is possible that he will attend to the business in person, but equally possible that other matters will persuade him to remain in the south.'

Rollo frowned. He knew there was no point in pressing Eleanor de Lacey for more. She'd told him what she knew, and now it was up to him to decide how to proceed. Go north, and hope to find the king and his party, make himself known to William and quietly merge with that large, powerful, well-equipped army and thus acquire protection from the agents hunting him? Stay where he was, and wait until he had uncovered more about William's movements?

An image of his lodgings flowed into his mind.

He didn't think he could bear to stay there any longer.

He thought about the practicalities: about getting out of Cambridge and onto the road north, and about how to avoid the sharp eyes of the men who sought to kill him.

As he always did, he thought about what was available to be used.

And he came up with an idea.

Reaching for the purse at his belt, he said, 'I shall need to commission some purchases.'

Eleanor de Lacey nodded. 'Very well.'

'I have a good horse, but I need to exchange it for another. Also, I require a second horse.' He counted out the necessary coins. Eleanor raised her eyebrows, but she didn't ask why he needed a new horse: without doubt, he reflected, she already understood.

A man on the run was identified by the horse he rode more readily than by almost anything else.

'Also,' Rollo continued, 'I require clothing for a gentlewoman. A gown, underlinen, leather boots and a warm travelling cloak of fine wool lined with fur.'

Eleanor nodded. 'And what size of person are these items of apparel to fit?'

Rollo hesitated. 'Would you mind standing up, please?' Eleanor did so. 'She is of a similar build to you, although perhaps not quite as tall.'

'Good,' Eleanor said. 'When I make the purchases, the assumption will be that they are for me. It is the time, after all, for the acquisition of warm winter clothing.'

Rollo counted out more money. 'Finally, two last things. I require food and drink for several days.'

Eleanor nodded again. 'That is easily achieved. I will furnish what you need from my own larders, and replenish the goods afterwards.' *Once you've gone*, hung unspoken in the elegant room. 'The other?'

'I would be most grateful if everything could be ready as soon as possible. Two days from now, if that can be managed.'

'It can.'

Rollo looked up from his counting and grinned. Eleanor de Lacey, he thought, was one of his better contacts.

* * *

53

With extreme care, keeping himself concealed at every corner and junction until he had checked that the way was clear, he made his way back to his lodgings. The dilapidated house and his own dark space within it seemed even worse after the luxury of Eleanor de Lacey, and the stink – unwashed flesh, filthy clothes, rotting food, vomit, faeces, urine, dead vermin – almost made him heave. *Not for much longer*, he told himself.

For he was going north, and, if all went well, he would go without attracting the eyes of the men who were hunting for him. They were looking for a man on his own, but when he left, he wasn't going to be alone.

He would go with the best disguise he could think of.

Lassair would be with him.

Jack Chevestrier made his slow, gasping and painful way along the track that weaved through the deserted village. When he reached the opening of the narrow little passage that curved round the base of the castle mound, he had to pause to catch his breath. He stood leaning against the high stone wall that formed its outer boundary, staring blankly up at the great earth rampart rising up on the opposite side of the alley. His legs were trembling and he was sweating heavily, and he'd walked no more than a few hundred paces.

When he felt better – not much better – he walked on, keeping his left hand on the stone wall for support. As the alley emerged onto the wide track that led up to the entrance to the castle, he stopped again, staring up at the great edifice on top of its mound. The king's father, he reflected, had known exactly what he was about when he'd commanded the construction of these monstrous wooden fortifications at strategic points in his new kingdom. In a land where hitherto men had lived in long, low halls, the castles high up on their man-made earth hills had inspired awe and fear even before the Conqueror had uttered his first oppressive orders.

Jack moved on, round to where the castle entrance glowered down onto the main road north out of the town. A flight of wooden steps led up to a small platform, across which a barrier controlled access. Two guards stood on it. Trying not to show how much the exertion was costing him, Jack climbed up to the platform.

The guards had recognized him. One of them gave a sort of bow – not much more than a dip of the head – and opened the barrier. The other reached out a hand as if to clap Jack on the back but, perhaps observing his frail state, thought better of it. He muttered, 'Good to see you here, chief.'

Jack would have liked to make a suitable reply, but, aware that he needed his breath for the far more challenging climb still to come, merely nodded.

The second flight of steps demanded almost more than he had to offer. When after an eternity he reached the top, his head was spinning, he felt very sick and it was all he could do to stay on his feet. Knowing that many pairs of eyes would be on him and quite a lot would be unfriendly, he forced himself to move on, after the briefest of pauses, and cross the narrow walkway that led from the top of the steps to the castle's huge oak doors.

Stepping into the chill of the interior, he felt the sweat cool on his skin and a huge shiver ran through him. But he couldn't weaken now, when he'd come so far. He forced his feet to move and, temporarily barely able to see, stumbled into the anteroom where he and his fellow lawmen habitually congregated.

There were four men within, two deep in conversation, one peering out of the high, narrow window, one lying along a bench and apparently dozing. All four turned to stare at Jack and, to a man, they came hurrying across the room to greet him.

He waved aside their expressions of dismay at how pale he was, but when they drew the bench forward and encouraged him to sit down, he all but collapsed onto it. One of the men thrust a mug of beer into his hands. He drank it, resisting the temptation to gulp it down. Even a few mouthfuls of weak alcohol tended to make his head spin, although he hoped it was only a temporary state.

He waved aside the anxious enquiries about his health and said with a grin, 'I haven't struggled all the way up here to tell you lot how I'm feeling.' He turned to the eldest of the four, a serious-faced man called Ned. 'I've been kept informed by Walter and the lads, but they've no way of knowing what's happening in there.' He waved a hand in the direction of the low arch on the far side of the room, where a closed door marked the entrance to the sheriff's private quarters. 'Is he present?' he asked in a low voice.

'No, we've not seen him today,' Ned said.

'Didn't see him yesterday, come to that, and only briefly the day before,' offered the youth who had been dozing on the bench. 'He's realized he's not the popular figure he always thought he was,' he added with a chuckle.

'It was the way the town turned out to tell him he couldn't possibly arrest you for murder since his precious nephew struck first,' said a large man who went by the accurate but unoriginal name of Lard. 'Reckon that until then he was planning on getting you strung up as soon as you could stand on your own two feet, and out of his hair at last.'

'Yes, Walter told me about that,' Jack said. Walter had in fact told him more than once, the tale growing with each repetition, although in fairness to Walter, the first couple of times he'd tried to impart the very welcome news, Jack had been delirious and lost in a world of frightening dreams and visions.

'Are you joining us again?' Ned asked. 'We need you and that's a fact. You know about these two murders? The young man found out on the road to the fens, and, night before last, the corpse we had to fish out from under the Great Bridge?'

'Yes, I do,' Jack replied. Walter was keeping him well informed. 'And I want to be back here with you, believe me,' he went on. 'But I am as

57

you see me. Simply climbing up here has all but knocked me out.'

'Nothing wrong with your head, though, is there?' Lard said shrewdly. 'If we were to report to you, let's say, saving you the necessity of exerting yourself overmuch till you're fit again, you could still be in charge of things.'

Jack looked at each of them in turn. His group of supporters led by Walter had said much the same thing. 'Is that what you want? All of you who answer to the sheriff, here in the castle?'

And all four men said, 'Yes.'

Jack waited while the wave of emotion ran its course. It was, he'd observed, another symptom of his deep wound and its aftermath, this tendency to be unmanned by sentiment that when he was in his right mind he wouldn't even have noticed.

'I need to know what's been happening within Sheriff Picot's inner circle,' he said. 'Gaspard Picot must have left family. I believe he was married, and he may have had children, although I don't know. What will become of them now that he's dead?'

'Why d'you want to know that?' the youth – Iver, Jack recalled now – demanded.

Jack turned to him. 'Because I killed their father and widowed their mother,' he said.

Something in the way he spoke seemed to stop further questions, although it was plain from the others' expressions that they too wondered why he was wasting his sympathy on the relations of a man as despicable as the sheriff's late nephew.

'I also want to know,' Jack went on, 'what Sheriff Picot plans to do. As you just said, Lard, he's had to endure a humiliation, and it's surely possible that he may retaliate in the form of far stricter and tighter control. He—'

'He may also bugger off and leave us alone,' Iver interrupted.

Jack smiled. 'Wishful thinking, I would say.'

'I can tell you about his family.' It was the fourth man, short, narrow-shouldered and with a dark aspect, who now spoke, breaking his silence. Jack turned to him, trying to recall who he was. 'Ranald, chief,' the man supplied.

'Yes. I'm sorry, I couldn't bring your name to mind.'

'No offence taken,' Ranald said. 'Like I say, I know a bit about Gaspard Picot, since a year or so back I was sent as part of the guard detailed to watch over the grand new house he was building for himself.' He grinned briefly. 'Seems that people in the neighbourhood didn't take to him, or, more particularly, to the way he was rubbing their faces in their poverty by putting up such a costly and luxurious dwelling cheek by jowl with their hovels. Building materials were disappearing from the site almost as fast as the merchants could deliver them, and we were set as Gaspard Picot's private watch.'

How typical of the man, Jack thought. 'And what of his household?'

'Servants by the handful, indoor and outdoor,' Ranald said. 'His wife is called Elwytha. Short, skinny, white-faced, self-absorbed, nervy sort of a woman, with that pop-eyed, lashless look

59

that puts you in mind of a rabbit. We all reckoned she went in awe of her lord, although that didn't stop her ruling her servants and those of us sent to guard the new building with a tough hand. She used the threat of a beating for even a small misdemeanour, and it was no idle threat, I can tell you.'

'And what of children?' Jack asked.

Ranald shook his head. 'None.' He hesitated, 'Go on,' Jack said.

'Well, I was going to say she didn't look capable,' Ranald said. 'Narrow hips, figure like an undeveloped girl, if you take my meaning.'

'No tits?' Lard put in helpfully.

Ranald grinned, aiming a cuff at Lard's head. 'I wasn't going to be so crude,' he said. 'But if I'd wanted a wife with a view to raising a home full of sons and daughters, I'd have looked elsewhere.'

'So why did Gaspard Picot pick her?' Iver demanded.

Ranald rubbed the tips of his fingers against his thumb. 'Work it out, lad,' he said, not unkindly. 'Why does a man ever marry a poorly favoured woman?'

'The lady Elwytha had wealth?' Jack asked.

'Her family has,' Ranald replied. 'She gives off the smell of money, too. Rich jewels, beautiful gowns, furs, haughty manner and nose in the air like she's avoiding a foul stench. And they say she clings on to what she has with a very tight fist. The family hold big estates up towards the Wash, and her grandfather and his sons were among the first to welcome the

60

Conqueror and his Normans when they—'
Abruptly he stopped. He knew, as they all did,
that Jack's father had been a Norman; a carpenter
by trade, who had been recruited by the present
King William's father into the vast army which
was dispatched to England to build the new
castles designed to remind his new subjects to
behave themselves.

'I see,' Jack said diplomatically. 'And presumably marrying a daughter of the house to a man
they perceived as powerful and important in the
new regime was useful to them.'

'Won't do them much good in the long term if
she's not a breeder,' Lard observed.

Jack nodded, the small movement making him
suddenly dizzy. *Time I left*, he thought. *Before I
pass out and they have to carry me home.*

Slowly he got to his feet. 'Come to me whenever you have something to tell me,' he said.
'Any time. You know where I'll be.' He made
his way carefully to the door. He sensed the four
men's eyes on him.

'Want a hand, chief?' one of them – Lard, he
thought – asked quietly.

'No,' he snapped. Then, as a wave of vertigo
hit, he said, 'Maybe.'

And, with Ned behind him and Lard in front
in case he stumbled, Jack made his way with
as much dignity as he could muster down the
two flights of steps. He dismissed his attend-
ants at the foot of the second flight. When he
reached the place where the narrow alley led
off around the base of the castle mound towards
the deserted village and home, he turned. Lard

and Ned were still standing where he'd left them. He gave them a wave and stumbled off down the alley.

Rollo's preparations were complete. In the space of only a couple of days he had acquired, thanks to Eleanor de Lacey, everything he needed. She had excelled herself, and he had silently handed her a bonus for her efficiency. The new garments and the leather boots were precisely what he would have chosen himself. While the quality of the wool, linen and fur was excellent and the cut expensive, the styles were subtle and understated, the beautiful colours muted: typical of the apparel of a well-to-do woman who did not feel the least need to flaunt her wealth. The horses, at present hidden away in stables on the northern fringe of the town, were good but not exceptional. The supplies of food and drink, neatly packed in two sturdy leather bags, were of the best.

Rollo was ready to set out. Now all that remained was to locate Lassair and persuade her to go with him. It was still early – he had been awake since dawn – and, once he had done his final checks, he could be on his way.

He went first to the deserted village behind the castle hill, concealing himself behind a half-ruined wall and peering out along the track. He had little hope of finding her there for he had already checked the house where he had previously seen her and there had been no sign of her. Nor of anybody else, for that matter. Had she nursed the big man back to health and then gone?

Rollo squashed the brief, worrying thought that perhaps she and the big man had left together. For sure, he told himself, the man had been far too unwell to travel.

Had she, then, lost her battle to save him?

Rollo felt a sudden, guilty lift of the heart.

Abandoning the quiet, lonely paths of the little settlement, he returned to the town. Keeping to the back lanes, pausing to watch at every corner and junction, he made his careful way to the narrow alley behind the market place where Lassair's mentor lived. As with the big man's house, Rollo had little hope of finding her here, for he had been watching this place too and, although the rotund figure of the old magician had appeared once or twice, hurrying off up the alley on some commission and returning to shut himself away once more, Lassair had not emerged.

There was only one other place where she might be; only one that Rollo knew, at any rate, and if she wasn't there he'd have to think it out again.

He returned to his lodging house behind the quay. Now that he was leaving, he could finally admit to himself just what it had cost him to put up there. For the last time he went back to the tiny room where he'd been living through these interminable days, collecting his bags and closing the door behind him. He'd put a new lock onto it on taking the room – a length of chain secured by a portable lock he'd acquired from a merchant in Troyes – and he removed it and stowed it in his pack. He gave the door a savage kick and it shuddered on its hinges.

He had paid when he took the room – it was the sort of place where payment was always demanded in advance; no doubt, Rollo reflected, because it was so horrible that people might quibble over the price after they'd been there a day or so – and now he was free to go. He made his way along behind the taverns, the brothels and the other lodging houses, alert, keeping to the shadows. He waited for some time before emerging to cross the Great Bridge, hiding behind the last of the big warehouses until the right moment came and then slipping out to join a large, cheerful group heading out of town onto the road north. He stayed with them until they reached the lane that led off to the place where he had stabled the horses, then left them as quietly and as unobtrusively as he'd arrived.

A short time later, he was mounted on one horse and leading the other, the bags on the second horse and firmly fastened. His bag of gold – only slightly lightened by his recent purchases and expenses – was in its accustomed place on his belt.

It was, to judge from the sun's position, an hour or so before noon. If he made good time, and if he remembered the way, he should reach Aelf Fen before dusk.

The paths and tracks around the south-eastern edge of the fenlands were in reasonable condition for the season, for the weather had been dry so far this autumn, and Rollo's progress was steady and uneventful. His anxiety eased off slightly as the distance between him and Cambridge

64

increased, although he didn't for a moment lessen his extreme vigilance. It would have been so much more convenient had Lassair been in the town, and sometimes, when he thought he heard or saw something suspicious, he was angry with her for not being there when he had such need of her.

He knew it was unreasonable. He told himself firmly that it was probably a symptom of his fear. For he was afraid; although he couldn't have said why he was so sure, he knew without any doubt that somebody wanted to kill him.

He came to a stretch of good road. He put his heels to his horse's sides and increased his pace, first to a canter and then, unable to quell the alarm coursing through him, a gallop.

He arrived on the higher ground above Lassair's village as the sun was setting beyond the waters of the fens to the west. He needed somewhere secure to tether the horses, not wishing to advertise his presence to the whole village by riding up to her door. He had already passed the hall where the lord and his household lived, down to his left between him and the water. Lakehall. The name popped up from his memory; Lassair must have told him. Now he was level with the church.

In a corner of the graveyard beneath a yew tree, a man was digging. Turning his horse's head, Rollo rode down the gentle slope and hailed him.

'May I leave my horses under your watchful eye?' he asked. He put a hand on his purse.

The man's eyes had gone straight to it. 'You

may,' he replied, 'although if you tether them too close to this yew, they'll not be fit for much when you return for them.'

Rollo had extracted a coin, which he flipped towards the man. Transferring his spade to his left hand, the man stretched out his right and deftly caught it.

Nodding his thanks, Rollo dismounted and tied the horses' reins to a stumpy alder well out of reach of the yew. Removing a heavy leather bag from the second horse, he slung its strap over his shoulder and headed down into the village.

He thought at first that she wasn't there.

The depths of his distress told him, if he'd needed telling, just how much he was depending on her help.

He spent some time – too long, for his state of mind and his desperate impatience – watching her aunt's house and the house where her parents lived. The dwellings were small, and when anybody opened the doors to go in or out, the interiors were visible. Lassair was in neither house.

Rollo retreated to the shelter of the huge old oak that stood on the upland behind the village. He'd stood there before, and knew it was a good vantage point. Also, he remembered he'd seen Lassair standing just where he now stood, the last time he'd come to the village. She'd been talking to a fair-haired young man. Irrationally – he was forced to admit he wasn't his usual self – he thought that standing in the very place she had stood might help towards the success of this mission . . .

And then it seemed as if the spell had worked.

For he saw the young man with the smooth fair hair, going into a house that stood on the edge of the row lining the track through the village. The man appeared from nowhere and was looking over his shoulder. Spy that he was, Rollo instantly recognized someone trying not to be seen.

He was tempted to wait until it was fully dark, but haste had him in a stranglehold and he found he couldn't. He hurried down the slope and, slowing his pace, crept up to the house. Raising his hand before he could change his mind, he tapped on the door. The door was opened a crack. The fair-haired young man, suspicion written clearly on his face, stared out at him through narrowed eyes. He had a cut on his forehead, healing and starting to scab over. He said curtly, 'What do you want?'

Rollo almost put his shoulder to the door to shove it open and burst in. But that wasn't the way to do it. Forcing himself to speak quietly, he said, 'I am looking for Lassair. I believe you are a friend of hers, and wonder if you could tell me—'

Then suddenly the door was wide open, for someone else had shoved the young man out of the way so that he no longer held it almost shut. In a flurry of swift impressions, Rollo took in a sweet-smelling, clean interior, bedrolls beside the hearth, cheap but well-made shelves of pots and platters, a fire over which a pot of something fragrantly savoury was bubbling. A woman knelt beside it, stirring, and she looked up at Rollo with pale, alarmed eyes.

Right in front of him, staring up at him as if she couldn't believe what she was seeing, stood Lassair.

She looked dreadful. His first thought was that she was ill, but swiftly he dismissed it for if she was, she'd have been in the care of her healer aunt. He couldn't begin to guess why she was here, in the house of the young man and the older woman. Had she come to the village for a rest? Had she worn herself out caring for the wounded man?

Was her haggard appearance the outer sign of her grief at his death?

He stared into her deathly pale face. She was thinner, and the loss of flesh emphasized her high cheekbones, which were casting shadows on her face. Her eyes, dark-circled, looked huge. The crescent moon-shaped scar on her left cheek stood out clearly. She staggered slightly – she was obviously exhausted – and he put out his hand, steadying her.

'Rollo,' she breathed. 'What on earth are *you* doing here?'

He glanced at the young man and the woman, both of whom were watching intently. 'I need to speak to you, in private,' he said very quietly. Leaning closer – he could detect her familiar, sweet fragrance – he whispered, 'I have urgent need of your help.'

She spun round to look at the two people within. 'I'm going out for a while,' she said.

The woman made a noise of distress; of protest.

'It's all right, Froya,' Lassair said. 'This is Rollo, and he's a friend.' Then she stepped outside to join him and firmly closed the door.

He led her up the slope towards the higher ground. Twilight was swiftly advancing, and he doubted whether anybody would have spotted them. Nevertheless, he went on to the shelter of the oak tree, only then turning to her.

'Tell me what you want me to do,' she said.

He was deeply touched. *Here I am*, he thought, *turning up without warning and, apart from one brief meeting, after months of absence, and I ask her to help me, and instantly she asks what she has to do.*

Briefly he closed his eyes in a swift prayer of thanks for her loyalty and her love.

He reached out and took her hand.

'I have to go north,' he said, 'and I can't go alone because men are hunting for me who I believe may wish to harm me.' He wondered whether to tell her the truth – that it was not a question of *they may wish to harm me*, more of *they are without doubt out to kill me*. He decided against it. 'They are, however, looking for a man on his own. If we travel together in the guise of a lord and lady—' He heard her swift intake of breath and, knowing what she was about to say, forestalled the protest. 'Don't worry, I have horses and fine garments. The men who search for me will not look twice at a man and his wife together, and—'

But she didn't let him finish. 'I can't,' she

said flatly. 'I've had—' She stopped. 'I've been unwell.'

'Yes, so I see,' he said, putting all the sympathy he could muster into his voice. 'I'm sorry, Lassair. I can see you've been suffering. But I really need you. I hate to insist, but I truly believe it is a matter of survival.'

'*Your* survival.' She managed a faint smile.

'My survival,' he agreed.

There was a pause. To Rollo, his anxiety mounting, it seemed interminable.

Finally she sighed. Then – and she took her hand out of his, wrapping both arms around her slender body – 'When do you want to leave?'

'Straight away,' he said.

She shook her head. 'No.'

'At first light, then, before the village is awake.'

She smiled again. 'Then we'll have to leave *before* first light. People work hard here, from sunrise to sunset.'

'You'll come with me?' He could hardly believe it.

'Yes.'

'One more thing.' He knew it was pushing his luck but he had to do it.

Her eyes met his. 'What?'

He held out the large leather bag. 'You need to hide this in the safest place you can think of.'

She raised an eyebrow, 'I do, do I?'

'I'm sorry, I didn't mean to sound as if I was giving you an order.' He paused. 'It's valuable,' he said quietly. 'I've recently collected it from an agent of mine who lives locally.' Eleanor de Lacey, in common with others in England, in

70

France and further afield, was the custodian of a portion of his wealth, kept against an urgent need of funds such as this one. He'd already transferred quite a lot of the bag's contents into the purse on his belt, and the remainder would be much more accessible hidden out here in the wilds than in a house in Cambridge.

There was only one list of the names and locations of all those who guarded his wealth, and, aware that he was going into peril, Rollo had left it in Eleanor de Lacey's keeping. In case it ever went astray, it was in code.

Lassair took the bag. 'It's very heavy,' she observed.

'It contains a great deal of gold,' he replied.

She stared at him.

He reached out and briefly touched her shoulder. 'Hide it well, and keep the location secret,' he said. Then with a grin he added, 'If anything happens to me, it's yours.'

She didn't answer.

After a moment she turned and moved off. Then, stopping, she said, 'Have you a place to sleep?'

She wasn't, then, going to invite him to share that warm and cosy little house and that appetizing pot of stew.

'I'll find somewhere,' he replied.

She nodded. 'Until tomorrow, then.'

And she walked away.

Five

When I'd wrenched the door from Sibert's hand and flung it wide open to see Rollo standing there, I'd thought I had entered into the sort of delirium that took hold of Jack during the dreadful days when he was on fire with fever. In the handful of heartbeats of simply staring at Rollo, I was diagnosing myself: *You've slipped a baby, you've lost blood, you're not sleeping, you're imagining it!*

But then I almost fell – I felt very faint and the feel of my pounding heart was too high in my chest, its noise too loud in my ears – and when he reached out to hold me, his hand was strong and warm. And very real.

But I still couldn't believe he was there.

In that moment, he seemed to be the answer to a prayer of intense, aching need that I hadn't even managed to put into words.

So I went outside to hear what he wanted to ask of me, and, because he was Rollo, because he looked so desperate, because he needed me, because I'd loved him – still loved him, perhaps – because I was so sad and didn't know what I wanted, I agreed.

He'd said that men were after him who he thought wanted to harm him, but it was far, far worse than that. I'd seen fear in his eyes, heard it in his voice, and somehow even *smelt* it on

72

him. Without his having to say so, I knew without any doubt that he was running for his life.

He looked faintly affronted when I asked if he had a place to sleep for the hours until dawn. Perhaps he'd imagined I was going to invite him to come to Froya's house and settle down with the three of us beside the fire. It did occur to me, briefly, but for one thing, it wasn't my house and, for another, the thought of being with Rollo with two pairs of interested eyes watching was so uncomfortable that it wasn't to be entertained for a moment.

I left him standing under the ancient oak tree.

The bag over my shoulder was so heavy that it was making my back ache. I forced myself to ignore the pain, for I had quite a way to walk. I was heading for the safest place I could think of, to use Rollo's words, to hide his gold.

Aelf Fen is a small community. Its people know each other's business, and live in very basic dwellings shared by a number of people. Their animals live close by, often in lean-tos attached to the houses. The idea of a safe hiding place in or close by any of the houses is faintly absurd.

So here I was, trudging off across the marshy ground towards the fen edge, where the dark water laps up against the bulge of land on which Aelf Fen grew up. There's a faint path that runs to and fro between the stumpy willow and alder, and I can follow it even when the light is fading; I can follow it with my eyes shut.

Many, many generations ago, my fenland ancestors had constructed an artificial island just offshore on which to bury their revered dead. It's said in the record kept by the long line of our family's bards that our ancestor Aelfbryga spoke with the spirits, who not only showed her the secret way through the perilous marshland to the spot that would become Aelf Fen, but also instructed her in the building of the island. Most of the villagers give it a wide berth, fearing the presence of its resident spirits. But I am a frequent visitor: the spirits are those of my ancestors, and their shades do not frighten me.

The latest member of my family to be buried there was my paternal grandmother Cordeilla. I was very close to her in life, and sometimes, to my joy, she speaks to me from wherever she is now.

I had reached the fen edge. The weather had been unseasonably dry, and to my relief the water level was quite low. I ought to be able to wade out to the island without getting wet any higher than my thighs. I took off my boots, gathered up my skirts and tucked them in my belt, hitched the leather bag higher on my back and set off. The water was deeper than I'd anticipated, but not by much. I reached the island safely, and, giving a bow of reverence to the lines of ancestors buried on the far side, hurried over to Granny Cordeilla's grave.

I knelt down. 'I have something that has to be very well concealed,' I said, after my usual greeting, 'and I hope you don't take offence but hiding it out here with you is the best I can come up with.' I waited. Nothing.

'It's a bag of gold,' I went on, leaning right

74

down over the ground and whispering for Granny Cordeilla's ears alone, 'and it belongs to someone I thought – think – I love, but then I met someone else, and I believe I love him too, and for sure he loves me, and, oh, Granny, I was carrying his baby and I couldn't tell him because he'd have insisted we marry and I wasn't sure I wanted that, but then two days ago I lost it and now – now—' I was sobbing so hard that I couldn't go on.

And now that the baby is lost, it's the one thing you want more than anything in the world, said Granny Cordeilla's kind, loving voice. *I know, child, I know.*

I stretched out across her grave, arms extended as if I was hugging her. Somehow – I know it is physically impossible, but this is how it felt – I was aware that she was hugging me back.

After a while, feeling very slightly better, I sat up. As if she'd been waiting, Granny Cordeilla said, *It is very hard for a woman to love two men, and until she makes up her mind or circumstances decide for her, she brings nothing but pain to all three.*

Granny Cordeilla spoke from experience; I knew that, and I imagine she was aware that I knew. Whatever else happens the other side of the veil, I'm quite sure the dead acquire a mystical ability to understand what's going on in their living loved ones' minds.

Thinking about what Granny Cordeilla had just said, I murmured, 'So it's up to me to decide.'

Granny Cordeilla made the impatient snort

that had been so very typical of her, and despite everything I smiled.

'I'm going away with the man who gave me this bag.' I held it up as if for her inspection. 'It's full of gold, and I think he's probably a very wealthy man. I'm going to hide it here, with you, if that's all right.'

Granny Cordeilla made no reply, so I took that for acquiescence.

Her grave is covered by a huge slab of stone, and in the years she had lain there, grass has encroached around the edges. I located one corner – one of the two at her feet – and very carefully scraped back the turf, trying not to disturb the grass roots. Then, lying flat on the ground, I put my shoulder to the slab and, bracing my feet, straightened my legs. The slab was reluctant to move, but after a muscle-creaking effort, at last, with a soft crack, it shifted. I went on pushing, and soon had made a space large enough for the leather bag.

I didn't pause to look at the tiny, linen-wrapped body. It was probably too dark now to have made out any details, but I didn't want to put it to the test. I did notice that there was a scent of flowers coming up out of the ground, and this made me smile once more.

Now I had to replace the stone slab. This was a little easier, and I managed it without causing myself too much additional pain. When it had settled back into its accustomed slot, I smoothed the turf back over it. I stood up to inspect my work. I reckoned nobody would know what I'd just done unless I told them.

And who was there to come and search? My family were the only people who came out to the island, and only on the rare days that had some significance in the lives of our ancestors here. When several people wished to make the crossing, there was a stock of planks that we used to make a temporary bridge, supported by bracing struts affixed to stakes of old dark wood that our forebears had driven down into the black fen mud. But the planks and the bracing struts were not kept anywhere near the island.

It had been dry, as I've said. As I gave my thanks and made my farewells to Granny Cordeilla and waded back to land, I turned to look out over the fen. Then I did something I've only done once before and then under Gurdyman's tuition, for it is deep magic.

I prayed for rain.

Rain, to raise the level of the fen and prevent anybody from even being tempted to make the crossing to the island.

When I'd finished, panting, sweating – spell-casting is far more exhausting than I could ever have imagined – I went back to the village.

As later I settled down to sleep beside the hearth in Froya's house, I reflected how odd it was that only a short time after I'd been out in the darkness spell-making, I was inside a snug little house being lectured by the kind-hearted, anxious woman who'd been looking after me. 'You shouldn't have gone out at all, Lassair, never mind for so long!' she'd whispered worriedly when I returned. Glancing at the sleeping figure of Sibert, she went on, 'Are you sure you have taken no harm? You're not in pain?'

I assured her I was all right. It was a lie, as I was in fact in considerable pain, but, bearing in mind what I was about to tell her, it didn't seem wise to say so.

'Froya, the man who was here earlier is someone I know very well,' I said very quietly. 'He needs me to help him with something he has to do, and I've agreed to do so.' She began to protest, as I'd known she would, but I took her hand and spoke over her. 'I must go,' I said firmly. 'Sibert is almost back to normal now, and no longer needs my care. You've been so kind to me, and I'll never forget it, but you know what's happened to me.' She nodded, wide, pale eyes intent on mine. 'There are consequences,' I went on, 'one of which is that I'm very sad, and very confused.'

'Of course you are,' she breathed.

'I can't make any decisions all the time I stay here,' I murmured. 'I can truly be of use to – to my friend, so I've decided I may as well do as he asks.'

'But are you sure you're well enough?' Her smooth brow crumpled into a frown.

'Yes,' I said firmly. 'We'll be riding, not walking, so it won't be all that demanding.' I almost believed myself.

'I can't stop you,' Froya muttered. 'I—'

'Then don't try.' I squeezed her hand. 'But even though you've already done so much for me, there's one last thing I need to ask of you.'

'Go on,' she said.

'I have to leave very early in the morning, and there won't be time to speak to my parents or – or to the rest of my family.' There was no need to mention my aunt Edild by name. 'Would you tell them I've left? That I've had a summons from a friend and have gone to assist him?'

'I will,' she said. 'Your kin are used to your absences,' she added. 'They appear to bear them with equanimity.' She shot me a glance. 'As long as you always come back.'

It was with that veiled reminder that people loved me and would grieve to lose me, and that I had a duty to them to take care, that she had left me to return to her own bed.

I was awake before dawn. I slid out from under the covers, folding them and placing them on top of the rolled-up mattress in their daytime place in the corner of the room. I put on my outer garments, slung the strap of my leather satchel across my body – it hadn't taken long to pack my few possessions – and picked up my cloak and shawl. I stood for a moment, looking at Sibert, then at Froya. I sent them my most grateful thanks, Froya in particular, and a blessing. Then I opened the door, closing it quietly behind me, and set out in the misty grey half-light for the oak tree to wait for Rollo.

I didn't wait long. I caught movement out of the corner of my eye, over behind the church, and presently three shapes emerged from the cloudy white veil that had rolled off the water to fill the lower ground. Rollo walked ahead, leading two horses. Both were bays and had a distinct look of having come from the same dam. As they drew closer and I could make out more detail I saw that one was a mare and one a gelding, and both were quite a lot bigger than any horse I'd ever ridden.

'Good morning,' Rollo greeted me. 'You're very prompt. Did you sleep?'

'Yes.'

He leaned closer, frowning. 'You still look very pale. Are you sure you're all right? We'll be riding for much of the day.'

'I'll tell you if I'm not,' I said shortly. I wasn't at all sure about my ability to ride at all, never mind *for much of the day*, but I wasn't going to say so.

'I thought you'd like the mare,' he went on, 'since she's slightly smaller, but you can have the gelding if you prefer.'

Up close, both horses looked huge. 'The mare is fine,' I said. 'What's her name?'

'Starlight.'

'Isn't that more appropriate for a pale-coloured horse?' The mare had shoved her nose into my hand, and I smiled.

'Push her mane off her brow,' Rollo said.

I did so, revealing a large white star. 'What's yours called?'

'Bruno.' He was busy with the bags, checking the fastenings. 'I have clothing for you – for us both – fit for our roles of a wealthy lord and his lady, but we'll ride for a while before we change into them. There's no need for disguises until we're going to be among other people.' He looked at me. 'We need to go north, eventually

80

joining up with the great road that runs up the east coast. Is there a way you can take us that avoids returning south towards Cambridge?'

I didn't much want to go anywhere near Cambridge either.I thought hard. 'It's possible in a dry season to go due west across the fens,' I said after a moment. 'You head for Ely, then across the marsh to Chatteris, and eventually you get to Peterborough. Although it can be treacherous and it's very hard to find, there is a safe way, provided the water level is not too high.'

He was staring straight into my eyes. 'I remember the safe way from Ely to your village,' he said very softly.

I drew in a sharp breath. Of course he did: I took him on it soon after our first meeting. Circumstances had forced my hand and given me no option but to try out the strange skill I seemed to possess, of finding things that were hidden to others' eyes. When I was a child, I'd used it to locate lost objects. That day, on the cusp between girlhood and womanhood, I'd used it to save three lives.[4]

I couldn't think of anything to say.

'It's been dry recently,' he went on in his normal voice. 'Will we come to grief if we take this secret path?'

'I can only do my best,' I replied.

'That's good enough for me.' He helped me up into the saddle, checked the stirrup leathers and the girths, and mounted the other horse.

[4] See *Mist over the Water*.

Then he extended his hand, palm uppermost in invitation, and said, 'Lead on.'

I remembered last night, when I had stood on the land facing the island and done everything within my power to bring on rain. Now, I sent up an even more urgent plea that it wouldn't begin to fall until we'd reached the far side of the fens.

I soon discovered that having something of vital importance to absorb every bit of my mind was just what I needed. From the moment when, off to the north of Aelf Fen, I led us down onto the first of the winding, narrow, perilous little paths across the marshland, everything else, including my own discomfort, melted away.

It's very hard to describe the dowsing ability – of which this finding of the secret way was, I suppose, a part – to someone who can't do it. You have to put your mind in a light trance state, deliberately emptying it. My aunt Edild, who first encouraged me to develop the skill, used to say, 'Breathe deeply. Put aside everything else and concentrate. The ways are there and will reveal themselves to you. Be calm.'

It helps, I find, to ask the spirits for their assistance. They are always there, although I don't know who or what they are. Here in the fens and close to my own village, I suspect they are the shades of my ancestors. It's a reassuring thought.

That day, with Rollo, the spirits were both listening and in a helpful mood. As we set out along the tricky little track – it appeared to be

82

the only ribbon of firm ground in a vast expanse of water and bog – I felt the tingle of their presence. And, as I stared ahead, I saw the path quite clearly, snaking ahead of me, twisting this way and that across the fen and lit by a very pale, blueish light. All I had to do was keep faith with those who I felt so close beside me and keep going.

It wasn't easy. At times our horses splashed through water, occasionally rising almost up to their bellies. At times the path doubled back on itself, so that I thought I'd missed the way and was about to get us fatally lost. But when that happened, I put myself deeper in my trance and let my guides take over. And, an unknowable amount of time later – the sun was quite high, so morning must have been well advanced – we were on a stretch of higher, firmer ground and Rollo, breaking a very long silence, said, 'I believe that must be Ely.'

He was pointing over to the south, to where the bulk of an island rose up out of the mist. I heard a song of triumph in my head, and for a moment felt relief flood through me. But then I thought, *We are less than halfway across, and the next part I have never tried*, and I didn't feel so confident.

It took us until the sun was going down, directly ahead of us, to reach the far side of the fens. We had passed Chatteris – I sent words of love to my dearest Elfritha, there in her convent living the life she had yearned for since childhood – and silently asked her to pray for the safety of whatever mission Rollo had persuaded

83

me to join him in. But I was in an odd frame of mind, in which it didn't seem to matter very much what happened to me. Then, perhaps six or seven miles after Chatteris, Rollo and I realized simultaneously that the watery crossing was behind us.

'Well done,' he said. 'I knew you were the person to do it, if anyone could.'

I looked at him. 'To get you across the fens without returning to Cambridge, you mean? Well, that's good. I'm glad I've been of use.'

He picked up the irony, and must have understood instantly that his remark hadn't been very tactful. 'Lassair, it's a bonus that you have this strange skill,' he said softly. 'It's not why I wanted your company. Of course it isn't!' he added forcefully.

I smiled, and we rode on.

We found a humble inn beside the track to spend the night. It wasn't much – it wasn't very clean, and the only accommodation was a couple of spaces on the straw of the communal bed chamber – but we were utterly spent, as were the horses, and neither of us wanted to ride any further. I sensed that the weather was changing. The skies had been clear all day but now clouds were building in the south-west. Besides, I was in quite a lot of pain – I'd only stayed on the bay mare for the last few miles by willpower and the anticipation of dosing myself from the remedies in my satchel as soon as we stopped – and anything would have done. As it turned out, the evening meal – shared with a handful of other weary travellers, the tavern keeper, his wife and his daughter – was very good (or possibly Rollo and I were very hungry), and the ale was excellent. I'd asked for hot water as soon as we'd arrived, and, the pain-easing draught having already taken effect, I was able to enjoy both to the full. When we stumbled our way to bed, I fell asleep almost as soon as I'd rolled myself up in my cloak.

Just before oblivion took me, I heard the rain begin.

We left early, not pausing to eat but taking fresh bread and a couple of slices of smoked ham with us to consume on the way. Rollo, I sensed, wanted to be off before anyone got a good look at us in daylight.

It was apparent that it had been raining for much of the night, although now it had eased off to a fine, soft drizzle that wasn't all that distinguishable from low cloud. I looked out over the water, just visible in the distance over to our right. Had anyone been attempting to follow the path we'd taken yesterday, they wouldn't have stood a chance. And I thought, as well, that the water level on the edge of Aelf Fen would also have risen, making access to the island far more difficult.

It was reassuring to feel that the spirits were still on our side.

When we'd ridden for perhaps two or three miles, Rollo led the way off the remote track we were on – we hadn't seen a soul – and under the shelter of a dense stand of pines. He dismounted, indicating that I should do the same.

We ate our bread and ham, drank some water, and then he unfastened one of the bags tied behind his saddle. 'It's time,' he said, drawing out rolled-up garments and a pair of boots in very shiny chestnut leather, 'to adopt our new personas.' He turned to me with a grin. 'You first, my lady.'

I watched as he spread my new clothes out on the thick carpet of pine needles. Underlinen, beautifully made, the fabric fine and delicate, with pin-tucking around the neck. A gown in soft, supple wool, in a shade of deep, brownish red that I'd never seen before, let alone worn. Those boots, as soft to the touch as their appearance had led me to suspect. And, last of all, a cloak, hooded, fur-lined, in a shade just a little deeper than the gown.

'I won't need that,' I said, pointing at the cloak. 'I already have one.' I held up a fold of the cloak that Jack had bought for me.

Rollo gave it a swift glance and said, 'Put yours away and take this one. It's warmer and of much better quality.'

He doesn't know, I told myself very firmly. *He cannot possibly be aware that Jack gave me my cloak. That hearing him dismiss it so decisively is hurting me like a thin blade in the heart.*

I was still holding Jack's cloak between my hands. Out of my memories I saw him, the day he'd presented me with it. He'd still been so ill that he couldn't even sit up, and I'd been trying to persuade him to eat, although he'd kept saying he felt too sick.

Jack.

You left Jack, I reminded myself.

I took off the cloak, rolled it carefully and gave it to Rollo to pack away. Then I picked up the beautiful garments lying on the grass and went behind a tree to change into them.

I forced myself to think of everyday, practical matters. I was now dressed as a lady, so I should brush out and re-braid my hair. One of my own white caps would do, since I made sure to buy the finest I could afford; they were, I felt, the badge I wore to show that I was a healer, and must be the best. I could draw up the hood of my dark red cloak over the cap, and look as fine as any lady riding out with her lord.

I stepped out from behind the tree. I didn't know why I'd been so modest; Rollo and I had briefly been lovers, a long time ago, and our bodies held no secrets for each other. But that was then, and this was now.

He too had changed into new, rich garments and he looked superb. He had shaved and his bright fair hair hung brushed and glossy to his shoulders. As he turned to look at me, his dark brown eyes widened. 'My lady,' he said, holding out his hand.

'My lord,' I replied, taking it.

He was still looking at me. When he spoke – he said, 'What shall we call ourselves?' – I had the sense that he was having to force his mind away from wherever it was.

'I've always liked the name Sybil,' I said. I was still holding his hand, and my blood was pounding. It was an effort to speak lightly.

'Lady Sybil,' he repeated. 'And I'll be Odo. I

87

look like a Norman, so I'd better have a well-known Norman name.'

'And where do we come from, if anybody should enquire?'

'If they do, we'll tell them to mind their own business. If they persist, we'll say London. We'll be on the road that leads north from London, so that'll be credible.'

'We're travelling to the home of my sister Hild,' I went on, 'who is newly wed to a fine young lord with estates near Lincoln, where I am to attend her in her first confinement.'

He grinned. 'And if and when we get to Lincoln?'

'We'll simply move my imaginary sister's location progressively further north.'

He helped me into the saddle. As I took up the reins, he frowned. 'I forgot about gloves,' he said. 'No lady rides without them, so, the first chance we get, I'll buy some.'

With that prosaic thought, we left our little pine wood and set out for the road leading into the north.

Jack Chevestrier was taking his daily exercise. Before she left, Lassair had told him – no, commanded him – to go out walking every day. She had explained how his body had become wasted after weeks of immobility, and she said the only way to restore himself to his former strength was to do a little more with each excursion.

It sounded sensible and sound. It was only once he'd begun putting the theory into practice

that he understood something rather funda-
mental: she hadn't told him how much it was
going to hurt.

But he persevered. By the time she returned
– again, the silent dialogue with himself allowed
no room for doubt that she *would* return – he
would be able to show her how faithfully he'd
been following her orders.

Today the air smelt sweet after the heavy overnight rain. He paused on the Great Bridge to
watch the water flowing slowly beneath. The
level, he noticed absently, was quite a lot higher.

He moved on, making his slow, painful way
along the well-used road that passed to the
eastern side of the busy centre of town and the
market square. He'd set himself a challenging
target this morning, for he was going to walk to
Gaspard Picot's brash new house, which was
some way beyond St Bene't's Church. By the
time he reached the church, he was wondering
if he'd been too ambitious. He was sweating
heavily, in a great deal of pain and feeling dizzy.
And I still have the walk back, he reminded
himself miserably.

Cambridge was overflowing with priests,
but just when he could have done with some
kindly and charitable cleric asking if they could
help and hurrying to fetch him a restorative
mug of cool water, none appeared. After a
while, Jack thought he felt sufficiently recovered
to proceed.

Finally, reaching his destination, Jack stood
beneath the shadow of a ruined wall – presumably
all that remained of a row of former dwellings

– and looked out at what Gaspard Picot had made for himself. He recalled what his fellow lawman Ranald had said about the sheriff's nephew having caused such animosity by building his grand new house so close to the meagre dwellings of the poor. Now that he was there, seeing for himself, Jack thought that Gaspard Picot's brutish offence was even worse, for it was quite clear he'd in fact destroyed quite a lot of lowly little houses to make room for his. The tendency to help himself to what he wanted without any consideration of the rights of others was clearly a trait that ran in the family; Jack remembered how Sheriff Picot had infuriated the burgesses of the town by taking over the common pastures for his own use. The monks had some choice names for the sheriff, of which *hungry lion*, *filthy swine* and *dog without shame* were some of the mildest.

Gaspard Picot's house was in the form of a long hall, with a private area for the family's use at the far end. Enclosed by a stout wooden fence containing a single gate, the edifice stood up high and proud, raised above ground level to accommodate the capacious cellars beneath, where, no doubt, Gaspard's vast supplies of goods were stored. A short flight of stone steps led up to the entrance, and the paired oak doors, heavily studded with iron, were firmly closed.

Noticing a narrow wooden bench set into the wall a short way off, beneath the sweeping branches of a willow tree, Jack went along to it and, with huge relief, sat down. The sweat cooled on his skin, and he shivered. He was just coming to the conclusion that it would be unwise to stay there much longer when, over to his right, he noticed a dark figure standing under a trio of apple trees. The man must have moved very slightly, for Jack had already studied the area quite carefully and had seen nobody. And, even though he now knew the man was there, he couldn't see him any more . . .

He leaned back against the wall. So someone else was watching the late Gaspard Picot's house. That had to be the object of the dark-robed man's interest, for there wasn't anything else here. The ruins of the destroyed hovels formed a cordon in the immediate vicinity of the big new hall, but nobody lived in them any more. The nearest alleys of inhabited dwellings were some distance back towards the town centre, and the dark figure had his back to them.

So, Jack thought, *two of us watch and wait.*

All thoughts of starting on his return journey having flown, he turned his attention back to the house. And just then, one of the great doors was opened and a small group of people emerged. Two men came first, one getting on in years and stout, the second younger and fitter-looking – servants, by their demeanour – followed by a woman, fussing and worrying at someone close behind her. Two more women brought up the rear. The serving men stood back as they reached the foot of the steps and Jack had a clear sight of the woman at the centre of the group.

He knew immediately that this was Gaspard Picot's widow. She wore a heavy veil in a sombre shade; black or perhaps dark grey. So voluminous

91

were its folds that, unable to see properly, she almost missed her footing and, with an impatient gesture, flung the veil back over her shoulders. She was just as Jack's man Ranald had described, down to the pale, rabbity eyes and the skinny, flat-chested figure. Head in the air, and an expression on her lean face that suggested she knew the whole world was beneath her.

The little party made its way across the courtyard before the hall and out onto the road, where more servants appeared, falling in before and behind their mistress. The lady Elwytha, Jack reflected, proceeded like a queen on a royal progress.

But then, ashamed, he arrested the critical thought. She was a veiled widow because Jack had killed her husband, and that was something he wasn't going to let himself forget.

He waited until the lady and her escort had reached a bend in the road, then gathered his strength and prepared to stand up. But then, once again, movement from over to the right caught his eye. He leaned back against the wall, concealing himself behind the sweeping branches, and watched.

The secretive figure was hurrying away, following the road taken by the widow Picot and her servants. He was intent on trailing them without being noticed, moving forward in short bursts of speed then pausing again to make sure nobody had turned round and observed him. He had little spare attention for anything else, and he was going to pass quite close to Jack on his bench.

As he approached, Jack studied him. He was of average height, and apparently not overly large, although because of the dark, enfolding garments it was hard to tell. The cloak had a deep hood, drawn forward so that the man's face was shadowed. He had arranged a fold of cloth across his mouth and chin. Jack had an impression of intensely dark eyes, narrowed in concentration.

The man was very near now. Some instinct told Jack that he must not be seen, and he sat totally immobile. The dark figure passed within perhaps ten paces of him, but he didn't once look in Jack's direction.

When he had gone – breaking into a run, for the sheriff's widow and her servants had now disappeared from view – Jack was quite surprised at how relieved he felt.

Six

Rollo and I rode northwards. We were on what looked like a fine, well-kept and regularly maintained road that I thought at first must be the most important and greatest-used one, although Rollo told me it was one of several and there were others of even better quality. It made me realize how unsophisticated I must seem, in his worldly eyes.

As the day began to draw to a close, I hoped Rollo was thinking about where we'd stay for the night. I was in pain and wanted very much to stop riding, dismount, eat and sleep. I should have been able to say this to him, but I couldn't. He seemed to have withdrawn himself from me. I guessed he was deep in his own mind, working out his plans, and, while fully understanding the peril he was in, nevertheless it irked that he was so uncommunicative. I had, I reminded myself, come along with him at his urgent request and purely in order to help him escape from whoever was hunting him. It surely wouldn't have hurt him to address a remark or two my way from time to time. He hadn't even told me who he was running from and why he was being hunted. He'd simply told me he was in danger, and needed my help, and that appeared to be all the explanation he was going to give.

As these resentful thoughts were running

provocatively through my mind, he turned and, with a smile, said, 'I'm sorry, Lassair, for being so silent. I've been working out what to do, and I forgot to include you. I'm far too used to travelling alone,' he added.

It was reasonable, I supposed. 'I understand,' I said briefly.

His smile widened, and I guessed he wasn't fooled by my frosty reply. 'I need to find out what King William is doing and where he is,' he went on. 'I have given him loyal service, and that entitles me to his protection. It's usually the way with kings and great lords that they reward—'

'I don't want to hear a lecture on the ways of the powerful and mighty,' I interrupted irritably. 'What I would like to hear, however, is a brief summary of who you're running from, why they wish to harm you and what you've done to annoy them, although on reflection the last two may amount to the same thing.' He began to answer but I was angry now and didn't let him. 'Presumably, since you're hoping for the king's protection, the person you've upset is his enemy, for otherwise there would be no certainty that King William would take your side over this other man's. Since I recall from our previous encounters that you act as an agent of some sort for the king, then I would further venture to suggest that whatever caused this person to set off in pursuit of you was in some way connected with the king's business. Since you've put yourself in danger through acting for King William, you're planning on asking him to protect you from the consequences, which seems only right and fair, although of course I can't speak for how kings see such matters and he may very well say that he pays you to take risks and isn't responsible when the taking of them puts you in peril.' I realized I'd run out of words and abruptly stopped.

He said after a moment, 'In essence, you have it, although there are one or two little details that aren't quite accurate. If I may, though, I will explain later, once we're – well, later.'

'Very well.' I didn't think there was any point in trying to persuade him. 'So, the king is in the north?'

'Possibly,' Rollo replied.

'*Possibly?* But if you're not sure, why are we heading that way?'

He grinned. 'That's what I was thinking about so exclusively and impolitely just now. Or, to be precise, I was wondering how to turn a supposition into a certainty.'

'And did your lengthy introspection come up with an answer?'

'Of sorts. I know a man in the village up ahead.' He nodded towards a collection of various-sized buildings huddled around a small church, just coming into sight around a gentle bend in the road. There was a fair-sized farm, a dilapidated manor house and perhaps fifteen or twenty single-roomed dwellings. 'This place is very close to the most frequented of the roads leading north, and the man of whom I speak – he's a priest, in fact – keeps his eyes open for movements up and down it, in particular, those of large bodies of men.'

'Such as armies, and kings at the head of great processions?'

'Precisely.'

We rode on for a few moments. Then I said, 'Rollo, will your priest also be able to offer us accommodation for the night?'

'Not personally, no, since what little space he has is always full of starving vagrants, but I'm planning to ask him about that, too. Don't worry,' he added encouragingly, 'without a doubt there will be households in the vicinity which will be willing to put up Lord Odo and Lady Sybil. And I bet you a coin to a kiss that we'll be more comfortable than we were last night.'

He put heels to the brown gelding's sides, kicking him to a canter, and set off up the road towards the church.

By the time I'd ridden at a more sedate pace to join him, he was already in conversation with his priest. The man was young, red-haired and bearded, broad in the shoulder and tall. As he turned to look up at me, the bright blue eyes confirmed his ancestry. 'My lady, welcome to Elsby,' he said with a smile. Holding out a hand, he added, 'I'm Father Oswald. May I help you to dismount?'

Once I was standing beside him, I realized he was even taller than I'd thought.

Rollo, clearly impatient with the priest's social manners, said, 'Please, Father, go on with what you were telling me.' Intercepting the priest's swift glance at me, he muttered, 'It's all right, you can speak in front of her.'

'Very well. As I was just saying, I've not noticed any large-scale movements on the road these past days and weeks. Nor any small-scale ones, come to that, other than local traffic, and usually I recognize people who go to and fro on a regular basis. There are the farmers, of course, and the merchants, naturally, and—'

Rather pointedly, Rollo cleared his throat.

'Yes, well, you don't want to hear about that.' He leaned closer to Rollo and, lowering his voice, said, 'But there was one particular party who'll interest you, or, rather, what they had to say. There's talk of a big row between the king and Malcolm of Scotland, and the word was that the Scottish king's done something to annoy King William, King William's reaction has angered Malcolm and he – Malcolm – has gone off in a cold fury to plan his retaliation.'

Rollo nodded. 'And where did this intelligence come from?'

'It was a party heading for Landsay. They stopped here briefly to water the horses. That's Landsay Castle, my lady' – courteously he turned to me – 'the home of our Lord Edwin, and, he being a loyal king's man, no doubt the party of which I speak were heading to Landsay to discuss what sort of threat is posed by the Scottish king's intransigence.'

Father Oswald, I reflected, could also describe himself as a loyal king's man, since, without apparently knowing more than the bare bones of this dispute between the two kings, he had come to the instant conclusion that it was Malcolm who was being unreasonable.

'When was this?' Rollo asked.

'Three days ago – no, four.'

'And did anyone in this party happen to mention whether the king was on his way north?'

'Not that I can recall. You'd be best advised to do as they did and head for Landsay Castle, since Lord Edwin is likely to be better informed. You know the way?'

Slowly Rollo nodded. Then, reaching into the purse suspended from his belt, he took out coins. 'Thank you, Father.' The priest held out his hand and there was a clink as Rollo dropped the coins into his palm. 'For the poor box.'

'The poor will be grateful, as am I,' Father Oswald said.

He was bestowing his blessing upon us even as we mounted up and rode away.

It was only some six or eight miles to Landsay, but our route took us north-east, towards the Wash. The ground became steadily more water-logged. After a while, the rain intensified. At times now the track was under water, sometimes reaching halfway up our horses' legs.

Whoever had built Landsay must have understood the locality and its particular problems and threats, for the castle – small, unassuming and isolated – stood on the only piece of raised ground for miles. The rise overlooked a waterway that wound its way off north-east towards the marsh and, eventually, the Wash. The stream would normally have been narrow and insignificant, but the overnight rain and the day-long misty drizzle had widened it. In places, it had burst its banks.

The castle was enclosed by a paling fence, in good repair, and the stout gate was watched over by a simple tower from which a couple of guards were looking out. Rollo gave our names and the gate opened. Life was easy when you had money and a lord's title, I reflected; wealth obviously trusted wealth, for this Lord Edwin had clearly instructed his men to admit anyone of his own station who came asking for shelter.

But I was cold, wet, tired, hungry and in pain, and I certainly wasn't going to complain about the injustice of the world when it was working in my favour. It would only be temporary, I was well aware, so I intended to make the very most of it.

Perhaps Lord Edwin really did know a man called Odo who looked a little like Rollo; perhaps he was merely being polite, or even pretending to recognize someone who in truth he couldn't remember at all purely so as not to appear dim; either way, he claimed to have a memory of meeting 'Lord Odo' at some wild-sounding festivity some time in the vague past, and greeted Rollo like an old friend. I was afforded the same warm welcome, and in my case, Lord Edwin included an embrace and a kiss on the cheek.

He also tried to include a surreptitious fondle of my breast, which I managed to foil by pretending to cough and swiftly putting my hand to my mouth, knocking his arm aside. Quite firmly.

I might not have had very much to do with the civilized and mannered world of lords and ladies, but I knew a lecher when I encountered one.

'Now you are wet and weary, so we shall offer you the chance to restore yourselves before we reconvene for our evening!' Lord Edwin said brightly. We were standing in his hall, on the lowest floor of the castle, and an archway behind us led away into the darkness of a passage. Lord Edwin turned in the direction of the arch and yelled out a command, and almost instantly two servants appeared: a tall, spare man clad in black and a sharp-eyed, skinny woman whose dark gown was covered by a clean white apron. 'Take Lord Odo and his lady up to the guest chamber,' he commanded. The tall man nodded and the skinny woman bobbed a curtsey, then, beckoning to us with a muttered 'My lord? My lady?' the man led the way out of the hall, along the passage and up a narrow, steep wooden stair.

The chamber was stunning.

A fire was laid ready in the hearth, and the woman knelt to put a flame to it. As the kindling caught, she went round the chamber lighting a couple of torches set in sconces on the wall, as well as lamps and some candles. Beeswax candles: the sweet scent was unmistakable. There was not a great deal of furniture in the room – bed, a chest or two, a bench and a chair beside the hearth – but everything was of excellent quality. The walls were hung with woollen hangings.

As was the wide, sumptuously dressed bed.

Lord Edwin, clearly, was a very wealthy man.

The tall man had gone off to fetch hot water and the skinny woman was spreading out our damp cloaks beside the rapidly growing fire. I felt Rollo's eyes on me. Spinning round, I saw that he was standing beside the bed.

Deep within me, I felt as if a gentle but strong fist had slowly clenched.

There was barely time to wash our hands and our mud- and rain-splashed faces, and for me to re-dress my hair and arrange a small veil, before we were summoned back down to the hall.

Lord Edwin kept a board that more than adequately fulfilled the promise of his wealthy abode. We were served wine in silver goblets, soft, fresh bread, meats, a wonderfully rich beef stew cooked with fruits – apples, raisins and dates – seafood in little dumplings, honey-glazed carrots, baked apples and a sweet, spicy custard. While we ate, Lord Edwin asked us where we were bound, and we told him our story. Then, clearly eager to impress us with his awareness of royal matters, he told us all that he knew about the king's present whereabouts, his plans for the immediate future and his state of mind. I guessed that much, if not most, of it was conjecture, for how could a rural lord living miles from any centres of civilization and government know so much?

'See, our William is angry with Malcolm because the king believes it's up to him, not Malcolm, to arrange a marriage for Malcolm's daughter Edith. And she's a spirited lass, by all accounts, and not a one to welcome a man telling her when and whom to marry, be that man her father or her king or both.' He frowned, momentarily having confused himself. He'd been drinking freely, and had reached the state of inebriation where you keep repeating yourself and get cross and red in the face when people contradict you. Rollo seemed happy to let him ramble on, and I guessed that maybe one utterance in a dozen might just be helpful.

'So Malcolm in turn has taken deep offence at William's cold refusal to meet him and talk it all over until Malcolm does right by him, by which he means he wants Malcolm to bend the knee, apologize and promise to be a better boy in future.' He hiccupped. 'It's a stalemate, that's what it is.' Lord Edwin nodded sagely. 'That's what I say: a *stalemate*.' He seemed to be rather pleased with the word, repeating it several times in a variety of voices and then falling into a fit of giggling.

'So you believe King William will amass a force of men and go north to meet the threat?' Rollo asked.

'No,' Lord Edwin replied. 'No, no, no, no, no.' Watching Rollo, I saw him suppress a smile. 'Doesn't need to go *himself*, does he?' Lord Edwin went on. 'He has good, loyal, fighting men in the north who are more than capable of dealing with Malcolm's border raiders, foremost among them . . .' He ground to a halt, his face the picture of perplexity, and raised a hand to scratch his head. 'Now what the devil's the man's name?'

Rollo and I waited.

'*Mobray!*' Lord Edwin shouted triumphantly. 'Robert Mobray, Earl of Northumbria! He'll be the man for this task, you mark my words, and

103

he'll protect William's borders for him from this threat, just see if he doesn't.'

'So where, do you think, is King William?' Rollo asked quietly.

'Gloucester.'

'What makes you say that?'

But Lord Edwin was busy yelling for more wine – the jug had emptied itself into his goblet – and didn't answer.

We all had our goblets topped up once again – Rollo and I had drunk little, although our caution hadn't held our host back – and I guessed he was as sober as I was. Then Lord Edwin raised his cup to Rollo. 'You look like a man who can fight,' he pronounced. 'You should go north and offer your sword to what's his name, the Northumbrian fellow. You'll be welcome up there.'

Rollo smiled. 'I should be glad to add my own small contribution to the fight,' he said smoothly. 'Before I can proceed to the border lands, however, I must escort Lady Sybil safely to her sister's house.'

'Her sister?' Lord Edwin looked confused for a moment, then his face cleared. 'Ah, yes, you told me earlier. The lady who is to have a child. And you're going to help, bless your kind heart!' He turned to me, picked up my hand and dripped a wet, clumsy kiss in my palm. I was very glad I wasn't seated near enough for him to kiss me anywhere else. 'Once that has been achieved, however,' Rollo was saying, 'then I will ride north.'

* * *

We lay side by side in the luxurious bed. The room was lit only by the soft glow of the dying fire, and the near-darkness was comforting.

I sensed the proximity of his strong, lean body. I could even have told myself I felt his warmth, but in truth the bed was wide and we were an arm's length apart.

I didn't know whether I wanted him to turn and take me in his arms or fall swiftly asleep and leave me alone.

I felt very, very sad.

After a while he said, in a very quiet voice, 'I'm sorry that he died.'

So lost was I in the confusion of my own miserable thoughts that, initially, I didn't understand.

'I'm not surprised, though,' Rollo went on. 'I know how skilful you are, and it was obvious you'd do everything within your power, but I saw with my own eyes how badly wounded he was, and how he bled. You mustn't blame yourself, Lassair, for—'

'He didn't.'

Rollo fell silent.

For what felt like a very long time, neither of us said a word.

Eventually it was he who made a move. He reached out and took my hand. Then, softly, kindly, he said, 'I was afraid you'd think me unkind and callous – and over-preoccupied with saving my own skin – because I didn't ask you about him straight away. I thought, you see, that your presence in Aelf Fen meant he was dead. When I saw how you looked – how deathly pale, how sick and tormented – I believed it served to confirm my assumption. Then I didn't know how to speak of him without upsetting you further. You agreed to do as I asked and help me – set out with me on this journey – and I thought you welcomed the chance to get right away from your memories.' He gave my hand a squeeze. 'I'm so sorry.'

My face was wet with tears. I didn't know whether I was weeping for Jack, who I had abandoned and from whom I'd withheld a very important truth, or for Rollo, shocked into accepting one reality when for quite a long time he'd believed in another.

'I'm sorry, too,' I managed to say. 'I should have explained.'

'He – you—' Rollo stopped and began again. 'He's better, then? Recovering? I'm only saying that because you're not with him. Because you'd felt it was safe to leave him and return to your village.'

'He's going to be all right.' I couldn't elaborate. If I let myself think about Jack, by himself in that isolated little house, dumped back in his lonely life, still far from recovered from a wound that would have killed most men, I knew I'd break down completely.

Through the waves of my own misery, I was aware of Rollo, tense beside me. I could tell his state of mind from the way he was holding my hand. I had utterly failed to tell Jack the truth he had the right to know; was I going to fail as abjectly with Rollo?

I wasn't ready to speak of the lost baby, but I owed him as much of an explanation as I could manage.

'Rollo, I don't really know how I feel,' I said after another long silence. 'About Jack or about you, I mean. You're right, in a way, when you said you thought I'd come with you to get away from my memories. It's not precisely that, but more that I undertook to help you because it was better than staying in Aelf Fen and not knowing what to do with myself.'

'Thank you for being so honest,' he murmured. I sensed he was smiling. But then, in a different tone, he said, 'I can tell you've been unwell. I won't ask' – I must have made some small sound – 'but I would like to say that, given that you're obviously in pain quite a lot of the time, I appreciate your company all the more.' He gave my hand a final squeeze and then let go of it. The bedclothes rustled as he turned on his side, away from me. 'And, much as I'd like for us to go back to being the lovers we once were, I understand that a lot of time has gone by during which I failed utterly to contact you, and also that, with no promises made, you were free to love another.'

Once again I was at a loss for words.

I thought he was settling for sleep. But, as I too turned on my side and snuggled under the covers, he said very softly, 'None of which means, of course, that I shan't be doing my utmost to persuade you to come back to me.'

I woke to daylight, and to the sight of Rollo seated beside the hearth, expression intent, apparently deep in thought.

I felt awkward about referring to our conversation of the previous night. Fortunately, it seemed that he did too. After wishing me good morning and asking how I'd slept – soundly and uninterruptedly – he said, 'I've been working out what to do.' He got up and came to sit on the edge of the bed, leaning close and speaking very softly. 'I believe there's an opportunity here that will assist us. If I, or in fact *we*, can persuade Lord Edwin and his household that we really are going north, there's a good chance that the men who are after me will find this out and set off after us. We won't be going north, of course, because Lord Edwin told us last night with utter certainty that the king's in Gloucester.'

'And you believe him?' I wondered why he'd take the word of a garrulous drunk.

He smiled, and I guessed the same thought had occurred to him. 'Well, he's not the first person who's told me that. And overall it makes sense. King William isn't likely to set out on a costly campaign when he's confident someone on the spot can achieve the same end.'

'So where *will* we go?' I demanded.

'We,' Rollo replied, 'will head for Gloucester, where I shall achieve my purpose of reminding my king how valuable I am to him, and hope to put myself under his protection until this present danger is past.'

I sank back into the pillows. Gloucester. I had only the vaguest notion of where it was and how long it would take to get there; even less idea of what on earth I was to do once we'd arrived.

But then, I reminded myself, nothing in this

world was certain, and there was little point in getting anxious about something that might not happen.

Heartened by that thought, I shooed Rollo off the bed and got up.

Seven

We didn't go anywhere that day, for the atrocious weather forbade it. As we ate our breakfast the wind increased to a howl, and even from inside the hall we could hear the rain drumming down on every external surface. Stepping to the doorway to look outside, we saw a solid curtain of water.

'Stay here!' Lord Edwin shouted happily above the fury of the elements. I'd already come to the conclusion that he didn't receive many visitors. Since he was a man who clearly enjoyed company, that must be hard. 'We've food and drink aplenty, and I'd welcome your company on a day when nobody will venture out of doors unless he has to!'

It was a good chance to put into practice our plans to mislead the household. Rollo sat in the hall with Lord Edwin and questioned him at length about the best routes north (although, I suspected, he probably knew the roads better than Lord Edwin). And I too did what I could. Returning to my room in the early afternoon on the pretext of resting in preparation for setting out the next day, it wasn't long before the skinny, sharp-eyed maid came sidling in, offering to brush my hair, wash out some small linens or scrub the mud from my boots. Accepting the last as the least intimate task, I slipped into the role of bored woman engaging in a cosy domestic conversation in order to help pass the long hours of a wet afternoon. I told her all about my imaginary sister and the sister's confinement, adding quite a lot of details garnered from tending other first-time mothers to enliven the story. I made sure to describe my sister's husband's beautiful house, close to the fine city of Lincoln, and, making my face droop with dismay, said how I dreaded the long miles on the road north, especially at a time when the weather seemed to be so uncertain.

The sharp-eyed maid lapped it all up, prompting me with a well-judged question whenever my narrative slowed. I had no idea whether she was simply a gossip or whether she was in the habit of extracting information from her master's guests in order to use it somehow to her own advantage. I did, however, rather suspect the latter. There was something about her that put my senses on alert, and I have learned to trust those senses since they seldom let me down.

And in addition, when I'd hurried back to the guest chamber the previous evening to fetch a piece of cloth to tuck in my sleeve – the fire was smoking and making my eyes water – I'd caught the skinny maid going through my bag.

Rollo and I set out next morning.

For some time we rode in silence. The day was fine so far, and Lord Edwin had sent us off with a good breakfast inside us and food and drink packed in our saddlebags. He had been so reluctant for us to leave that it had actually been quite hard to get away.

111

A weak, pale sun was shining muzzily behind the clouds and from its position in the sky I saw we were heading almost due north. The road was narrow and quite winding, but in reasonable repair. It clearly wasn't the great road north, however. I wondered how long we would ride before turning off it.

'Rollo, are we going northwards all day?' I asked eventually.

He spun round to frown at me, his brown eyes dark with some emotion I didn't understand. 'What? No, of course not.'

'So when do we turn south for Gloucester?'

'South-west,' he corrected absently. 'Soon.'

I was rapidly running out of patience with his brooding silence. 'You can share your thoughts with me, you know,' I said coolly. 'I'm here to help, remember?'

He gave an exasperated sigh. It seemed my questions were interrupting some deep thought process. 'I'm being followed by a man or men who wish to kill me,' he said with exaggerated patience. 'The purpose of my repeated statements to Lord Edwin and his household to the effect that I'm heading north is to persuade my pursuers that I am somewhere that I'm not. If I leave the north-bound route too soon, anyone keeping an eye on my progress will see straight through the ruse. I will change direction, but only when I—'

'*Me, my, I!*' I cried. I couldn't stop myself and the angry protest burst out of me, far more shrilly that I'd have liked. 'In case you've forgotten, Rollo, there are two of us!'

Fury flashed up in his face and I thought for

112

a moment that he would retaliate. But then it was gone. He even managed a faint smile. 'Two of us, yes,' he said quietly. 'It's very rare for me to travel with someone else. If I forget, and revert to planning just for myself, I hope you'll understand and forgive me.'

Then he turned the brown gelding's head and rode on.

It was easier said than done to find a south-westwards turning off our road, or indeed, for quite a long time, any turning at all. We were deep in the countryside now, sometimes woodland, sometimes arable, and the late autumn day appeared almost empty of people. Much of the land to our left was low-lying and waterlogged, with not even the suggestion of a safe way through. I was far from my own home ground now, and I didn't dare trust to my skill to find us one.

It was not until well after midday that we finally left the north-bound road. For some time we made good progress in our new direction, for the track was good and, again, very little used. We passed wagons, carts, horses, people on foot, but never in great numbers.

The misty morning and its feeble sunshine gave way to a gradual build-up of heavy cloud, at first bright, fluffy white but soon turning to ominous greys and black. The rain began, and straight away our progress slowed right down. Soon it was clear that a terrible storm was coming, and we were riding straight into it.

Rollo turned to me. 'It's not safe to go on,' he said over the howling of the wind. 'I've no idea

113

where we are but I think we should stop at the first dwelling we come to and beg shelter.' I nodded my agreement. My face was so cold that I wasn't sure I had the mobility in my jaws to speak.

The light began to fade. It might have been simply the effect of the ferociously lowering clouds, or it might have been evening creeping on; I'd lost track of the time. By now I was starting to feel very afraid. I could hear thunder in the distance, and huge forks of brilliant light were striking the ground ahead of us. I'd have gladly crawled into the meanest, dirtiest, most tumbledown barn if one had presented itself. Anything would have done, to get out of the rain and give the illusion of shelter.

We didn't find a barn but we did find a monastery.

It barely warranted the name. It consisted of a very small, timber-framed and reed-thatched dwelling – a hovel, really – with a tiny chapel beside it. It stood a little back from the track, and it was sheltered from the prevailing wind by a small copse of alder and willow. A path wound away through the trees, behind which could be made out a long, low structure that looked like stabling.

Rollo dismounted and ran up to the timber-framed house. The door opened, revealing a tall, thin-faced, black-clad monk. There was a brief exchange, then the monk nodded and pointed down the path through the trees. Rollo hurried back to me. 'They'll take us,' he panted. 'Gather up what you need and go in – I'll see to the horses and then join you.'

114

I didn't need more than what was in my leather satchel, and that I always carry slung across my body. As well as my healer's materials, I'd also packed my favourite shawl and the shining, magical, mysterious scrying stone that I inherited from my forebears. Leaving the larger bag attached to the saddle, I slid off the mare's back, my legs so cold that they were numb. Rollo put out a hand to steady me. 'I hope they have a fire,' I said, my teeth clattering.

His mouth turned down. 'So do I, but I'm not expecting it.'

I grabbed my cloak around me and made for the door. It opened as I reached it and a dark-clad arm reached out and drew me inside. I stood dripping on the step and looked at the community.

It consisted of three monks: the thin-faced man who had just admitted me, a lad of no more than twelve or thirteen, and, propped on a pile of dirty blankets in the far corner, a very old man. His vacant expression and wandering, blank gaze suggested he was senile.

'Come to the hearth,' the thin-faced monk said. There was no welcome in his voice. 'You should try to dry your outer garments and your boots, for if you do not, you risk sickness.'

His tone suggested that if I was so foolhardy as to do that, it would be entirely my fault and *he* certainly didn't welcome that outcome as it meant he'd have to look after me till I was better.

'Thank you,' I replied with as much grace as I could. I stepped forward to the hearth, where a reluctant fire glowed. As I advanced, the lad drew

115

back, an expression of dismay, or perhaps fear, on his face. He'd obviously been taught already to avoid women. Undoubtedly the thin-faced monk was drumming into him that my sex was the devil's instrument, put in men's way to tempt them from their purity.

Judging by the heady mixture of bodily stenches in the small room, there wasn't all that much purity here in the first place. It was stinking and foul, with all too apparent evidence of the animals that had the run of the place.

Presently Rollo came in and joined me beside the hearth. I turned to him and briefly met his eyes. 'There's no option,' he breathed, so softly that nobody else could have heard.

Just then a huge blast of thunder crashed almost overhead, and simultaneously the world lit up in a vivid lightning flash. Reluctantly I had to agree that Rollo was right.

Soon after sunset, there was a pause in the onslaught. Rollo got up and peered outside, then turned and beckoned to me. 'The rain has stopped, although I fear there's more to come,' he said. 'Shall we go outside for some – er, to stretch our legs, my lady, while we have the chance?'

'Yes,' I said, scrambling up. I glanced at the monks. The senile one seemed to be asleep, and the boy was peeling onions. One more pungent smell to add to the mix. The thin-faced monk said nothing, merely staring at us out of cold eyes.

Rollo and I walked into the copse. As well as the path that led through to the stable, there were smaller tracks winding between the trees. We followed one, presently coming to a small, hurrying stream. In summer, or on any better day, it would have been a pretty spot.

I climbed down a shallow slope and stood on the bank. 'Plenty of fresh water,' I observed.

Rollo came to stand beside me. He'd obviously picked up my thought. He said, 'Yes, and the stable is reasonably clean, with water for the horses and fresh straw. Maybe they've taken some cranky vow that insists they have to live in squalor because it's good for the soul.'

I smiled. 'Perhaps, or maybe they've just lost the will to—'

Just then I heard voices. A man's and a woman's. Rollo put his hand on my arm, but there was no need for him to warn me to keep silent.

Now we could hear hoofbeats. From where we stood, down beside the stream in its little valley, we would not be seen from the track through the trees. We knew from the sounds that the newcomers were heading for the stables. We waited.

'The stables aren't too bad,' the man's voice said. 'There are two horses here already.'

'Yes, that zealous-looking monk muttered something about having to stretch their food many ways,' a woman replied. 'Dear Lord above, Henry, I'm not looking forward to tonight.'

'I know, and neither am I, but we cannot go on. Both of us are drenched, the horses are worn out and it's almost dark. I do not believe the storm is yet over, and we dare not risk being caught out in the open when it resumes.'

The woman gave a deep, heartfelt sigh. 'I know,

and you are right.' She said some more, but they were almost out of earshot now and I couldn't make out the words.

Rollo and I waited. Quite a lot of time passed – the newcomers were surely tending to their horses – and then we heard them return on foot through the trees and back to the monastery. When we were certain they would neither hear nor see us, we climbed up the stream bank and stared after them. From what I could make out, they were around our own ages, and well dressed in fine travelling cloaks. Each carried a good-quality leather bag.

Rollo watched as they opened the door of the monks' dwelling and went inside. He was frowning.

The guilty had to die.

The man who was going to ensure that the ultimate penalty was paid was very clear in his own mind. An eye always paid for an eye, a tooth for a tooth. *Lex talionis* insisted upon that. And the Bible said that as a man is injured, so shall injury be done to him.

He had set out on his great task and he hadn't deviated from it; not for a moment. This, he felt, was a tribute to his courage and his resolve, for the road had not been easy and more than once he had followed wrong trails and been misled into making mistakes.

He had been so very sure, that first time, that he'd allowed his fury to overcome him. Discovering his error had made him a little more cautious, but even so he had again been misdirected and the wrong man had died. He had been too eager; so impatient to strike the great blow that he hadn't taken the time to make absolutely sure. He'd have probably killed the third one, too, if he hadn't been disturbed.

Two dead, one attacked, and not one of them the man he sought.

But he didn't allow himself to think about that.

If he did, if he permitted the luxury of remorse and sought to unburden his overloaded conscience, then he knew without even thinking about it that it would be the end. The end of his mission and the end, probably, of him.

So instead of lamenting where and how he had gone wrong, he used his errors as lessons. Building on what he had learned over the past few intense days and weeks, he drove himself on. And he knew that experience had greatly improved his ability: he was capable of achieving his purpose now, and nothing was going to stand in his way.

It had been such a long, lonely road.

He wasn't yet at the end of it, but it wouldn't be far now.

He had been watching the skies for a break in the cloud. There had been one around sunset but that had been too early, for there was still a little light. Then, as night came on, the rain had begun again.

Rain made his task more difficult, although not impossible. He had made a slightly amended plan for wet weather, and now, standing in the meagre shelter of the band of trees, he

119

understood that he would have to use it. Very well, so be it.

He guessed that it was around midnight, although in the absence of any sight of the stars, he couldn't be sure. It didn't really matter.

He closed his eyes and began his prayers.

He always prayed before he went into action. It calmed the mind, and, far more importantly, it was a tribute to God. *This is for You*, it seemed to say. *What I do is for Your greater glory.*

He had evolved his own form of prayers. For quite a lot of his life he had lived with the deeply devout. There was some confusion in his mind – how could everyone be right, when they said different things were true? – but he always did his best to obey the rules and the laws.

He was in no doubt that what he was about to do was not only the right but the *only* thing to do.

His prayers completed, he moved forward, silent as a shadow, out from the trees and across the open ground to the monastery.

He crept right in under the deep overhang of the thatched roof. Out of the rain, he withdrew an item from under his cloak. He felt it anxiously with his free hand. It was dry; dry enough, anyway. He sent up his thanks.

From the pouch on his belt he took out a small piece of flint. He laid the object he'd been carefully keeping dry on the ground. It was a length of wood, as long as his outstretched arm and about as thick as his wrist. At one end, he had fastened a large bunch of loosely bound

120

straw. Kneeling over it, repeatedly he scraped the point of his knife swiftly against the flint. Sparks appeared. He scraped harder, and now the sparks were flying off into the dry straw.

Before long, it caught.

Slowly, patiently, knowing he must not rush, he blew gently on the little glowing patches. Soon they grew into small flames. He blew some more, and now he had to pull away for already the heat was uncomfortable on his face.

He stood up, holding his flaming torch in his hand.

He looked up at the thatched roof stretching up above him. It was a pity it was so wet.

He went round the side of the building to the door. Quietly he opened it and edged inside. The fire had died down and gave out barely any light, so he held up his torch.

There was an old monk in the corner, huddled deep in his blankets like a burrowing animal. A lad in monk's robes lay on a thin straw mattress close beside the old man. A third monk lay on his back on the bare earth floor, well away from the hearth.

The hearth and its meagre warmth, it appeared, was reserved for travellers begging shelter.

And there they were.

The man nodded in satisfaction and allowed himself a smile.

Already the monk on the bare floor was stirring, his eyes fluttering open, a frown of perplexity on his thin face.

With no further hesitation the man thrust his flaming torch up into the underside of the thatch.

Here within the building, it was dry. Then, even as the quiet crackle told him it had ignited, he went calmly around the small space, thrusting the flame into anything and everything that looked as if it would burn.

Then he went out, closed the door and fastened it firmly with the length of leather hanging beside the latch.

He stepped back. One pace, two; then, hurriedly, eight, nine, ten, a dozen, twenty.

For the fire had taken hold with terrifying swiftness, and anybody standing too close would suffer the same fate as those trapped within.

And they did suffer.

The man stood at his safe distance and breathed in the screams. They did not continue for very long.

'The sight and the sounds of hell,' the man said quietly. 'So perish sinners; so must suffer all who break the laws of God and man.' His face contorted in a moment of deep emotion. 'Who *betray*,' he spat out viciously.

After a time the roar of the fire began to abate, for it had used up most of the available fuel. The thatch had long gone, and the timbers that had held it up were almost burned through. As the man watched, the main one collapsed into the ruins of the monks' dwelling.

He thought he might as well go.

For a moment he felt strangely flat. His mission had driven him on, riding him so hard that he'd willingly foregone food, sleep, comfort, companionship, to achieve his end. But now his task was done, and he felt almost bereft.

But then he remembered there was something else he had to do.

With a purpose once more – with something to live for – he turned and walked away. Soon he broke into a run. He was in a hurry now, for there was a long way to go.

Eight

Jack lay on his bed listening to the rain beating down. It was late, and he was exhausted. To take his mind off worrying about how much damage the water was probably doing to the little lean-to next door – temporarily without a roof, since earlier, on returning from his mission to the widow Picot's house, Jack had taken a variety of heavy tools to it and pulled the whole ruined, rotten structure down – he did a mental overview of his body and listed every bit that hurt.

His wound, of course, gave the worst pain. He knew it was folly to have worked so hard today. Whilst he could clearly remember Lassair ordering him, in addition to his daily walking, to begin moving his upper torso as soon as he could, she'd said nothing about swinging a heavy axe into ancient roof beams. Yes, the wood had been half-rotten in places and hadn't put up much resistance, but all the same, she wouldn't even have allowed him to pick up the axe if she'd been there. Then, when he'd done with the axe, he'd got going with the pitchfork, dragging away a small mountain of stinking old reed thatch, and, after that, he'd broken apart an intransigent tangle of old rafters and supports with his pickaxe. Finally he'd fetched a broom, and all but made himself pass out with pain and fatigue as he swept the debris out of the derelict dwelling and down the alley to the midden.

By then it had been getting dark. Returning to the clean, neat interior of his own house, he'd been long past making himself anything to eat. He had washed the filth off his aching body in the trough outside, then gone in, taken a long draught of water and collapsed on his bed.

Where now, some time later, he lay documenting his hurts.

The long list was depressing. He told himself it had been worth the pain. For one thing, he'd proved to himself that he was still sufficiently strong to take on such a hard, heavy task. For another, he had the enormous satisfaction of knowing that the rotten, filthy roof was now gone, taking with it its foul stench and its assortment of vermin, their nests and their droppings. Even the continuing heavy rain could be seen as an advantage, he reflected, since it would be achieving for him, with no effort from himself, what he'd otherwise have to bring about with countless pails of water. In the morning, or when the rain eventually stopped, he'd return with his broom, sweep out the puddles and be left with a clean floor.

To take his mind off Lassair, and how she'd approve of how thoroughly he was preparing the ground for the new dwelling space, he began to think how he'd go about rebuilding the roof.

Quite soon, he was deeply asleep.

He woke stiff and sore. He got carefully out of bed, and, ravenously hungry after the previous day's

125

exertions and having gone to bed with no supper, prepared a huge breakfast. Then he went into the adjoining dwelling to see what a night's rain had done.

As he had hoped, the beaten-earth floor looked as if the entire top layer had been washed away, which it probably had to judge by the earth-coloured little rivulets still trickling away into the alley outside. Decades of dirt and detritus had been washed away too; Jack saw with satisfaction that the floor now looked newly tamped down.

Glancing up into the sky, he could see that more rain would soon fall. It was no day to begin rebuilding the roof, for, apart from the unpleasantness of working in a room open to the elements when it was raining, it was also necessary for the interior to dry out. He'd be affixing beams and rafters to the existing wooden framework supporting the walls, and he couldn't do so if everything was soaking wet.

So, back in his own house, he set aside his labouring clothes and put on a better tunic, hose, cloak and boots. Then he set out on his daily walk.

He avoided the castle. He was still uncertain of his precise status there: his men, and indeed most of the townspeople to whom he'd spoken, seemed to take it for granted that he'd be back in his post as soon as he was fully fit, and, in the meantime, was busy doing what he could for the forces of law and order. Jack was quite happy with that. It remained to be seen whether Sheriff Picot was too.

For now, Jack's men knew where to find him, and he was aware, without anyone actually having to say so, that they'd come to him if they needed him. He was all but certain that he could make a similar approach to them, which was fortunate since he was formulating a plan which would require the assistance of at least one of them.

He strode on, increasing his speed until he was panting but not allowing his pace to slacken. Avoiding the market square – too many people around, and quite likely at least one of them would stop him and delay him by lengthily passing the time of day – he headed on towards his destination. And soon, out beyond St Bene't's Church, he was standing beneath the shelter of the trees that overhung the old wall and looking up at Gaspard Picot's house.

Coming here had become a daily ritual. Jack wasn't certain why he felt compelled to keep up his vigil, for he had only seen the dark-clad figure on one other occasion after he'd first spotted him, and, on the face of it, there was nothing suspicious about somebody standing looking up at a grand house. Possibly, he'd told himself, he was one of those who had been chucked out of their hovels and been forced to witness those same hovels smashed apart, utterly destroyed, so that Gaspard Picot's ugly, flamboyant and self-aggrandizing edifice could be thrown up in their place. It was enough, Jack thought, to make anyone want to stand staring at the imposing house and wish evil to those within.

For, although he had no proof and nothing whatsoever to confirm that he was right, Jack was absolutely sure that the cloaked figure's interest in the house of the late Gaspard Picot was far from benign.

As he stood there beneath the sweeping branches of the willow tree, concealed from view unless anyone looked really closely, Jack wondered at his certainty. He wouldn't have said he was a man given to whimsy. Wouldn't have said he believed in magic, or superstition, or the ability of evil to permeate the air in detectable form, as if it were a foul smell or a toxic emanation. Yet here he was, keeping watch on the house of a man who most people would have judged to have been his enemy, solely because he feared a mysterious, shadowy figure somehow meant harm to the house or its occupants.

Perhaps, he concluded with a faint smile, he'd been spending too much time with Lassair.

He moved over to the bench and sank down onto it. He was encouraged to find he felt less exhausted than he'd felt the last time he'd walked here. He was definitely making progress, and soon—

He could see the dark-cloaked figure. He was standing perhaps twenty or thirty paces away to his right, as still and almost as well concealed as Jack was. Jack narrowed his eyes, trying to make out details. As before, his attempts were foiled by the voluminous, enfolding cloak with its deep hood. *But why shouldn't a man wear a heavy cloak?* he thought in frustrated irritation. *It's about to rain.*

He was cross with himself for taking such

trouble to watch someone who in all probability was doing no harm and had no intention of doing so, purely on a whim.

Nevertheless, he went on watching. And when the dark figure melted away – it seemed to Jack that melted away was exactly what happened, since one moment he was there and when Jack next looked, although only a few heartbeats had passed, he wasn't – Jack knew what he was going to do.

He allowed sufficient time to pass for the cloaked figure to have got well away from the Picot residence. Then he set off for home. Before returning to his house, however, he called in at the tavern which he had always used as an unofficial meeting place for his group of especially loyal and trustworthy lawmen. It was on the quayside and the tavern keeper, whose name was Magnus, could be relied upon to pass on messages between Jack and his men. Jack ordered a mug of ale and a pie – his appetite seemed to be increasing with every day – and, when by the time he was ready to leave none of the men he sought had appeared, he asked Magnus to tell whoever he saw first out of Walter, Ginger, Fat Gerald, Luke or, at a pinch, even young Henry, that Jack wanted a word.

Then, nodding a farewell to Magnus and his pretty wife, Jack went home to wait. And – he had to admit it to himself – to have a much-needed rest.

He was deeply asleep when the knock on the door came, so deeply that it took Walter and Henry several attempts and even then Henry had to slip inside and shake Jack's shoulder before he stirred.

'You wanted to see us, chief,' Walter said once Jack was on his feet. He didn't seem to be able to meet Jack's eyes; discovering his superior sound asleep in the middle of the day appeared to have discomfited him.

Jack decided the best course was to ignore it and proceed immediately to the reason for the summons.

'I did.' He sat down on one of the circles of tree trunk that served as stools, waving a hand to two others. Walter and Henry sat down on the opposite side of the hearth. 'I've been concerned about Gaspard Picot's widow, the lady Elwytha, because—'

'Yes, chief, we know,' Walter interrupted quietly. 'Ranald and Lard told us.'

Jack recalled his first exhausting visit up to the castle, and the conversation he'd had with the four men in the guard room.

'Yes, of course,' he said. With a grin, he added, 'I'd almost forgotten how the lot of you gossip over your evening mug of ale.'

'We wanted to hear about you,' the lad Henry put in disingenuously. 'Ranald only told us about your interest in the widow Picot because we asked what you were doing with yourself all this time.'

Walter leaned over and lightly cuffed the lad. 'We asked nothing of the sort,' he said curtly. 'He's convalescing, that's what he's doing with himself, and we'll have less of your cheek.'

Jack looked from one face to the other. Did his loyal men really believe he ought to be making more of an effort? Perhaps they were right . . .

130

He turned to Henry. 'I want to resume my role among you as soon as I can,' he said. 'Believe me, I'm building my strength up again but it takes time. You have my word, Henry, that as soon as I'm sure I can work all day and pull my weight as a full member of the force, I'll be there.'

Henry had blushed furiously. Now, temporarily robbed of speech, he just nodded.

'I've been keeping an eye on Gaspard Picot's house,' Jack went on, 'and three times now I've seen someone else doing the same.' Briefly he described the dark figure. 'It's not much to go on, and the man may have his reasons. I wondered, for example, if he was one of the people driven out of his home in order that Gaspard Picot's house could be built, and—'

'That could mean he had a grudge against the Picots and a desire to do harm!' Henry piped up. He had, Jack thought with a quiet smile, recovered his usual buoyant spirits.

'It could, Henry,' he replied.

'You said a dark figure,' Henry pressed on, eyes alight. 'Perhaps this man's a wizard and he's putting an evil spell on the house and its inhabitants, so that they—'

'Or perhaps he's not,' Walter interrupted crushingly. 'Perhaps he knows there's gold and riches inside and wants to get his hands on some of it. Shut your mouth and listen, lad.'

Henry subsided.

It was strange, Jack thought, that Henry should have mentioned evil spells. Hadn't he himself had the strongest sense that the dark figure's interest in the Picot house was malicious?

131

'I can't in truth say what makes me suspicious,' he said after a moment. 'There could be no cause for concern, but I think we ought to keep a watch.'

'If this dark man notices we've got our eye on the place he'll probably give it up and slink away,' Walter said.

'True,' Jack agreed, 'but I think we should try to find out more about him and his purposes. I will undertake to keep watch in the mornings at least, and possibly again later as well, since I'm already in the habit of walking out that way each day, getting myself fit for duty.' He grinned at Henry. 'If you can arrange between you to have eyes on the house at other times of the day – and night, I suppose – let's keep at it for the rest of today and tomorrow, then meet in the tavern the following evening to report on what we've seen. If anything,' he added grimly.

Walter and Henry got up, and Jack went with them out into the alley. Evening was drawing on, and the light had begun to fade.

Henry called out a cheerful farewell and led the way off up the path. Walter, following, turned back, his face creased in a frown.

'She's not your responsibility, you know, chief,' he said softly.

Jack knew who he meant.

'She's a widow because of me,' he replied.

'She's a widow because her thieving cheat of a man attacked you and all but killed you,' Walter said bluntly. 'And,' he added, 'it's not as if his death has thrown her into penury, is it?' He turned away again and a faint 'Night, chief,' floated back.

Jack returned inside and closed the door, leaning thoughtfully against it for a few moments. Walter was right; the lady Elwytha had been born into wealth and it wasn't going to be taken away from her now that she was widowed. And, from all accounts, she was a self-serving, uncharitable soul who clutched her riches to herself like a miser.

Jack sighed.

It was folly, perhaps, but nevertheless he recognized that some impulse within him wasn't going to let this go.

He resumed his vigil for a spell late that evening, and was back at his post the following morning. Perhaps he was losing his powers of observation, or maybe the dark man was getting better at concealing himself; perhaps he had simply given up. He returned briefly in the evening, still with no success, and finally, as darkness closed in and worn out from the extensive walking and the tension, he went home, ate a bite of supper and fell into bed.

With a start of alarm, Jack woke from a brief, deep sleep.

He knew he hadn't been asleep for long because the couple of small logs he'd put on the fire when he went to bed had still not burned right through.

He wondered what had woken him. His heart was beating hard, as if he'd sensed danger. Then, like an echo out of a dream, he remembered smelling smoke.

Yes, that was it – he'd been dreaming of fire.

He'd heard the hungry roar, seen the great billowing clouds of white smoke rising into the dark night. Fear returned, and he felt the sweat break out on his chest.

He sniffed, once, again. Other than the usual background aroma of woodsmoke that was always present inside his house – inside everyone's houses, so that nobody really noticed it – the air was clear. No wild blaze, no smoke, no danger.

He sank back and tried to make himself relax.

He was tired – exhausted might be more accurate – and his bed was snug and warm. He should try to go back to sleep. He knew he needed his rest. Lassair had told him that the body used the sound sleep of deep night to heal, and he was well aware he still needed to heal. Although he was slowly building up his strength – as well as everything else, he'd managed to do quite a lot of work on the new roof today, and his muscles weren't burning with quite so much pain as the last time he'd made such an effort – he was still a long way from being his former self.

His body was relaxed but he couldn't still his mind.

Lassair filled his thoughts, as she so often did. At first, thoughts of her made him smile. But, as always seemed to happen, soon his optimism began to fade. She'd been gone so long. When would she come back? *Would* she come back?

As his thoughts set off down the dismally familiar track, he forced himself to contemplate something else. And, for want of anything better, he returned to the reliable distraction of planning in his mind how he would complete the construction of the new roof.

There was no sign of the dark-cloaked figure the next morning, either. By the end of that day, when Jack had stayed at his post far longer than he usually did and become thoroughly cold and very grumpy, he was ready to tell Walter and the others to quit. He had little hope that any of them would have had more luck than he had, and went along to the meeting at the tavern that evening wishing he could stay at home by the fire.

Seeing his faithful band huddled in their usual corner, however, raised his mood, especially when one after another they got up to greet him, and even more when Fat Gerald thrust a mug of ale into his hand. They were settling down again, shoving each other along the benches and pulling up additional stools, when the door opened and two more men came in.

'We heard you were meeting tonight,' Ranald said, 'so me and Lard here thought we'd come and pass the time of day. Ned and the lad Iver are on duty, else they'd have come too.'

'It's good to see you,' Jack said. 'Thank you for coming.'

'We want you back, chief,' Ranald said bluntly. 'We know you'll be with us soon as you can, and in the meantime, we're prepared to come to you.'

Made awkward by the men's confidence and trust, Jack hastened to the purpose of the meeting. 'We've all been keeping watch on Gaspard Picot's house,' he said. 'I for one have seen no sign of the dark figure in the cloak for the last two days. Anyone else got anything to report?'

There were shakes of the head and mutters of 'No' and 'Same with me.'

'They're saying she's increased the guard,' Ranald volunteered.

Jack turned to him, recalling that, when he'd first raised the subject of the widow Picot, it had been he who had provided information. 'How do you come to know about her?' he asked.

Ranald grinned. 'I know one of her maids. Not like that!' he added quickly as various suggestions of greater and lesser crudity were made. 'She's a comely lass, I'll admit, but she's sweet on one of the manservants. She's my cousin's wife's sister, and when my kin get together, we like to talk.'

'And is there any reason for this increase in security?' Jack asked.

Ranald shrugged. 'Other than the obvious one – that she's now a woman alone, sitting in a rich man's house with a wealth of costly possessions – can't think of one.'

'Maybe she's spotted the dark figure,' Henry suggested, eyes wide. 'She'll be frightened if she has, because I reckon he's—'

Walter dug an elbow in the lad's ribs and he subsided.

'What d'you want us to do, chief?' Lard asked. 'Keep up the watch?'

Jack hesitated. On the one hand, he remained certain in his own mind that the dark-clad man meant harm to the household. Theft perhaps – the general opinion seemed to be that nobody, excluding herself, would lose much sleep if the widow Picot were to be relieved of a little of her fortune – but it was always possible that there was something else. His instinct went on telling him there was, but was it fair to impose extra duties on these hard-working, willing men simply on his instinct?

'We'll stand down,' he said eventually. 'It may be that, observing our interest, the dark man has quietly given up and slipped away. In that case, you'd all be wasting your time, and I don't want to be the cause of that.'

It was evident, he noticed with a wry, private smile, that nobody protested.

'We could make sure to keep the house on our rounds for a few days more,' Walter volunteered. 'Wouldn't hurt to pause for a while and cast an eye over the place.'

'Thank you, Walter,' Jack replied.

It was time, he decided, to move on.

To repay the men for their time, he ordered more ale and some food. The least he could do, having kept them from returning to their well-earned rest at the end of another hard day, was to send them home with full bellies.

Jack couldn't sleep. Earlier, he'd been so certain that keeping vigil to watch out for the cloaked man was a total waste of time. Now, alone in the darkness and the silence, he wasn't so sure. Why? What had changed?

He tried to still his thoughts, to see if that would leave space for whatever was troubling him to make itself known. And, straight away, in his mind he was seeing the house of Gaspard

137

Picot's widow. Images of the rabbit-eyed woman, the extravagant, vulgar house and the mysterious man lurking outside filled his head and wouldn't go away. He knew, *knew*, something was wrong.

Impatiently he flung back the bedding, reached for his leather tunic and drew on his boots. He fastened on his sword belt, feeling the weight of the steel dragging on his left side. He put a dagger in his belt and a smaller knife in a stout leather sheath in the small of his back, tucked into his belt and concealed by his tunic.

Then he set out.

The night was clear. For once it wasn't raining, and the stars bright above him suggested it wasn't going to in the near future. He strode on, fatigue driven out by purpose. Something was going to happen. He was all but certain.

He kept a look-out for patrols, but, other than hearing evidence of a small band of marching men in the distance as he passed by the deserted market square, didn't encounter any. The town, it appeared, was fast asleep.

He hurried on, increasing his pace as the unreasoned sense of urgency tightened its hold. And, soon, the huge bulk of Gaspard Picot's house rose up before him.

He stood panting in his usual place, beneath the willow trees overhanging the tumbledown wall. At first it seemed that all was quiet, and his unease misplaced.

Then, standing absolutely still, his breathing now returned to normal, he heard it: a long, thin, drawn-out scream of fear, of horror, of shock.

He didn't pause to think but sprang straight

138

into a hard run and made for the steps up to the iron-studded doors. He raised his fist and banged on them. The screams from within paused briefly, then resumed at an even greater intensity.

Then there was the sound of bolts being drawn back, and the doors opened. A deathly white face peered out, and, taking in the rest of the man, Jack recognized the stout servant who had been among those escorting the lady Elwytha on her excursion.

'What has happened?' Jack demanded. 'I'm one of the sheriff's men, I'm here to help.'

The man's face crumpled and tears filled his eyes. 'Oh, come in, for the dear Lord's sake, come in! Oh, thank God you're here!'

'What is it?' Jack repeated. 'What's the reason for the screaming?'

The man, busy mopping his streaming eyes and running nose, set off at a trot, beckoning to Jack to follow. Other than a strange, distressed gulping, he didn't seem capable of making another sound.

He led the way along a passage, stone-flagged, with ornate oak chests set against its sides. By the light of torches set in sconces, Jack made out the bright, lively colours of tapestries hanging on the walls. On the top of one of the chests, the flames reflected in a range of exquisite silver: goblets, platters, something that looked like an ornamental shield. There was more wealth in this one corridor, he thought, than in a whole street of the small, cramped, inadequate dwellings of the poor. Than in a dozen streets.

The corridor opened out into a high, wide hall, in the centre of which a fire burned in a huge hearth. More chests lined the walls, as well as a long, narrow oak board on which was arranged more silver.

But then the plump servant stood aside, and Jack saw what lay on the stone floor on the far side of the fire.

It was the blood that first caught the eye. There was a lot of it, pooled on the flagstones and glistening like garnets in the light of the flames. As always, he was overcome with amazement that the body should hold so much, and at how quickly it leaked away when the flesh was irreparably breached. It was an awe-inspiring, dreadful sight, even to him who was used to the appearance of violent death. For the young girl kneeling over the still figure, wringing her hands and still screaming, it was a horror straight out of hell.

Turning to the stout servant, Jack said, 'Send for someone to take that poor child away, or do it yourself. She'll scream herself hoarse otherwise.' *And I'll need to talk to her soon*, he could have added. 'Get a woman to sit with her and comfort her,' he went on; the plump man hadn't moved. 'She needs a hot, sweet drink and some kindness!' he said more forcefully, and at last the plump man jerked himself out of his shock and did as he was told.

Alone in the hall, Jack knelt down beside the victim.

It was a woman, and he was already fairly sure who she was. She lay on her front, however, and he needed to confirm his suspicions. Gently he took hold of the shoulders and turned the body over.

Even looking into the dead woman's face, logical assumption had to take the place of a firm identity. For the woman had been attacked with such savagery that her forehead had collapsed, her nose was splattered across her cheeks and her lower jaw hung loose.

It was the eyes that gave the only real confirmation; those small eyes, with their *pop-eyed, lashless look that puts you in mind of a rabbit*: from the depths of his memory, Jack recalled Ranald's description. Now the eyes were wide with horror; with fear; with agony. The lady Elwytha hadn't died easily.

Jack tore his gaze away and methodically inspected the rest of the body. His questing fingers detected a bump on the back of her skull; perhaps the initial blow had been from behind. He pushed back the long, elegant, lace-trimmed sleeves of the undergown and inspected the thin stick-like forearms. Both left and right had bruises, marking the deathly white flesh like broad stripes. *She tried to fight him off*, Jack thought.

He continued his examination. It was quiet in the great hall: having noticed the strange silence, he wondered at it. And why, too, was he still here alone? He seemed to have lost track of time, but he was fairly sure that rather a lot had passed since he'd entered . . .

He sat back on his heels. His hands, he noticed, were covered in blood. Looking around for something with which to wipe them, he saw a small pile of linen cloths on the oak board. He got up and fetched one.

He had just finished cleaning up when there were footfalls in the corridor leading to the doors. Two sets. Three . . . No, more.

He turned to see who was approaching.

First came the younger of the two manservants he'd seen escorting the lady Elwytha. Next came a well-built young man – an outdoor servant, or perhaps a groom – who had armed himself with a cudgel, and who had presumably accompanied the serving man for protection when he went for help.

Bringing up the rear was a trio of lawmen, all three of whom Jack recognized. He nodded to them, and two of them murmured greetings.

Between the servants and the lawmen, puffing slightly as he hurried into the hall, came a short, barrel-shaped figure dressed in a dark robe, over which he had wrapped a brightly coloured shawl. His round face was topped with a bald head, circling which was a halo of pure white hair. Two brilliant blue eyes sparkled with intelligence.

Flooded with relief – although he didn't stop to ask himself why – Jack stepped forward to take the man's hands. 'I am very glad to see you,' he said feelingly. 'I should be most grateful for your help.'

And, giving Jack's hands a squeeze before releasing them and stepping forward to crouch beside the corpse, rolling up his sleeves and already staring in fascination at what lay before him, Gurdyman said, 'And I am here to give it.'

Nine

Gurdyman studied the corpse for only a few moments before turning his attention back to Jack and beckoning him close. Standing over him, Jack sensed the great effort it took to interrupt his fascinated examination even for an instant.

'You should go,' Gurdyman breathed in his ear. 'Sheriff Picot is on his way.'

Of course. Jack frowned, angry with himself. The lady Elwytha was the widow of the sheriff's late nephew. The sheriff would see it as his personal duty to investigate and avenge her murder.

Whilst Jack recognized the folly of being found here when Sheriff Picot arrived, nevertheless he wanted to stay . . .

'You're sure of that?' he asked.

'Oh, yes,' Gurdyman replied firmly. 'The man who came to fetch me had been dispatched by the sheriff himself. He told me Picot was coming. He will be here as soon as he's finished barking out unnecessary orders to men who function perfectly well without him.'

But Jack had only taken in the first few words. 'He sent someone to fetch you?'

Gurdyman smiled briefly. 'Don't sound so surprised. It's far from the first time that Sheriff Picot has commanded my assistance in determining how and by whom murder has been committed, and this of all victims' – he glanced dispassionately down at the body – 'is a case that will require of him all the expertise he can muster.'

'I want to—'

'You want to remain. Of course you do, Jack, but you can't.' With surprising strength for a short, tubby, elderly man prone to breathlessness, Gurdyman shoved Jack away, so that he was forced to take a step or two back. 'Go home, try to rest, and come to see me in the morning.'

He turned back to the body, and Jack sensed that already there was no place for himself in the old man's mind. He paused for a brief word with the three lawmen, then marched back along the passage, out of the door and down the steps.

His pace increased as he strode away from the house. He was furious at having had to leave the scene of the brutal assault. He knew there would be so many small details to uncover, and he had no faith that anyone else could pick them up as well as he could. *Arrogance*, he told himself. *Pure arrogance. Gurdyman has a far better eye than you.*

But that, really, was no comfort at all.

Suddenly he heard marching feet, coming straight towards him. Berating himself for the preoccupation that had driven all thoughts of self-preservation from his mind, he understood instantly just who was hurrying towards him and what would happen if they were to come face to face. He glanced around. He was on the main track that looped in a shallow curve round to the immediate east of the middle of the town, and

144

on his left several small, dark alleys and passages snaked off into the concentration of dwellings to the east of the market square. Choosing one at random, he ran down it for a few paces. Then, leaning back against a wattle-and-daub wall, he drew into the shadows and looked back out at the track.

Where, only a few moments later, Sheriff Picot strode past, at the head of a group of ten or a dozen men with flaming torches held aloft, his head up, his shoulders squared and a sword in his hand.

And much good a drawn sword would do now, Jack reflected, when the lady Elwytha lay dead and rapidly cooling on the floor of her own hall.

He waited until the last of the lawmen had passed, then eased himself away from the wall. He was about to return along the narrow little passage and back onto the main track when he heard something.

He stopped still. He turned his head from side to side, listening. The night was fine, and there was hardly any wind. There was no movement of air at all here, in this maze of alleys that turned this way and that between the walls of the houses. Despite the silence, however, whatever sound had alerted him had ceased.

He started to walk away. Then it came again.

It emanated from deeper in the mass of dwellings. Without pausing to think, Jack went towards it. What was it?

He stopped to listen. Closer now, he could hear it more clearly.

It sounded – it sounded like a lament. It was

a cry of sorrow; of despair. The pitch rose and fell, and it was almost singing; chanting, perhaps. There were words to the mournful sounds, although he couldn't make them out. He thought they were in a language he didn't know.

He felt cold suddenly. He told himself it was no more than the sweat of exertion cooling on him, now that he was standing still. But he didn't believe it.

There was something eerie about the lament. Something visceral and profound, that seemed to go right into the deep heart of his humanity and command him to mourn, to grieve, for what was life but the path to death?

With a huge effort he drew himself back.

And stood, trembling, shaking, as if he had stepped away from the abyss.

He knew he should go, for whoever was floating their grief on the night air was dangerous to him.

He turned and began to walk away.

And then – either starting up as an accompaniment to the lament or replacing it, he couldn't be sure – there came another sound: that of weeping, so harsh and raw that it surely threatened to tear asunder the heart of whoever was making the awful, racking sobs.

Now, as if released from some spell, Jack ran.

As he pounded down the alley and emerged, panting, onto the main track, the sounds of the weeping faded and died. His spirits instantly lifted and he set off for home.

* * *

He was knocking on Gurdyman's door early the next morning.

It was not easy to be there, even standing outside in the alley, for the house was indelibly associated in his mind with Lassair. He had stood here on the step several times, waiting for her. *And I shall do so again*, he told himself firmly.

The heavy old door opened a crack and Gurdyman's bright blue eye peered out. 'Jack!' he exclaimed, opening the door widely. 'In you come!' Jack stepped up into the long, cool hall and followed Gurdyman towards the light spilling in at the far end, where there was a little enclosed courtyard open to the sky. Whenever the weather permitted, it was where Gurdyman habitually sat when he was not in his workroom, down in the crypt deep beneath his house, and it was furnished with benches and a small table. This morning, although the skies were lowering, so far it was fine and the temperature mild.

'So,' Gurdyman said, settling himself with an involuntary sigh on one of the benches, 'you wish to hear about the body of our victim, the lady Elwytha, widow of Gaspard Picot.'

'I do.'

Gurdyman paused, gazing into the distance. 'It was an attack of great savagery,' he began, 'as you will have seen for yourself. There were many blows, and she was not killed by the first ones.'

Jack nodded. 'The bruises on her forearms, yes, I noticed those.'

'You will not have noticed other evidence of the infliction of pain before the killing blow, however,'

Gurdyman went on, 'because I didn't either, until I had her maid unfasten her garments.' He shot a quick glance at Jack. 'She had been struck repeatedly across the breasts and the lower belly, so hard that I am all but certain three of her ribs had been broken.'

Lower belly and breasts . . . 'Was there any sign of a sexual assault?'

Gurdyman nodded. 'I too wondered that, the areas of her body being those associated with a woman's sexuality. However, as far as I was able to ascertain, her undergarments were all intact and she hadn't been touched in the genitalia.'

'You can't be sure?'

Gurdyman said, with a trace of asperity, 'It is not easy to conduct an intimate examination of a woman's body when her late husband's uncle is standing over you breathing hot, angry air on the back of your neck and demanding that you hurry up with some answers and refrain from disturbing the dignity of the corpse.'

Jack grinned briefly. 'The two aims can't be achieved together.'

'As I tried repeatedly to tell him.'

'What did you make of the extreme damage to the face?' Jack asked.

'Much the same as you, I imagine,' Gurdyman replied. 'I would say it indicated true hatred; that the killer's desire – need – to be rid of the victim extended to a powerful wish to obliterate her entirely. Our faces are where we display our identity,' he added, leaning forward, his expression eager. 'It is a matter to which I have given much thought. Where do we reveal our nature, Jack? In our appearance or in our deeds?'

'Too large a question for an autumn morning,' Jack said shortly. 'Please, do not misunderstand me' – Gurdyman's face had fallen – 'I am fascinated by what you just said. But—'

'But other matters must take precedence. Yes, quite right.' Gurdyman leaned back once more. 'So, if we agree that the victim had aroused intense hatred, perhaps we should now ask ourselves whether the hatred was specifically for her – for the woman she was and the things she had done – or for the man who had been her husband.'

'Gaspard Picot,' Jack said quietly.

'Yes, who, on the face of it, was far more likely to have aroused the impulse to violence than his wife. But then we must ask ourselves what sort of a man takes out his fury at a man already dead on his widow?'

'You think it was definitely a man's hand that killed her?'

Gurdyman looked up in surprise. 'I had assumed so, because of the blows to the breasts and belly. But, now you mention it, I believe a powerful woman could have wielded whatever club or cudgel did the damage. Why do you ask?'

The question had appeared to materialize in Jack's mind of its own volition. 'No particular reason.' He paused. 'But there's something you should know.' He went on to tell Gurdyman about the dark-cloaked figure he had observed watching the house.

'Aaah,' Gurdyman said slowly. 'A thief, do

149

you think, looking for his chance to break into the house? And perhaps the lady Elwytha disturbed him as he prepared to help himself to her treasures?'

'It's possible, although she had a houseful of servants and one of my men informed me she'd recently increased the guard. If she'd heard a noise, she'd have sent one of them to investigate.'

Gurdyman nodded. 'Will you continue to watch out for your dark man?'

'I'm not sure there's much point,' Jack admitted. 'If he was there for some innocent reason, he'll soon find out what's happened and keep well away before he's hauled in for questioning. If it was him who killed her, he'll be miles away by now because, again, he'll fear falling under suspicion.'

'And if the purpose of his presence here in the town was to kill the lady Elwytha, then that has now been achieved and so there is nothing to keep him here,' Gurdyman added.

There was a brief silence as both of them contemplated that bleak prospect. Then Jack said, 'I had overlooked, what with my preoccupation with the widow Picot and her household and now her death, that—'

'Preoccupation,' Gurdyman put in gently. 'Yes, I had noticed.'

'It was I who—'

But, again, Gurdyman interrupted. 'Stop, Jack. Stop the remorse, stop the guilt. Gaspard Picot was an evil, corrupt man and the world is well rid of him. He tried to kill you and in defending

150

yourself – as is your right under the law – you took his life. Let that be an end of it.'

Sitting there in the soft light of the courtyard, with a weak yellow sun sending a kindly ray down upon him, Jack slowly became aware that something had changed. It was as if a weight he'd been carrying on his shoulders had suddenly been lifted off. He could sit up straight, open his chest, breathe the good air.

It was far from the first time that well-meaning friends and colleagues had told him Gaspard Picot's death was not his fault. It was, however, the first time he truly believed it.

He met Gurdyman's bright blue eyes. 'Thank you.'

'You are most welcome. Now, you were saying that you have overlooked something?'

'Yes. I was thinking of those two earlier deaths, the body found out beside the road to the fens, and the one that got caught up beneath the Great Bridge.'

'Two good-looking young men, both with longish fair hair, their dead bodies discovered within the space of a couple of days.'

'You saw them both?'

'I did.'

'And no progress made, or so I believe, as to who killed them,' Jack mused.

'There was in fact a third attack,' Gurdyman said, 'although fortunately it didn't result in a death.'

'Who was the intended victim?'

Gurdyman paused, as if weighing something up. Then he said, 'It was a young man called Sibert, the son of my friend Hrype.'

151

'From Lassair's village.' The words were out before Jack could stop them. 'You've spoken to Hrype recently? Has he news of her?'

Gurdyman reached out and put a steadying hand on Jack's arm.

'Hrype comes to see me quite frequently. The most recent occasion was only shortly after Lassair went back to Aelf Fen,' he said kindly. 'He had no news other than that she had arrived safely.'

Jack stared at him.

'She will return,' Gurdyman said very quietly. It sounded as if he was intoning the words.

'You can't *know* that.'

But Gurdyman, smiling didn't reply.

With a great effort, Jack dragged his mind back. 'So is Sibert all right?'

'Fortunately, yes. He has a tough skull, it appears.'

'Was he able to describe his attacker?'

'No.'

'Could he say anything that might be of use?'

'Only one thing, and this is at third hand, mind, for it was something that Sibert told someone, that they repeated to Hrype and that Hrype told me.'

'I'll bear that in mind,' Jack said wryly.

Gurdyman didn't appear to have heard. 'It seems the attacker was trying to find out something from Sibert, or perhaps holding him culpable for something he thought he'd done. Punishing him for this imagined crime, possibly.'

'And two other similar-looking young men were also attacked, but in their cases the damage was fatal.'

'Quite so. There was some suggestion, it seems, that the assailant heard Hrype coming – he'd gone to look for Sibert – and fled.'

But Jack barely took it in. Speaking softly, voicing thoughts even as they formed in his mind, he said, 'They were all similar in appearance. It's almost as if the killer was searching for someone he hated so much that he didn't much care about making sure he was attacking – killing – the right one.' He shook his head. 'But that's absurd.' He fell quiet.

'Hate,' Gurdyman said. The single word dropped into the silence.

Jack looked up swiftly. 'As with the murder of the widow Picot.'

'Precisely.'

'I heard a strange thing last night, as I hurried away from the Picot house,' he heard himself saying. He was mildly surprised, having decided this morning, in the clear light of day, that he might well have imagined the whole thing. He described the eerie, spine-chilling lament, and the heartbroken weeping that had followed.

Gurdyman listened intently. Then, when Jack finished speaking, he nodded slowly. 'A lament for the dead,' he said slowly.

'You believe, then, it pertains in some way to the murder of the lady Elwytha?'

But, with a shrug and a spread of his hands, Gurdyman said, 'I have no idea.'

Ten

Rollo and I were running for our lives.

Two nights ago, we had come so close to losing them that I still dreaded to think about it . . .

Rollo watched as the two newly arrived, well-dressed travellers opened the door of the monks' dwelling and went inside. He was frowning.

'What's the matter?' I asked. I was worried, for I sensed his sudden tension. 'Do you recognize them? Is it the man who's after you?'

He didn't answer for a moment. Then he said, 'I can't be sure. I don't know what he looks like.' He paused, the frown increasing. 'I think we won't go back to join the brethren just yet.'

I thought I understood his reasoning. 'In case one or both of that pair are looking for news of you?' He nodded. 'But surely it won't be a man and woman travelling together, on your trail? I'd have thought it'd be a man alone, or perhaps with a male companion, or – oh.'

He nodded, smiling briefly. 'Quite.'

He had disguised himself by acquiring a woman – me – to travel with him. It was entirely possible that the man chasing after him had done the same. I was about to comment but he went on, 'I wouldn't have expected that he'd ride in the company of a woman, and the pair of them looking so prosperous and fine, but then I've concealed myself by riding with you, and dressing us up as a lord and lady, so why shouldn't he?'

I didn't appreciate the reminder that I was only there with him to help to blur his identity, but I didn't think it was the moment to say so. 'What do you want to do?' I asked him. 'Do you think we should fetch the horses and ride on? It's not raining now, although I believe there is more to come.'

He looked up into the sky. 'So do I, and we'd be fools to ride off when a storm is threatening and risk being caught in the open, especially when in all probability I'm worrying about nothing, and those two travellers are perfectly innocent. But all the same . . .' He didn't finish the sentence. He was still frowning.

'Why don't we sleep in the stable?' I suggested. 'If it's sound enough, it'll keep us dry when the rain starts again, and there's probably straw to keep us warm. We've got our cloaks, too, and it's not cold tonight.'

He smiled briefly. 'Yes, there's straw, and it's reasonably fresh. In fact, I do believe we'd be a lot more comfortable in the stables than in with the monks. The smell isn't nearly as bad, for one thing.'

So instead of returning to the monks, we set off down the short track that led off behind the monks' house and through a clump of trees to the stables. The newcomers' horses – of fine quality and well cared for, I noticed – were in a stall at the end of the short row, and ours were at the opposite end. Fortunately, the three smaller stalls in between were empty. The straw wasn't in too bad a state, and Rollo had been right about the smell.

The wooden walls were, to the casual glance, in no worse a state of repair than those of the monks' house, and possibly slightly better. We had our own food with us, and I was sure it was better than anything those poverty-avowed monks could have offered us. All three of them had looked on the verge of starvation, and I was beset by pangs of guilt as I tucked into my pie.

As we finished the food and made ourselves comfortable, side by side and wrapped in our cloaks, I said, 'Do you think we should go and tell the monks what we're doing? They might wonder where we've got to and worry about us.'

'Let them.' Rollo spoke through a yawn. 'We'll explain in the morning.'

We settled down to sleep. The storm had renewed its ferocity, but the wind and the rain were sweeping up from the south-west, and the night was mild. Wrapped in my cloak, a blanket draped over me, I was snug and warm.

I was wide awake.

I'd been deeply asleep, dreaming some muddled and vaguely disturbing dream, and suddenly I was sitting bolt upright, pushing back my cloak and blanket, senses alert. Beside me, Rollo slept on.

I got up, moving carefully so as not to wake him. If it had been not a real danger but something in my dream that had shot me out of sleep, there was no need to disturb him.

I crept out of the stall. At either end of the short passage all four horses were restless. They too, then, sensed something was amiss.

I emerged from the stables and took a few hurrying steps along the path. I was just registering that the storm had moved away and both rain and wind had eased right off when the first waft of smoke drifted towards me. Simultaneously, or so it seemed, I heard the dreadful crackling sound and saw the orange glow.

I flew up the path.

As soon as I came out from the stand of trees I saw it: the ramshackle wooden dwelling that comprised the monastery accommodation was on fire. Very well on fire, and even as I raced on I was struck by the oddness of that. It had been raining very hard for most of the day, and the roof and walls of the structure would surely have been saturated . . .

I skidded to a halt about fifteen paces from the monastery, on the fringe of the trees. My heart urged me to go on, *go on*, I might be able to help. But my logical head stopped me. For one thing, if I'd gone any nearer I'd probably have begun to burn too. For another, there was absolutely no chance that anyone inside that white-hot hell might still be alive.

So I moved back several paces and simply watched. I thought about the people inside, but very soon closed my mind to their fate. It was too dreadful to contemplate and I prayed fervently that death had been swift. After a while, I sensed Rollo coming up behind me. He muttered something – it might have been a prayer, too – and put his arms round me, drawing my head down onto his shoulder. It was immeasurably comforting.

He said softly, 'We should leave. I'll fetch the

horses and—' But then suddenly he stiffened. Gently but firmly, he edged backwards, pushing me before him, until we were right back under the shelter of the trees. 'Stay here,' he said right in my ear.

'Why? Where are *you* going?' I hissed back.

'Lassair, someone else is watching the fire. He's standing quite still, at a safe distance right over there' – he pointed – 'and he has his back to us.'

'He's *watching*? But how long has he been there? Why didn't he try to—' But then I thought I understood. 'He set the blaze, didn't he?' I whispered.

'Well, he has an extinguished torch in his hand, so yes, it looks like it.'

Both of us as still as stone, we waited.

Then Rollo started suddenly.

'What's the matter?'

'I'm missing an opportunity,' he said, and I sensed that he was cross with himself. 'He has no idea we're here, so I must take the chance to get a good look at him.' He set off, walking with such softness that even I could detect no sound. 'Go back, *very* quietly,' he whispered over his shoulder. 'Pack up our luggage and get the horses ready. Take them right over to the far side of the copse, down that path' – he indicated – 'and stay well out of sight. I won't be long, I promise.'

He was gone for quite a while. I did as he said and prepared the horses, then led them through the trees until we were almost on the other side. Then I stood beside my mare, tightly wrapped in my cloak, leaning against her friendly flank and taking what comfort I could from her solid warmth.

He came back.

'What did you see? Has he gone?'

'Yes. He had a horse, tethered right over on the other side of the copse, and I watched him ride away. He went south, as far as I could tell, and he was obviously in a great hurry, judging from the way he whipped up his horse. I don't think he'll be back.'

'What did he do? Did he – did he go right up to the monastery?'

Rollo shook his head. 'Not quite, no, although he went as close as he could and stood looking for some time. Then he checked the stables and found the horses belonging to the travellers. He let them loose. Don't be concerned,' he added, picking up my unasked question. 'They'll soon make their way to someone who'll welcome them and they'll be well looked after. Come on, we must go.'

The fire was still smouldering and I could smell the overpowering stench of the smoke. Fear had hold of me, that ancient deep-seated terror that is in all humans, and I wanted to run. To mount up, put my heels to the mare's sides and get away, as fast and as far as I could.

But I was a healer.

'Stop,' I said.

Either he didn't hear or he was ignoring me. '*Stop!*'

Already in the saddle he drew rein, so harshly that the brown gelding jerked its head in distress. 'What?'

'The monastery's still on fire, but it must be dying down now.'

'So?' Even the one short word expressed his impatience.

'We've got to go back, Rollo! We've no choice! I – we – might be able to help, and anyway I—'

'You can't!' he cried harshly. 'You and I both saw the blaze. Nobody could have survived in there!'

'But I have to check!' I yelled back.

'What for?' he shouted.

'Because I'm a healer, and if I don't at least try – even if that means no more than ensuring they're all dead and tending the bodies – I won't be able to live with myself.'

He stared at me. Then, after what seemed an age, he shrugged.

'Very well. You're not going to see sense, are you?'

'If by that you mean I'm not going to give in and come round to your opinion, then no.'

I wasn't sure, for the light was poor, but I thought he grinned.

We made sure our horses were securely tied to a couple of the alder trees, then set off through the copse to the ruins of the monastery.

The wild, fierce blaze had indeed died down, but very soon I had to admit that Rollo had been right, and there was no possibility of entering what remained of the building. The roof was gone, two of the four walls had also vanished, totally consumed by the flames, and the remaining two were little more than lines of charred upright posts, some leaning at strange angles.

160

I went as near as I could.

The five skeletons were visible, among and beneath the piles of detritus that had fallen upon them. The senile old monk who had sat in the corner looked as if death had taken him as he slept, for his position was exactly as it had been when I'd last seen him, when he was still alive. One of the other monks, too, lay on his side, his body curved as if sleeping. I knew it was a monk because, strangely, a portion of the black habit was unburned. The three other bodies, however, all gave signs of having died in terrified agony. One was on its knees, brow touching the blackened ground, as if praying. Its hands were curled into claws, positioned in front of the grinning skull face as if about to fight off an enemy. From the solidity and size of the bones, I thought this was probably the male traveller; I'd had the impression he was a big man. The last two corpses were entwined, as if one had been trying to help the other when the fire overcame them. I told myself this was probably the zealous monk and the woman.

I wanted to help. I wanted to go in, draw their bodies out of their fiery tomb, lay them on the ground, wash and anoint them. Prepare them for burial.

But I couldn't.

Without realizing it, I'd been moving forward, closer to the ghastly sight before me. The soles of my feet were already uncomfortably hot.

I felt Rollo's arm round my waist. 'Come away, Lassair,' he said. His voice was very tender. 'There's nothing you can do for them.'

I let him lead me away. I didn't know why I was crying, but I didn't seem to be able to stop.

We planned to ride a long way during what remained of that first night. Both of us urgently wanted to get away, and it made sense to make the most of the darkness.

But we had to decide where to go.

We drew rein and discussed the options.

'Wouldn't it be best to carry on with the plan to go to Gloucester, where you'll be able to put yourself under King William's protection?' I said.

But Rollo shook his head. 'I don't believe that's the right option any more,' he said thoughtfully.

There was quite a long pause. 'And are you going to tell me why?' I asked presently.

He turned to me, and I sensed he was coming out of some deep thought. Reluctantly.

'Lassair, that fire was no accident. We wondered at first if the two travellers who arrived after us were the ones hunting me, but that can't be right.'

'Because they have now been killed, you mean?' He nodded. 'Killed because the man who set the monastery on fire believed they were you and me?' He nodded again.

'*Oh!*'

It was a dreadful thought. I tried to drive it away with another question.

'So who were the man and the woman?'

'I would say they were innocent travellers, and nothing whatsoever to do with me. With us,' he amended, not quite quickly enough. 'The man or men hunting for me possibly paid for information

162

from someone at Lord Edwin's castle, and knew they were now hunting not a man alone – me – but a man and a woman travelling together, well dressed and on good horses.'

'Us.'

'Us, yes. But the pair who arrived after us fitted the description equally well. The man who burned down the monastery followed the wrong couple.'

'And killed them,' I whispered.

'Yes.'

'But I don't see why that makes you dismiss the option of going to Gloucester,' I protested. 'Surely the safest place in the whole land is under the king's protection?'

He looked at me for a long moment. 'The killer is close,' he said tonelessly. 'He almost caught us. If – when – he finds out he's slain the wrong man, he'll be back on our trail. It's a long way to Gloucester, and I don't know the secret ways.'

The echo of his words seemed to stay in my head.

Secret ways. Secret . . .

I said, 'I think I may have an idea.'

For the remainder of the night we made our way south, gradually turning towards the east. I wasn't entirely sure where we were, and Rollo could offer no help other than that the monastery had been roughly south-west of Peterborough. I was travelling pretty much blind, navigating by the stars when we could see them through the clouds, and fervently hoping that sooner or later we'd come to somewhere I recognized. As dawn broke

– and I was greatly relieved when the growing light on the horizon confirmed that we were going in the right direction – we found ourselves on the edge of a pine forest, bordered on its eastern side by what looked like a fairly major road.

'I hope very much,' I said as we drew rein on the edge of the tree line, 'that's the Cambridge to Peterborough road.'

'It is,' Rollo said. 'About five miles that way' – he pointed to his left, where the road curved in a loop round the north-east side of the forest – 'there's quite a reasonable inn.' He must have seen my face light up for straight away he went on, 'Where we won't be putting up, because, for one thing, it's in the wrong direction, and for another, our intention is not to be spotted by anyone else on the roads and bigger tracks.'

I had dismounted and was already leading the mare in under the trees. 'I've slept in pine forests before,' I called back. 'As long as we can find a dry spot, we'll be comfortable enough.'

The place we selected wasn't entirely dry – nowhere out of doors was truly dry after all the rain – but it was adequate. We piled up pine needles and spread out blankets, and, wrapped in our cloaks, we were warm enough. There was a fast-flowing rill close by, and we watered and fed the horses, then hobbled them. We ate a few mouthfuls, then settled to rest.

It was very hard to force the images of the burned monastery and what lay within from my head, and it took all the willpower I had. But I was exhausted. I slept.

When I woke, the sun was dropping to the

western horizon. I'd been asleep for most of the day.

Rollo was already up, and he'd made a small fire. He'd used old, seasoned materials and there was little smoke.

'Is that wise?' I asked as I sat up.

He shrugged. 'We're deep in the trees and I've seen no sign of human life since I woke soon after noon. It's a slight risk, but I thought we could both benefit from hot food. And I was hoping you might have some supplies of one of your better restorative herbal drinks in that satchel of yours.'

'I have.' I reached for the satchel and selected a couple of small packages. He had water on to heat, suspended over the fire in the small can he carried in his baggage. As I went to test it to see if it was hot enough, I noticed he'd put chunks of meat on sticks and these were roasting over the low flames.

'Have you been hunting?' It wasn't a skill I associated with him, but then, I recalled, he made many journeys in the wild lands.

He smiled. 'I'd love to say that while you were sleeping I caught, skinned and prepared a hare, but it would be a lie. It's some of the salted pork that Lord Edwin ordered to be packed up for us. He was very generous, and there's plenty left. There's some very dry bread to eat with it, and a couple of apples.'

It was probably because I was very hungry, but our scrappy little meal in the pine forest on the edge of the fens was one of the best I could remember.

* * *

When it was fully dark, we set out again. We had to wait until nightfall, because, while up to now we'd been travelling cross-country and had been able to keep to small paths, animal tracks, field edges and wood margins, now we had no option but to take to the road.

But I was on familiar ground now, for we would be going round to the north of Cambridge, heading at first due east, then turning north-east. I knew the roads and the byways quite well, and there was no danger of losing our way because, after we'd slipped past to the north of the town, we'd simply be following the fen edge. The danger didn't come from any natural peril: it was entirely man-made.

I had planned to go round the town on one of the smaller, less-frequented tracks to the north of the road that most people used. But I'd reckoned without the recent heavy rain, for much of the land north of the road was waterlogged and, in many places, flooded.

Rollo, understanding the difficulty, said in a low voice, 'Can you not find a way across the water? If there's a submerged path there that you've used before, could you not get us onto it?'

I hesitated. I'd had the same thought, but I just didn't trust myself in the dark. Part of me knew I could do it, but the problem was that, in view of the horrors of the very recent past, I was pretty sure I wouldn't be able to detach my mind and slip into the semi-trance state that would be required.

It was too complicated to explain all that so I just said, 'No.'

He accepted it without protest, for which I was very grateful.

We stayed on the road for a heart-thumping, palm-sweating four or five miles. I was expecting some ferocious, well-armed figure to leap out at us at every turn and, judging by Rollo's fast breathing and his intense watchfulness, not to mention the sword in his hand, I guessed it was the same for him.

Eventually, after what seemed about half my lifetime, we came to the place where the road went on north-east and the little track I'd been searching for branched off almost due north.

'Here,' I breathed on a huge sigh of relief. 'This is where we leave the road.'

He muttered something, which I thought might be a prayer of thanks, and followed me as I set off up the path.

I knew I couldn't find the place I was heading for in the darkness so, once again, we stopped to rest until dawn. But there was no hope of a dry bed that night, for we were right on the fringes of the fens and the ground was soggy, squelchy and uncertain. We found a tiny hummock of slightly raised ground, topped by a couple of willows. We put our saddles on the ground and leant back against the tree trunks where, cold, uncomfortable and increasingly damp, we waited for daybreak.

And so the second night passed.

Now, on the morning of the third day since the monastery had burned, I had to get us safely to the place I'd remembered; the place deep in the secret heart of the fens where I thought nobody would find us. I'd thought it would be relatively easy. Now, faced with the actuality of fulfilling my plan, I wasn't so sure.

After an hour, I stopped.

'Are we lost?' Rollo asked calmly.

'Not exactly lost,' I replied. I slipped from the mare's back. 'Hold my reins, will you?'

I'd only been to the place I was looking for once before, but that had been a few weeks ago and the memory was fresh. Two details, however, had changed: the water level was considerably higher now, and the previous time I'd come, I'd been on foot.

I'd also been with someone who knew the way, but I didn't allow myself to dwell on that.

I couldn't do anything about the water level, but I was hoping that the altered vantage point of being down at ground level instead of up high on the mare's back would help . . .

And, after far too long – I could sense Rollo's growing impatience, snapping and snarling along the track behind me – it did.

I emerged onto a sort of beach, on the edge of the land and with the black fenland water spread out before me. A little way to my right was the place I sought.

I wanted to cheer. Instead I hurried back to Rollo, informed him I'd found it and, mounting once more, told him to follow me.

We shoved our way through onto the shore together. Stopping, I pointed.

He stared at the place I was indicating.

'But it's an island,' he said. 'And, unless you can magic one up, we haven't got a boat.'

168

'We don't need one.' My confidence had returned. 'There's a causeway leading out to it from there.' I pointed again. 'It's not really an island because actually there's a narrow neck of land about three paces across that connects it to the shore. Come on!'

I kicked the mare, and, with Rollo splashing along behind me, we went along to the place where the connecting causeway began. I dismounted, bending down to inspect the ground.

I was back in my own territory, and now the tension and fear were controllable. Straightening up, I looked out over the dark water. And, quite soon, I knew exactly where the safe path went.

I took off my heavy cloak and flung it across the saddle. Then I gathered up my skirts and tucked them securely in my belt. I spoke some calming words to the mare, who was a little nervous, and she relaxed. She gave a soft whinny, and nudged me affectionately with her nose. With one hand on her neck, hoping that the warmth of my touch would go on providing reassurance, I set off into the water.

It wasn't as deep as I'd feared, and even having negotiated the lowest point I was only wet to halfway up my thighs. Relieved that I wasn't going to get soaked, I raised my eyes and looked ahead.

The island was much as I remembered it, and just as dark and forbidding. Like the fen edge behind me, the vegetation here grew dense and profuse, forming thickets of alder and willow in which grew the occasional ancient oak tree. Beneath the canopy of the trees there grew the thick, all but impenetrable carr made up of a

169

tangle of bushes and shrubs, some of them peculiar to the marshes. Under the carr grew the marsh fern, rusty brown now.

On the island there was a house. It was small and simply constructed, with wattle-and-daub walls and a reed-thatch roof. It consisted of one main room, behind which there was a separate workroom. Other than the privy, that was all.

I had a mental picture of the main room, and I was hoping that once we'd lit a fire and driven out the damp it would be cosy enough.

I'd reached the far end of the causeway. I led the mare up onto dry ground, and she shook her head as if in relief, making her long mane fly and her harness jingle. I moved out of the way so that Rollo could step onto the island as well.

Silently I handed him the mare's reins. I walked forward, right up to the low door. I raised the latch and, before my courage failed, flung it open.

I went in, coming to a halt just inside the door.

I held my breath.

Nothing happened.

I gave a gasp of relief.

For, while I had recognized this house's value as a hiding place, nevertheless I feared it. It had been Gurdyman who, only a few weeks ago, had brought me here. He too had used it as a place of sanctuary; somewhere to hide when he feared his life was threatened.[5]

It had protected him from the danger that he knew about, but in going there he had encountered a far worse peril. So, because of him, had I.

[5] See *The Night Wanderer*.

But that peril had gone now.

And as I stood there in the open doorway it seemed to me that this house, whose solitary inhabitant had once been a force for good, was now welcoming Rollo and me as if we were long-lost children.

He had lost them.

Furious – with his prey but even more with himself – the man drove a hard, bunched-up fist into the tense muscle of his thigh. He had been so sure. He'd been proud of having picked up their trail again when they left the fens and headed north. He'd thought he'd lost them, but some instinct had told him to try that road; to pause in that out-of-the-way hamlet, stitch on a smile and pause for a pleasant word with the red-haired priest. Who had told him, with hardly any prompting, precisely what he wanted to know. Then there had been that dismal, miserable day of waiting in the rain, only for the reward of the glorious moment when he picked up the trail again and followed it to the monastery.

He'd been so sure it had ended there; he'd left, hurrying on with all speed to do what he had to do next.

Now he knew.

He was after the man again, and this time he wouldn't let himself be fooled.

Eleven

Late in the day after his lengthy discussions with Gurdyman, Jack met his loyal lawmen at the tavern on the quay. As he had anticipated, the murder of Elwytha Picot was the sole topic of conversation. Sheriff Picot, Jack learned, was incandescent with rage and searching desperately for someone to blame for his late nephew's wife's savage death.

'I'm not sure it matters if they're guilty or not,' Fat Gerald observed. 'He wants a hanging, and if he can come up with a slower and more painful method of execution, he probably will.'

His remark silenced the group for a moment. It was, Jack thought, looking round at the men's faces, as if every one of them – himself included – recognized the truth of it.

'I'm not pointing the finger at you, chief,' Walter said quietly, 'but the sheriff's sore as a whipped hound that he can't hang anybody for the death of his nephew. I reckon Gerald's right, and whoever he picks on for the lady's death will be made to pay twice over.'

'Has the body been removed?' Jack asked, more for the sake of moving the talk away from Walter's remark than because he really wanted to know.

'Yes,' said Ned. 'They brought it up to the castle early this morning and put it in the sheriff's private quarters. It's being prepared for burial.'

'And *that* will be no small affair,' Lard offered. He grinned briefly. 'They say the sheriff was none too fond of his niece by marriage, and had little to do with her when she was alive, yet all the same it seems he's intent on making a lavish spectacle of her death.'

Who will there be to mourn her? Jack wondered.

He remembered the gaggle of servants dancing attendance on her, the morning he'd watched her walk out.

'What of the household?' he asked.

He'd spoken too abruptly, and one or two of the men were exchanging glances. 'Not too sure, chief,' Walter said. 'I don't suppose they'll stay, though, with nobody to serve and nobody to pay them.'

'If I were sheriff I'd have a team of men standing by to search them as they go,' young Henry said, eyes bright with fascinated speculation. 'I'd wager that they'll have helped themselves to one or two easily portable and very valuable little treasures.'

'Aye, and who would blame them for that?' Ranald replied roughly. It was him, Jack recalled, who was vaguely related to one of the serving maids. 'The master and mistress of the house were hard on those beneath them,' Ranald went on. 'From what I hear, they did nothing to earn the loyalty, respect and devotion of those who served them.'

'Go on,' Jack said.

Ranald turned to him, a faint smile twisting his mouth. 'I guessed you'd want to know the latest, chief, and I've just come from a lengthy chat with

173

my cousin's wife's sister.' He paused, gathering his thoughts. 'Nobody who worked in the household was happy there. Many of the lowest servants were little better than slaves, since their only payment was their lodging and their food, and there was never enough of that.'

'Why did they stay?' asked the lad, Iver.

Ranald turned weary eyes on him. 'They had no choice, boy. When Gaspard Picot put up that great house, he demolished other people's homes to make room for it. They'd have been no better than half-ruined hovels to one such as him, and he'd probably said, if he'd troubled to think about it, that he was doing the town a favour by getting rid of an eyesore.' He shrugged. 'Eyesore or not, those houses were home to the folk who inhabited them, and when Picot destroyed them, many decided that they had little option but to accept his terms and go and work for him.'

'He was a hard master?' Jack asked.

'He was. Maudie – that's my cousin's wife's sister – says she was spared the worst of him, because she was the lady's maid, and the lady had separate quarters. But her man, he served the master, and that man was cruel in so many ways you wouldn't be able to count them, and the whippings and beatings weren't the worst of it.' Ranald paused, gazing across the room, clearly thinking. 'Best way I can sum it up, from what Maudie told me, is that Gaspard Picot could make you believe there was no hope, and that breaks a man's spirit.'

Again, silence fell as they all thought about

174

that. Then Fat Gerald said, 'In that case, I don't blame them for making off with a treasure or two.' There were nods and grunts of agreement.

They were ordering more ale when the door of the tavern opened and Ginger came hurrying in. 'Get one for me, will you?' he called out to Magnus's pretty wife, and she nodded, smiling. 'The weather's closing in,' Ginger added, shoving Iver up the bench so that he could sit down. 'There's a mist rising and it's no night to be out.'

'Are you just off duty?' Jack asked. Ginger, busy with the first draught of ale, merely nodded. 'Where have you been?'

Ginger swallowed and wiped his cuff across his mouth. 'At Gaspard Picot's house,' he replied.

'We were just talking about that!' Iver cried.

Ginger gave him a scathing glance. 'Now there's a surprise.'

'What's happening over there?' Jack demanded.

'The house is deserted,' Ginger said. 'The sheriff made quite sure of it. He had ten of us go through every chamber, hall and cellar, investigating every cupboard, chest and dark corner. Then he made a great business of locking and barring the doors. Some of the outdoor servants have organized temporary quarters in the outbuildings, but they'll all have to be gone soon. The sheriff has only allowed them to stay because he's ordered them to stop anyone trying to break in.'

'Where will they go?' Fat Gerald asked.

Ginger shrugged. 'No idea. Many are locals, though,' he added, 'so with any luck there'll be some relative or friend who'll help out.'

175

Jack was only vaguely aware of the conversation continuing around him. His thoughts had turned to those two earlier murders. He was sitting beside Ned, one of the senior of the lawmen based inside the castle, and now, leaning closer to him, he said quietly, 'Has any progress been made on the two young men found dead?'

Ned shook his head. 'Not that I know of, chief. We've nothing at all to go on, that's been the trouble. As far as I can tell, Sheriff Picot has decided that neither of them are our concern since both were strangers, one travelling by land and the other by water but both merely passing through.'

'So we're just to put them out of mind?'

'That's about right,' Ned agreed tonelessly. 'Both have been buried and will soon be forgotten.'

'You don't – it's not thought that the two deaths could be connected with the widow Picot's murder?'

Ned shrugged. 'Don't see how or why they should be, chief. Other than the timing, where *is* the connection? The young men were killed out in the open, the lady in her own hall.'

'All three bodies were savagely beaten,' Jack said.

'Aye, but then so are many of the murder victims we deal with.'

Jack had to acknowledge the truth of that. He leaned back against the wall, deep in thought. So the general view was that the two earlier deaths had nothing to do with the lady Elwytha's murder . . . He shook his head. Although as yet he couldn't rationalize it, Jack

176

kept on returning to his suspicion that there had to be a connection.

Jack was having trouble sleeping. After a night consisting of a few brief periods of dozing and a lot of lying awake, he rose just before dawn and set out, down the path through the deserted village, out onto the road and then left towards the town.

It was still dark, and the total blanketing-out of the stars suggested a cloudy sky. He was struck by the strange absence of noise: stopping just past the construction site where the new priory was nearing completion, he realized that the silence was absolute. The morning was mild, damp and still, and as he moved on down the gentle slope towards the river, he walked into a dense cloud of mist rising from the water. As he crossed the Great Bridge, he could barely see a pace in front of him.

He strode on, round to the north-east of the town. He was finding that walking along a road shrouded in mist was disturbingly eerie, and at times he was moving almost blind. He noticed that the mist also muffled smells; used to the various stenches of the river and the town, he was struck by the lack of them. The mist had a smell of its own . . . Pausing to sniff, he tried to describe it to himself. It smelt of the earth; of mud; of darkness and hidden things.

He strode on, dismissing the rambling of his thoughts.

Sometimes the total silence seemed to drum against his ears until it was almost painful. But

177

the deadening effect of the mist was not, he discovered, total; once or twice, unlikely and surely far-off noises such as the cry of an early risen boatman and the bang of a heavy door suddenly rang out with sharp clarity, so that they seemed far closer than they could possibly be.

Jack was beset by the weird sense that this wasn't the world he knew and understood.

Ruthlessly he crushed his apprehension and forced himself to walk faster.

By the time he reached the Picot house, the mist had cleared a little. He made out the ruined wall beneath which he had sat and watched, and the overhanging branches of the willow. He could just see the gates in the paling fence, firmly closed, and the house up on its rise beyond.

As he had done so many times before, he sank down on the bench – it was wet to the touch – and watched.

I have no idea why I am here, he thought after a while. *It's cold, my bum's damp, I ought to be snug and warm in bed and still sound asleep.*

Cross with himself and his own folly, abruptly he stood up and began a slow pacing, up and down, following the line of the old wall.

He kept his eyes on the house on its rise, looming out of the mist and, as its intensity varied, sometimes clearly visible, sometimes obscured. But then suddenly a great pall of white billowed upwards and outwards, and for several moments he couldn't see the house at all . . .

He smelt smoke.

And, starting to run although he had no idea

where to, he realized that what he had taken for a sudden intensity in the mist was actually a huge cloud of smoke.

He ran right into it, and instantly began to cough. The violence of the action, deep in his chest and right across his ribs, forced his wound to stretch and contract with such vigour that he cried out in pain. Doubled over, he moved away as quickly as he could.

When he could breathe again, he straightened up and stared back at the fire. It had taken hold now and sheets of flame rose high in the air. The gates had been flung wide and several figures were emerging onto the road, running from the flames and the smoke just as Jack had done. Some carried bundles, some helped others. A man cried, 'Is everyone out?' and someone else yelled back, 'Yes, I was the last!'

Jack moved back into the deep shadow of the ruined wall and, just like the others, watched as Gaspard Picot's vulgar, braggart, extravagant house burned.

And, knowing that nobody was inside, that those who had been sheltering in the outbuildings had all escaped, he felt a savage joy flood through him.

Suddenly, out of the corner of his eye, Jack caught a movement: small, swift, so that he wasn't entirely sure he'd really seen it. But, tiny though it had been, it had registered in his mind and he knew he must check. It was over to his right.

Precisely where he'd spotted the dark, cloaked figure before.

Keeping right up against the wall and trying to be quiet, he loped towards where he'd seen the tiny shimmer in the darkness. He thought he must have been mistaken, for, although anyone hiding there must surely have seen and heard his approach, there was no further movement.

Until, when he was right upon the place, a dark-cloaked figure shot out of the depths of the shadows, elbowed him sharply in the ribs and fled.

The elbow, on top of the damage caused by his smoke-induced coughing fit, almost finished Jack. But he couldn't let this chance go by, and, gathering all his reserves, he set off in pursuit.

In front of him, the dark-cloaked man suddenly turned off into the narrow, convoluted alleys of the community that Gaspard Picot had razed to the ground. It soon became apparent that he knew his way, and Jack understood now that he must have been hiding in here; living, probably, in one of the better of the tumbledown dwellings. He seemed to flit through the maze of alleyways and passages, as springy and light-footed as a deer. Nevertheless, for a while Jack was gaining on him.

But Jack was tiring. He was not nearly fit enough for such a chase. He was gasping for breath, sweating, his lungs burning. In desperation, seeing the dark-cloaked man starting to increase the gap, he forced himself to make one last, desperate effort. And, to his surprised satisfaction, he drew closer, closer . . .

As soon as he judged that he was near enough, he launched himself at the fleeing man. His arms fully extended, his hands reaching out, he grasped his prey firmly around the upper legs and felled him.

For a brief moment both of them lay still, stunned by the force of the fall. Jack had fallen fully on top of the dark figure, and he'd heard the whoosh as the air was driven from his body.

But then, recovering far more swiftly than Jack would have believed possible, the man wrenched both arms free and, bunching his hands into fists, began punching Jack: ribs, chest, shoulders and jaw all took a hit, and as his sore, vulnerable wound was attacked yet again, Jack let out a yell of fury. Using his weight to hold the man down, he grabbed first one and then the other wrist in one hand. In one hand . . . Before he could think about that, with his free hand he shoved back the deep hood of the cloak and pulled down the scarf tied high around the man's face.

But it wasn't a man.

It was a woman.

In the waxing light of day, he could make out the features of her face quite clearly. She was in perhaps the mid-thirties, and the most striking first impression was her ferocious and intensely dark eyes. They were large, set at a slight slant, fringed with thick black lashes. And looking at him as if she wanted to kill him.

Her skin was olive, her hair – what he could see of it, for it was drawn off her face and secured somehow beneath the hood – was black. She had a strong nose, the nostrils deeply etched. Her mouth, wide, mobile, beautifully shaped, was busy hissing a stream of curses at him.

181

A dozen thoughts flew through his head, so quickly that he barely had the time to register them all. Uppermost was the memory of Fat Gerald's shrewd words about Sheriff Picot, last night in the tavern: *He wants a hanging, and if he can come up with a slower and more painful method of execution, he probably will.*

The woman writhing and struggling beneath him might well have started the fire, and in all probability had. But nobody had been killed; all that had happened was that a monstrous house had been destroyed. If, as he had to admit seemed likely, she had also murdered the lady Elwytha, then that was a different matter.

But *seemed likely* wasn't enough to throw her into Sheriff Picot's vengeful hands; it wasn't for Jack, anyway. If he let her be taken by the sheriff's men, her guilt for both the fire and the murder would be assumed without question simply because she was found in the area, without one single question being asked or an iota of proof or evidence being demanded. As Fat Gerald had pointed out, Sheriff Picot was desperate to lay blame and anyone vaguely suitable would do.

This woman, fighting him so hard even as he felt her strength fail, would serve only too well.

Keeping firm hold of her upper arms, he got to his feet and dragged her up after him. Then he drew up her hood, bundled her cloak tightly around her and, one arm around her waist and the other encircling her wrist, he led her away.

He noticed, as he handled the heavy folds of her cloak, that there was no strong smell of

182

smoke on her. She could, he thought, have lit the fire and made her escape before it took hold. On the other hand . . .

He urged her down the road that rounded the town centre, hurrying now for already there were sounds that the townspeople's day was starting. She whispered, 'Where are you taking me?' He didn't reply.

They were heading over the Great Bridge now, and the mist was clearing away as the sun rose. Up ahead, the castle was visible on its mound. Her face paled and a gasp escaped her.

'Don't worry, we're not going there,' he said curtly. 'Not yet, anyway.'

She cursed him again, something she seemed to be able to do in more than one tongue. He understood, in the jumble of words, that she was hurling serious doubt on his legitimacy, and she definitely referred to his mother in a term not designed to flatter. Briefly he tightened his grip on her wrist and felt her wince in pain. He muttered, 'We'll leave my mother out of this, if you don't mind.'

They took the path that led round the base of the castle and on through the deserted village. They reached Jack's house, at the far end of the alley, and his geese set up their alarm. Quickly he hushed them. He opened up and pushed the woman inside. He closed and barred the door – it was the only way in and out, the windows being too small and too high – and stood with his back to it, staring at his captive.

Then he said, 'I found you skulking close to a burning house, where the night before last a

183

woman was brutally murdered.' Her expression changed, and for an instant she looked as if she was in great pain. 'Now I do not necessarily assume that you're guilty of either crime,' he went on, 'but the evidence against you is strong. I need you to tell me who you are and why, for the past week or more, you've been watching the house of Gaspard Picot.'

'It was burning fiercely,' she said dully. 'Soon nothing will remain.'

He noticed, as he had in a fleeting impression when she spoke before, that she didn't sound like a local woman.

'You are a stranger here?'

Slowly she nodded. She was looking at him warily. She didn't speak.

'Well?' he demanded. 'Where do you live? Why have you come to Cambridge? What's your name?'

Still she didn't speak. With a faint sigh, as if this was all too much to bear, she glanced around the room, her huge dark eyes resting on the shelves with their neatly arranged mugs and platters, the hearth and its recently swept surround, the clean floor. The small room beyond the archway, where the bed stood with folded blankets.

'Good enough for you?' Jack asked. She either missed or didn't understand the sarcasm.

In frustration he stepped up close to her, pushing her so that she stumbled and fell. Instantly she drew up her knees and encircled her body with her arms, protecting the vulnerable parts of her body, making herself a smaller target. Her eyes fixed on his were full of terror.

And he knew, by that instinctive gesture of self-protection, that she was a woman who had suffered brutality at a man's hands. With the realization came shame. Jack had seen what happened to a woman – even a brave one who would fight as long as she had breath – when she was beaten. Sooner or later that high courage got used up. And, spirit broken and ashamed, there would be nothing left.

He sat down beside her. 'I'm sorry,' he said. 'I shouldn't have shoved you, and I didn't mean to throw you on the floor.' He sensed her relax, very slightly. 'It's not my intention to hurt you,' he went on. *In fact,* he could have added, *I'm trying to help you.*

But it was too soon to promise that.

'It seems to me,' he went on when still she didn't speak, 'that you have two options: either talk to me, by which I mean tell me who you are and why you're here, and what Gaspard Picot's widow and her house are to you, or else—' He stopped. *Or else I'll give you up to our deeply unpleasant and untrustworthy sheriff, who happens to be related to the dead woman and whose nephew built that ghastly house, who is baying for blood and who will be very happy to shove you in a filthy, stinking dungeon until he takes you out and hangs you for murder and arson.*

No. He couldn't threaten that, for he wasn't at all sure he could bring himself to do it.

'You should know that I'm a lawman,' he said roughly. 'It's my duty to apprehend those guilty of crimes, and it may well be that here in my own house I'm harbouring one.' He had her

185

attention now, and her eyes didn't leave his. 'Oh, and we had a couple more murders not long ago which remain a total mystery,' he added. 'Had it been a less impartial officer of the law than I who happened to apprehend you, no doubt he'd have remembered those earlier deaths and found it convenient to ask himself if you were responsible for those, too.'

She had gone deathly white. Every drop of blood seemed to have drained from her flushed face, and she swayed where she sat.

He thought it was because of his threat, and while part of him regretted causing her such terror, another rejoiced because at last he seemed to have got through to her.

But, as haltingly she began to speak, he realized that her fear had quite another cause.

'Two more murders?' She muttered something under her breath, briefly closing her eyes. It sounded like a desperate prayer. Opening her eyes again, her expression pleading, she said, 'Please, who were the victims?'

'Two men, both quite young, both with smooth, fair hair. They were—' He had been going on to relate the details of where and when the two bodies had been found, but she was no longer listening. She had buried her face in her hands and she was sobbing.

Tentatively he reached out and touched the back of her hand. She didn't seem to notice. Her distress seemed to intensify, and soon she was rocking to and fro, gasping for breath.

At a loss to know what else to do, Jack put his arms around her.

Instantly she turned into him, her hands clasped into fists resting on his shoulders, her head on his chest. And something inside her seemed to collapse, so that she clung to him as if his solid presence alone was keeping her alive.

He let her cry.

When it stopped – she appeared to have worn herself out – he made her comfortable on blankets by the hearth and stoked up the fire. When it was going well, he put water to heat and made her a drink from one of Lassair's herbal preparations. Then he fetched bread and a hunk of cheese. She gulped down the drink but pushed away the food, so he forced her. She looked half-starved.

When she had finished – after the first reluctant bites she tore through the simple food as if her life depended on it, which he reckoned it might well have done – she gave an enormous yawn and lay down on her side, curling up her legs. He tucked her cloak and a blanket around her. Soon her eyes closed and she sank into sleep.

He watched her for a while. She began to snore gently.

Quietly he slipped out, closing and firmly securing the door behind him.

He made his way through busy early morning streets and alleys to Gurdyman's house. Once he'd managed to make the old man hear his pounding on the door and admit him – Gurdyman explained that he'd been absorbed in a particularly teasing problem concerning arsenic – he was given the usual welcome.

187

They settled in the little inner courtyard. It was chilly out there, but Gurdyman explained that the alternative was the crypt, which was unfortunately rather fume-filled just then.

Jack told him about the fire, about the woman, about his fear that, handed over to Sheriff Picot, she would not live long.

Gurdyman nodded. 'She would be a most convenient choice as perpetrator of both crimes,' he agreed. 'An outsider – you say she's not local – and a woman on her own.'

'I didn't say she was alone!' Jack protested.

'I think, however, that we may construe it,' Gurdyman replied. 'You have seen her keeping vigil outside the Picot house. She was there around dawn this morning. A married woman, a family woman or a servant would surely not be able to absent herself from her domicile so regularly and at such an unlikely time as the early hours of the morning.'

It made sense, Jack had to agree. 'You may be right,' he said.

Gurdyman was eyeing him, a small smile on his wide, mobile mouth. 'Wasn't it risky, to leave her alone?' he asked. 'She'll surely be gone when you return.'

But Jack shook his head. 'I don't believe she will. When I mixed a hot herbal brew for her I included one of the sleeping draughts that Lassair prepared for me. If my own reaction is anything to go by, she'll still be asleep when the sun starts to go down. And just in case it fails to work for some reason,' he added, 'I locked her in.'

Gurdyman was still watching him. 'Do you believe her guilty?'

'Yes. Probably. No.'

Gurdyman smiled. 'I see.'

'There was something else that I found strange,' Jack said, breaking a short, thoughtful silence.

'Yes?'

'When I was trying to persuade her to tell me who she was and what she was doing in the town, I told her there had been two other murders and that she might all too readily be held responsible for those too, once she came under suspicion of the killing of the widow Picot and the firing of the house.'

Gurdyman gave him a reproving look. 'And is that really likely?'

'That she killed the first two victims, no. That she'd be suspected, yes.' He spoke roughly, for Gurdyman was making him ashamed of his tactics.

'How did she react?' Diplomatically, Gurdyman moved the talk on.

'She went very white,' Jack said. 'She said a prayer – at least, I assume that was what it was, although I couldn't make it out – and asked about the victims.'

'And you told her?'

'Yes, upon which she suffered some sort of collapse and cried as if her heart was broken.' He saw her again in his mind. Felt the desperation with which she had clung to him.

'Interesting,' Gurdyman murmured. 'How old is she?'

'I'm not sure. Maybe in the middle thirties?'

'And the two young men?'

'Younger by a decade or so, I'd say.'

'Hmm. She is too young to be the mother, and perhaps a shade too old to be the wife, lover or mistress.'

'You're thinking of a connection to *both* the fair-haired men?' It seemed far-fetched to Jack, especially in view of the fact that no link had been established or even suggested between the victims. They looked vaguely alike; that was all.

But Gurdyman was shaking his head. 'No, Jack, I'm not. I'm wondering if somebody is hunting for a man who is of a certain age, with fair hair worn smooth, long and well cut. And—'

'And you think the woman locked in my house knows a man answering that description,' Jack finished for him, 'and now fears he's just been murdered.'

Twelve

As Rollo and I went through the doorway and into Mercure's house, the sense of welcome seemed to increase. The main living room was clean and smelled fresh. I ran my fingers across the top of a small side table, and to my surprise there didn't even appear to be any dust.

I heard Rollo drop the bags on the floor and I was aware of him unpacking. But my mind had gone back into the recent past: to the time when I had come here with Gurdyman, not long after his friend Mercure had left his home for the final time.

He and I had searched both this room and, more importantly, Mercure's workroom, hidden away behind the main building and reached by the covered way leading off from the rear door. Although Gurdyman had been well aware that Mercure's house was difficult to access, even given you could find it in the first place, so well camouflaged was it, he hadn't wanted to take any risks. For Mercure had also been a magician, a wizard: the title doesn't really matter, and neither man ever used such names themselves. Men like him and Gurdyman employ, are familiar with and experiment with many dangerous substances which, handled by the curious, the unwary or the foolhardy, are extremely dangerous. Poisons. Substances that suddenly and unexpectedly burst into flame or explode, or both. Strange and exotic materials, brought from far-distant lands, which, combined with one another, release powers that are too great for anyone who is not an adept to handle. Even the adepts sometimes come to grief, as I know from life with Gurdyman. So together he and I made the short journey out here to Mercure's house, and, walking in silence beside my mentor, I had the sense that it was a pilgrimage, of a sort; a final devotional act performed in honour of a man who I suspected had probably been a lifelong friend.

We came up with quite a haul. Gurdyman had sent me out to rummage around in the little row of outhouses for something with which to transport our finds, and I'd discovered a small but functional handcart. We stowed our unlikely treasures very carefully – there was a wooden barrel of a particular black powder, for example, which goes off with a bang and a cloud of foul smoke if it's dropped – and covered the load with an old blanket . . .

'Shall I set out the bed rolls in here, by the hearth?' Rollo's voice interrupted my thoughts. I turned to look at him, smiling.

'Sorry,' I said, 'I ought to be helping. Yes, good idea. This room is snug enough, and will be quite comfortable once we've got the fire going.'

Rollo spread out the bedding, then straightened up and said, 'The firewood's outside?'

'Round the back.' I pointed. Mercure, I recalled, kept fires both in his living room and in his workroom, and stored his fuel between the two.

Nodding, Rollo disappeared outside. Presently I heard the sound of an axe striking a block. He was, I guessed, making sure we had a good supply. We might, I realized with a shock of dismay, be here some time.

In which case, I told myself firmly, I should stop standing there daydreaming and feeling anxious, and get on with sorting out anything and everything that Rollo and I could use.

Mercure had lived a solitary life but, as I'd already suspected and as now was verified, he'd looked after himself well. The room was surprisingly comfortable – a stack of good wool blankets and some pillows were neatly stored in a big wooden chest, with a couple of straw mattresses tucked away behind it. The hearth stones were large and sound, and there was a space close by where the day's firewood could be stored, the fire's heat taking the damp out of it so that it was less likely to smoke. Everything was neat and tidy; Mercure, I surmised, had made sure of it. But then, I thought, it was likely that this pleasant, spacious living area was little used; that Mercure, like Gurdyman, had spent most of his life in his workroom.

I suddenly realized how tired I was, and I sat down on the wooden chest. We were safe, for the time being at least, and a wave of relief at having found this hiding place washed through me. But I didn't sit there for long, for my stomach gave a great growl and I got up again to see what food supplies I could muster.

We still had some of the provisions Lord Edwin gave us, and I laid them out on the long board running along one side of the room. The meat had been well salted and would be good for some time yet. The apples were wrinkly now, their crisp juiciness slowly drying out, but they were still edible and retained some of their goodness. The onions would keep all winter . . . At the mouth-watering thought of the sharp, appetizing taste of onions flavouring a stew, I glanced round and spied a cooking pot, set on a set of shelves over on the far side of the hearth. As soon as Rollo had a good fire going and we'd fetched water, I'd make a start.

Beside the shelves there was a small door which I hadn't noticed. Opening it, I discovered Mercure's store cupboard. While there was of course no fresh food, there was plenty that we could use: good supplies of oats, rye and barley flour; salt, pepper and a variety of dried, powdered spices; dried yeast; poppy and flax seeds; honey; bunches of herbs. Dried peas. A string of onions. A couple of barrels of apples. *Two* barrels of apples? I checked, and discovered that the second barrel contained ale.

Mercure had contrived a little shelf set high up at the rear of the cupboard, close to a small window. Putting my hand up to it, I felt a cold draught. I paused to orientate myself, and realized the window, and indeed this wall, faced north. On what was in effect a cold shelf were stored a stone jar of butter, well salted and still good, and a hard-crusted cheese. I closed the cupboard door and, smiling, went to crouch beside Rollo, putting my hands to the blaze he'd encouraged to flare up in the hearth. I told him what I'd discovered, and, as I'd anticipated, he was particularly happy to hear about the ale.

'Did you not think to take this good food away with you when you came here before?' he asked.

'We didn't even find it,' I admitted. 'We were here, as I told you, for a very different purpose.'

I went out for water, filled the cooking pot and suspended it over the fire. 'We're not going to starve,' I said, 'but, all the same, I think I should go out foraging. The pools and the reed beds are full of fish, and I could probably find clams and even try to net some eels, although it's late in the season.'

'Yes, good,' Rollo said absently. But I didn't think he was really listening.

I waited, and after a while he looked up and said, 'We have a stronghold here. A place where we can prepare ourselves for whoever comes hunting for me. Where we can stop running away and go on the attack.'

'We can?' I was dismayed, for if I'd thought about it at all – and I hadn't very much – I'd assumed that, safely hidden, we'd simply wait here until the danger had passed. But then how could we say when that would be? Were we facing an enemy who would give up when he didn't succeed, or one who would carry on relentlessly right till the end?

I had an unpleasant feeling that the man who was dogging our steps, the man who hadn't hesitated to burn down a building knowing there were five people inside, of whom, or so he'd believed, only one was the man he was trying to kill, wasn't going to stop.

As if he'd read my thoughts, Rollo said sharply, 'You'd thought we'd just hide here? Until when, Lassair? Until the man hunting me down gives up and goes away, or we all die of old age?'

I'd have liked to say that simply waiting it out sounded like a fine idea to me, but I didn't. I knew that Rollo was a fighter; used to taking the initiative, he must have hated this skulking in shadows, this endless running. I had to accept that I had a stark choice: either go along with what he wanted to do or else leave him to it.

The second wasn't really an option at all.

'So what do we do?' I asked.

He shot me a grateful look.

Then, glancing at the water starting to steam in the pot, he said, 'Let's get some food cooking, then you and I shall sit here beside the hearth, broach that barrel of ale you so cleverly found and I'll tell you all I know of our enemy and why he is so intent on claiming my life.'

About time, I thought. But, since he was on the point of responding to all the questions to which I'd so long wanted answers, I didn't. Instead I got up, went to look over the remainder of our meat supply and, throwing a string of onions at Rollo, said, 'Very well. You can peel and chop these.'

'So,' I said, when, with a salt meat, onion and herb stew bubbling fragrantly over the fire and mugs of ale in our hands, I could wait no longer, 'who do you think it is who so badly wants to kill you?'

Rollo must have been preparing what he was

going to say, for he immediately began to speak, and he was fluent and unhesitating.

'I'm not sure how much you've put together from the little I've told you,' he said, not meeting my eyes, 'but during my very long absence, I was far away in the lands in the east. There's no reason why you would know anything of the world beyond the fens, but—'

'In fact I do know a little,' I interrupted calmly. His head shot up and the amazed look in his eyes made me smile. 'Don't forget that I am Gurdyman's pupil,' I added. 'He has a head full of knowledge and he is a very good teacher. But go on.'

Looking at me with a little more respect now, Rollo said, 'There is going to be a war, quite soon, over who controls the Holy Places; the land where our lord Jesus Christ was born, lived, ministered, died and rose from the dead. The Christians believe it is their right to come and go as they please, but now that those whose lands surround and, indeed, include the Holy Places have discovered their own strength, they beg to differ. Already there have been fights, local battles, tales – probably exaggerated – of the torture, mutilation and murder of pilgrims wishing to walk where Jesus walked.' He paused, then, too quickly for me to comment, went on, 'The powerful ruler of Constantinople feels himself to be in the greatest danger, for his is, in effect, the last Christian kingdom that stands between the west and the Turks. As his enemy's strength grows, he will look – is already looking – to the lords of the west for help. He will ask them to summon a vast army – the biggest ever seen – to march east and help him fight the infidel and reclaim the Holy Places for the Christian faith.'

'But what about the lands surrounding these Holy Places?' I asked. 'Won't this huge army overrun those, too? That doesn't seem right.'

He was watching me, a wry smile on his face. 'Yes it will, and no it doesn't,' he said quietly.

'Maybe it won't happen,' I said. 'It must cost a fortune to create an army and march it so far, so perhaps the western monarchs will do no more than agree how dreadful it is but do nothing.'

He shook his head. 'I wish it were so. But it will happen, Lassair. For one thing' – he lowered his eyes – 'I've seen it, in a sort of dream, or vision. For another, I've been to Constantinople and I'm in no doubt that, sooner or later, Alexius Comnenus – that's the name of the man who rules there – will be forced to summon help. And, before you protest again, it'll be answered. Be in no doubt whatsoever about that.' He paused, and I sensed we were coming to the secret heart of the matter. 'I travelled east in order to find out for the king how matters stood,' he said, so quietly that I had to strain to hear. 'I returned, told him what I had discovered and was paid for it.' He paused again. 'Then I went to Normandy, to the court of Duke Robert – he and the king, of course, just happen to be both brothers and ferocious rivals – and sold the same information to him.'

My first reaction was disappointment.

I suppose I had built up an image of Rollo as

a hero; a brave, solitary soldier utterly loyal to the king and fighting those secret, shadowy battles for him that required intelligence and sharp wits rather than might, muscle and a show of arms.

But in all my imaginings, it hadn't really crossed my mind that he'd serve more than one master.

'Why?' I asked after quite a long silence. 'Didn't the king pay you well enough?'

He had the grace to look ashamed. 'He is extremely generous. I have no complaints.'

'Why, then?'

He met my eyes briefly, then shrugged, looking away. 'Because it's what I do, Lassair. I don't think I can give you a better answer. It's probably the one thing I can do, and I'm very good at it.'

'Not that good, if you're telling me what I think you are and some irate lord or whatever from Duke Robert's court caught you at it and is now after your blood.' The words were out before I could stop them, and, too late, I saw their effect.

He set down his mug of ale and put up both hands to his face, rubbing it. 'I must be losing my touch,' he muttered.

Silence fell once more. When he didn't break it, I said, 'Is that it, then? Is it someone from Normandy who is hunting you?'

He lowered his hands. 'Yes. I can't know for certain, but it's the only logical answer.' He paused, as if wondering if to go on. His eyes slid away from mine. Then he said quietly, 'I don't wish to boast, but I've been doing the work I do for a long time and I'm not easy to follow even for a day, let alone all the way from Rouen to the fens. Whoever has managed to do so is really not to be underestimated.'

I didn't want to think about that but there was no choice. 'So,' I said, my mind working hard, 'this man saw you with Duke Robert and knew why you were there, then, because somehow his suspicions were raised, he followed you when you left, suspecting that you were really working for King William and hoping to prove it by following you back to wherever the king is.' It all sounded rather vague. 'Is that right?'

He was smiling. 'More or less, although I would assume that whichever of Duke Robert's close circle suspects me in fact employed someone else to hunt me down.'

'And Duke Robert paid you adequately too? Yes, of course he did.' I answered the question before he had a chance to. Rollo, I understood, didn't do anything unless he was going to be well paid. 'Couldn't you just give back the money? Hand it to the man who's after you?'

He was looking at me with a wry smile. 'No, Lassair. I don't think that would really work.'

My mind was racing again. 'So he must have followed you across the sea,' I muttered, 'or else he's an agent for the duke on this side of the Channel and has taken over the pursuit on orders from Robert's agents on the spot – do such men exist?'

'Yes,' he said briefly.

'So, either in Normandy or else wherever it was you landed in England, he picked up your trail and you became aware of him. Where?'

'Not until I was in Cambridge.' He must have

seen my surprise, for he quickly went on, 'It was the first place where I stayed for more than the time it took to eat or sleep. The man on my trail is very good at following without being seen, but less good at keeping out of sight when his quarry remains in the same place.'

I nodded. 'So you sought my help in order to change from a man alone to one accompanied by his wife. We set out over the fens, then laid a false trail for him by letting it be known at Landsay Castle that we were heading north. He picked it up and followed us north, and then noticed that we'd left the north road and turned south-west. He knew we were staying at the monastery and he burned it down with us inside. Or so he thought.' I glanced at Rollo. 'He's good, isn't he?'

'He's good.'

'We saw him there – at the monastery – or rather you did!' I exclaimed suddenly. 'What did you observe? Did you recognize him?'

He shook his head. 'No. I don't think I'd ever seen him before, not as close as that. As to what I observed of him . . .' He closed his eyes, as if bringing images to mind. 'Dressed as if he was well used to travelling, in practical garments. His boots were obviously sturdy and sound as he didn't hesitate to run through shallow water. He had a heavy cloak, although he wasn't wearing it when he set fire to the monastery and I only noticed it when he went to fetch his horse. It was a good horse. The man moved freely and swiftly, with a certain elegance, and I'd say he was young rather than old, but I didn't get a good enough look at his face to be certain. I have the impression he was dark, although that might have been because of a black or brown head covering of some sort – a hood or a scarf – than because he was dark-haired.'

'He knows his way around,' I said.

'What?'

'He's had no problem following us, even though we've used lesser tracks and paths wherever we could. He managed to extract information about us from someone in Lord Edwin's household. He's' – I hesitated – 'he's familiar with our ways,' was the best I could do.

But Rollo was nodding. 'Yes,' he said slowly.

Something struck me. It wasn't a welcome thought, but I thought I'd better share it. 'Rollo, perhaps he is to Duke Robert what you are to King William. A spy, who has travelled in many lands, who knows his way about in them, who blends in with the local people.

He looked at me, a wry sort of look. 'Yes,' he said again. 'I very much fear you're right.'

'So what do we do?' I asked, hoping I sounded more confident and optimistic than I felt. In truth, I was beginning to fear this shadow of an enemy, who followed us despite our best efforts, whose skill in the mysterious, secret ways of the fens – and this was what really frightened me – equalled or exceeded my own.

'We make our plans and we lay our defences,' Rollo said firmly. 'We amass our weapons, and we search this house and the outbuildings for everything that can be employed in attacking our enemy. We set a trip wire across the causeway so that we have warning if he tries to approach. An island joined to the mainland only by a narrow and usually flooded path is a fine place to defend,' he added encouragingly.

'But he might have a boat,' I said softly.

He sighed. 'Yes, he might.' He was quiet for several moments. Then he said, 'Which is why we must draw him to us. We will prepare, then we will let him know where we are. When he comes for me, which undoubtedly he will, we shall be ready, and he will be – disposed of.'

'You're going to kill him.' I knew it; what other outcome was there than that one would kill the other? I didn't even want to allow the possibility that it might be the other way round to enter my head.

And slowly Rollo nodded.

They were near.

He knew they were. It was as if he had grown a new sense; it seemed to operate via his skin, so that he felt a sort of light prickling when he knew he was on the man's trail.

He was worried, although he tried to ignore it.

But, try as he might, he couldn't quite tamp down his unease. It was the fens: he didn't understand this region where water ruled, where firm land changed without warning into marsh, bog, quicksand; where you could look out at what appeared to be good green grass, only to find, when you were upon it and it was too late, that the green grass was brilliantly coloured weed, and that all there was beneath your feet was water.

And the man he was hunting, curse his crafti-
ness, had gone into these fens. He had a woman
with him who seemed to know her way, and,
coward that he was, the man was depending on
her for his safety.

'It may appear that they may have vanished
from the face of the earth,' he said softly to
himself, 'but that cannot be so. They are there,
somewhere out on the water, and where they
have gone, I shall follow.'

As yet, he didn't know how. But he would
think of a way.

For now, though, there were other matters for
his attention.

With great relief at the respite, for all that he
knew it would only be temporary, he turned his
back on the watery half-lands and headed for
the town.

Thirteen

Leaving Gurdyman's house and heading home, Jack took a detour and went up to the castle. As he flew up the steep side of the artificial mound on which it was built, it suddenly struck him that he was running: he was puffing and there was the beginning of a stitch knifing into his right side, but nevertheless the fact stuck him as something about which to be optimistic and even tentatively cheerful.

Perhaps it was a profound and almost subliminal awareness that he was recovering that was driving him, for, if he had stopped to think about it, this new determination to set things right, to step out of the shadows and sort out his life – his official status – would definitely have struck him as rash, if not downright foolhardy.

I am a lawman of this town and I am good at my job, he told himself as he strode up to the narrow walkway linking the top of the slope with the heavy, iron-strengthened main door of the castle. *If I need proof of that, I have only to think of the many townspeople who were prepared to swear that Gaspard Picot struck first, and calculate just how many of them were committing perjury.*

That made him smile briefly, but it was a good thought to keep in mind as he raised a fist and banged on the door.

The two armed men who admitted him were old friends. 'The sheriff's busy with something in his inner room, so you can slip into the guard-room unseen,' one said quietly, 'Ned, Ranald and some of the others are in there and they'll be—'

'I am not going to visit Ned,' said Jack.

Aware of the guards' astonished faces, he strode across the anteroom where people wishing to see, or, far more often, furiously summoned by, Sheriff Picot were always made to wait. On the far side was a solid oak door studded with iron, set in a low arch. With the most cursory of taps, he opened it and went inside.

Sheriff Picot, interrupted in the act of pacing to and fro across the creaking wooden floor-boards of the ill-lit room, stopped dead and spun round. 'Fuck off! Who gave you permission to come in here—' Then Jack moved forward into the lamplight. 'Oh. It's you.'

'It is,' Jack agreed pleasantly.

Anticipating a battle – verbal if not physical, and probably both – Sheriff Picot's reaction to his unexpected presence took him aback. Instead of the stream of foul-mouthed abuse, Picot fumbled behind him for his big wooden chair and sank into it. His plump and habitually red face had paled, and beads of sweat stood out on his forehead. The thinning gingery hair, Jack observed, was more sparse than he remembered, the few strands carefully arranged across the big bald dome failing to achieve the desired effect.

Jack stood still, looking down at the sheriff. Realizing he had put himself at a disadvantage by sitting down, Picot struggled up again, dragging his tunic down over the large hump of belly. But that was no better, since Jack was considerably the taller. With a sigh and a muttered, 'Oh, what in hell's name does it matter?' he subsided again. He ran a hand over his face and said, 'What do you want?'

Several things ran through Jack's mind. *What do you want?*, he reflected, was that sort of a question.

He wasn't even sure what his purpose had been when he'd taken the decision to face Sheriff Picot. Now, as his thoughts gathered into a cohesive whole – as if a sensible, wise part of himself had quietly assumed control – he believed he knew.

He also knew that he was never going to get an opportunity like this again.

'You have been in the habit of allowing other hands to hold the reins here,' he began. 'You had by your side a younger man, closely related to you by blood, who was raised in your own image, and you encouraged him to pursue the methods you yourself brought into being. Your system panders to those who have wealth, influence and power, and the hard-working men and women of the town who do not possess these things stand helpless in the face of the cheating, coercion, dishonesty and bribery that are the whips you use to rule.' He paused, waiting until he was sure his temper wasn't about to get the better of him. He hadn't realized quite how angry he was. 'Your late nephew Gaspard Picot, typical of the worst sort of rich man who always wants more, was a thief, caught in the act of hiding the stolen goods inside his clothing.'

'He—' the sheriff began feebly.

Jack didn't let him go on.

'It was I who stopped him,' he shouted, 'and in his desperation to escape, he attacked me and, but for the care I received, he would have killed me. As he threw himself on me, he landed on my own weapon, and the blade opened a wound in his throat.'

He seemed to be losing his battle with his better nature. Moving close to the cowering sheriff, leaning over him with his hands on the arms of the big chair, he said coldly, 'Perhaps, had there been one shred of respect or affection for Gaspard Picot, he would have been as lucky as I was, and some skilled, compassionate healer would have hurried up and stopped his life's blood flowing from his body. But as men sow, so do they reap, Sheriff Picot. Your nephew was universally loathed and feared, and not a woman or a man in that crowd wanted him to live.'

The sheriff gave a low moan.

And, hearing the echo of his furious, cruel words, Jack straightened up and stepped away.

For a while there was silence in the room. Once or twice the sheriff emitted a quiet sound, whose significance Jack didn't at first understand.

Then it occurred to him that he just might be weeping.

Is it grief for his lost kinsman? he wondered. *Or is his distress because he has been forced to confront unpleasant truths?*

He decided to give the sheriff the benefit of the doubt.

'You grieve for your nephew, I am sure,' he said.

Only someone who knew him well would have detected the faint irony. 'His death, moreover, has both left you isolated, since you have lost the man who stood at your right hand, and served to show you emphatically just how unpopular you are.' He met the sheriff's close-set eyes. 'Yes, I've been told just how many honest townspeople hurried here to tell you they saw your nephew strike first, and that I acted in self-defence.'

'Half of them were lying!' Picot spat out. Jack said nothing. 'They *must* have been!' he went on, drips of spittle on his thin lips.

'How could you possibly know?' Jack said calmly. Before the sheriff could think up an answer, he went on, 'Whatever opinion your town may hold of you, however, is irrelevant, for you are the appointed authority and nobody may question that.' Briefly Picot's mouth twisted into a cunning little smile. 'But no man can hold power alone,' he went on softly. 'Before, when together you and your nephew were strong enough to draw ambitious and like-minded men to you, you could do as you liked. Now that the voice of the town has spoken, those who saw matters rather differently have found their courage, and I do not believe you will find life quite so easily bent to your will.'

Sheriff Picot stared up at him with a face full of hatred. 'Just you wait and see!' he hissed. 'I'll – men will—' But he seemed unable to go on.

Jack moved to the side of the room, where a stout board set upon trestles bore sheets of blank vellum, rolled documents, quills and ink horns. He perched on the edge.

'This is what I propose,' he said, making his tone reasonable. 'I am almost fit for duty, and as soon as I know I am fully restored, I shall return. I have a group of capable, loyal and trustworthy men whose wish is to serve this town as it deserves to be served, and they will work with me.' He fixed the sheriff with a hard stare. 'Don't tell me that it's you who's in charge and who ultimately controls how the law is upheld here, because I already know. You will, I believe, find it a challenge, however, to continue in your old ways. If we are to work together, I suggest you think about what I've just said. There have been recent crimes of great violence, and answers will be sought. I do not refer solely to the death of your niece by marriage and the burning down of your late nephew's house, for, although these are without doubt the offences that most disturb you' – *and for which you most urgently require somebody to blame*, he might have added, *whether this person is in fact guilty or not* – 'let us remember that even before the widow Picot met her death, two young men had already been murdered.' He stood up, moving towards the door. Without turning round, he said, 'And if you're planning to have me arrested and thrown in a dungeon for insubordination, I will merely remind you that there are just two of us in this room, and nobody to bear witness to what has just been said. The only men who even know I'm here are loyal to me.'

He went out, ducking under the low archway and quietly closing the door. As he strode off across the anteroom, there was a loud thud: Picot, it seemed, had hurled something heavy at its sturdy planks.

Grinning, Jack emerged into the light. Apart from the sheriff, nobody other than the two guards had seen him; pausing briefly at the top of the steep slope, he muttered to one of them, 'I was never here.'

Quickly mastering his surprise, the man replied, 'Course you weren't, chief.'

Walking home, buoyed up by euphoria, it was only when he had almost reached his house that Jack wondered what on earth he was going to do next.

He stopped. Looking ahead, he stared at the closed, locked door. He felt a surge of relief: had he suspected, then, that the woman he'd shut up inside might have broken out?

He thought about her, and about his own actions. Any other lawman, finding her so close to Gaspard Picot's burning house and having seen her watching the house several times before, would have arrested her without hesitation. Now she'd be locked in a cell, being questioned with a greater or lesser degree of harshness, depending on who was asking the questions, and she wouldn't be left alone until she'd given an explanation.

I have just challenged a corrupt man who applied the law the way he wanted to, he thought. *Is it any more right and honourable for me to bend the law according to my own views, even if that bending is not towards cruelty and dishonesty but towards leniency?*

'The law is the law,' he muttered.

Then he marched up to the house, unlocked the door and went inside.

He could see her in the dim light of the further room. She was lying on the bed, the covers folded tidily back. Hearing him, she sat up, supporting herself on her arms as if her body was weak.

'I do not know what you administered to me,' she said, the husky voice holding a note of accusation. 'I try to make myself rise, but each time sleep overcomes me.'

'It was nothing that I haven't taken myself,' he said curtly.

He caught a gleam from her large, dark eyes as they reflected the light streaming in through the door. Abruptly he closed and barred it.

Observing him, she said, amusement in her tone, 'You think I shall try to force my way past you and flee?'

'You're not going anywhere until you have told me who you are and what your business is with the house and the kin of Gaspard Picot,' he said. 'Now, I'm hungry, and I dare say you are too, so, while you work out what you're going to say to me, I shall prepare food.'

She stayed where she was while he set water on to heat and put together a simple stew of oats, root vegetables and beans. For flavour, he was about to add a piece of ham bone, to which quite a lot of salted meat was still attached. The very handling of it made his mouth water. But, as he leaned towards the hearth she said quickly, 'Not that. Please.'

He nodded. He had encountered people before

212

who, for reasons of faith, did not eat certain foods. He would, he decided, carve off the last of the flesh and add it to his own portion once he'd served the food.

He heard her get up off the bed, and she asked for water to wash her face and hands. He provided a pail. There was another need that she must surely need to address before she washed: 'The privy's outside,' he said. 'If you wish, I will show you.'

She nodded, and he escorted her out to it, waiting until she was ready to re-enter the house. She went back into the rear chamber, and he heard splashing.

Presently the food was ready. As he ladled it into two wooden bowls, she emerged once more and sat down on one of the sections of tree trunk that served as stools. She accepted her bowl with a murmur of thanks, eating swiftly but daintily until the bowl was clean.

'And now,' he said when he too had finished, 'you start to talk.'

She stared down at her hands, folded in her lap. 'I have nothing to say.' He detected a tremor in her voice. 'I did not kill the lady of the house and I did not start the fire.'

He refused to allow his annoyance to show. 'I found you there, beside the house,' he said tonelessly. 'Where I had also seen you on previous occasions. You surely would not have me believe you were there out of innocent curiosity.'

She had no answer for that.

'You appear to know your way around the settlement of razed houses,' he went on, 'and from that

I guess that you have been here in the town for some time.'

'I was—' she began. Then she closed her mouth.

'You were undoubtedly here when the first two murders were carried out,' he went on. He was watching her closely.

'No! No, I—' Again she stopped. He had the sense that the words had burst out of her before she could prevent them.

Sensing a very slight opening, he persisted: 'You knew one of those young men,' he said harshly. 'Knew him and cared deeply for him, for I observed your reaction when I spoke of them last night. They were similar in appearance, those two poor men, and it seems likely that the first was killed because the murderer had mistaken him for the other. Which one, I wonder, was the man you loved? The one struck down on the road to the fens, or the one whose body was thrown into the river? Both had been savagely beaten, and had suffered greatly before the mercy of death took them.'

She had dropped her face in her hands. 'Stop,' she said. 'Please, stop.'

A harsh demon in him was urging him on, and he very nearly obeyed. But then, leaning over her, about to hit her with more cruel words, suddenly he saw another handsome woman, cowering on the beaten earth floor of this very house as a brutal man coerced her into doing something against which her very soul revolted . . .

He drew back. Then – for this woman in his memory and his heart was still far too near – he stood up and went to lean against the door.

After a time, his withdrawal seemed to penetrate the dark woman's awareness. She lowered her hands, revealing a deathly pale face. Her glittering, slanting eyes searched his face. Just for an instant, he thought he saw a different expression flash in her eyes, but he could have been mistaken.

He knew he should go on, pushing her, bullying her, for he had sensed a weakness in her and it was there for the using. But he couldn't.

After a time, he resumed his seat by the hearth.

She was studying him. 'You are a man who has seen violence done to women,' she said very softly. 'You do not approve, I think.'

'What I've seen and what I don't approve of are nothing to do with you,' he said with force.

'I beg to differ,' she countered, 'for here I am, a woman, in the power of you, a big, tall, strong man. I think that the—' she paused, thinking '—the *nature* of you, how you treat a helpless woman who is your captive, is very much to do with me.'

Absurdly, he laughed. She looked at him, the strong dark brows raised. 'Whoever or whatever you are,' he said, still laughing, 'I do not believe you to be helpless.'

She smiled. 'Perhaps not, but nevertheless it is you who has control here.'

There was a brief silence. It was, Jack thought, a more friendly silence than before.

Presently she said, 'Your mother, is it?'

He felt as if he'd been struck. '*What?*'

She smiled again, but now it was an expression of tenderness. 'I have been here in your house all

215

day and for much of the preceding night,' she said. 'Although it is true that I have slept for much of that time, my sleep has been filled with images and dreams. It is as if I have sensed a presence here; a woman, kind, strong, generous, loving. A woman who suffers, because she is alone in a harsh world and she has children who need her for their very survival. A woman who, faced with a terrible choice, made the hard decision to—'

'Stop.' It was his turn to give the command.

She cannot know, he thought. *She has perhaps sensed a presence, or, more likely, she merely observes the clean tidiness and order of this house and detects the hand of a careful, diligent woman.*

For this stranger to have seen his mother, to have detected her brave spirit when he who had loved her could not, was not to be countenanced.

She said after a while, 'I am sorry. I did not mean to hurt you.' Then, when he didn't answer, she added, 'Would it not be good to tell me?'

Everything in him shouted *no*. But, all the same, he heard himself start to speak and he didn't think he could – didn't think he wanted to – stop.

'She was a local woman,' he began. 'Her name was Rowyn, and her father had a boat in which he ferried goods around the fens. When the Conqueror came, he brought not only the soldiers but also engineers, blacksmiths and carpenters to build the castles with which he was to curb his new subjects. One of his carpenters was my father. He had fought at Hastings, for William the Bastard habitually selected men with more than one skill.' He paused, an image of his father floating up from his memory. 'He and my mother fell in love, despite the fact that he was a part of the invasion force. They were wed and they settled here, in this house, for it was one of the dwellings put up for the workforce who were building the castle. She conceived her first child, but soon after that child's birth, my father was sent away to work on other castles, and he was repeatedly away in the years that followed, although he earned good money and was able to provide adequately for his wife and son.' He paused. It was painful, looking back. 'Then he came home to stay, and his wife conceived again, this time bearing a daughter. But before that child was a year old, my father died. Then the bad times began, for the money dried up and, careful and frugal though my mother was, she—'

But he couldn't continue. The story was there, locked away deep inside his heart, and now he was seeing the images that he had tried so hard to forget. The little sister, sickening, feeble. His mother, trying remedy after desperate remedy, yet, without the money even for food, unable to go to the best apothecaries and buy what she needed.

His own efforts to find work and bring in money, lying about his age – for he was tall and powerfully built – and persuading them to let him join the army. Discovering too late that, although his new job earned him the money his family needed so badly, it also took him away. Far away, so that, when his mother did what she had to do, he wasn't there.

And, last and most haunting image of all, his sister lying dead, and his mother, who had endured so much for her child's sake, dying.

'You came!' she had whispered to him when he had finally managed to get home. 'I knew you would, my son.'

Her poor, bruised, skeletal face was still beautiful in his eyes; her smile the same loving smile that had always warmed his heart and made the world seem better.

'I'm so sorry!' he had whispered. 'I should have been here, I could have—'

But, with a huge effort, she had raised her hand and gently put it to his lips. 'It is not for you to be sorry, for there is nothing – *nothing* – for you to regret,' she said firmly. 'You took on a man's role when you were a boy, and, but for you, we would have starved years ago.'

'But—'

Once more she stopped him. 'You are here, son. In answer to my prayers, here you are. Let us not waste what time we have left.'

He had put his arms round her and held her until she died.

Later, when he had seen both his mother and his little sister safe in the earth, he had sought out the man. And he'd killed him.

It was not the first life he had taken, for he was a soldier and that was part of his job.

It was the one, however, over which he had never had the least regret.

He came back to himself. The dark woman was watching him intently. For a disconcerting moment, he wasn't sure how much he had told her; how much had remained in the secret spaces of his memory.

Then, with huge relief, he heard the echo of his last words.

'My mother died,' he said shortly.

'And your sister, too,' she murmured.

He wasn't going to let her go on doing it; go on making him believe she had some sort of vision into his soul. 'Obviously she did,' he said crushingly, 'since here I live, alone.'

Again he saw that tiny glimpse of something else in her eyes. But she simply smiled gently, and said, 'Of course.'

He found he couldn't look at her. It was as if her big, dark eyes had some power to make him speak of matters that were no concern of hers; no concern of anybody but him. He was amazed at himself, for having fallen into her trap and told her even as much as he had done. The *why* of it was something he must think very hard about, but not now.

He was a man of the law, he had in his sole custody a woman who, even if his instincts were right and she wasn't guilty of murder and arson, was probably involved and without doubt knew a great deal more than she was telling him.

The violent demon that lived inside him was shouting to be heard now. Fixing her with a hard stare, forcing himself to put up invisible barriers against the power of her eyes, he said softly, 'Now, unless you wish to be taken straight to the castle and locked away deep under the earth while the sheriff decides what to do with the woman upon whom the crimes of murder and arson could quite easily be pinned, I think you should talk to me. For a start, you can tell me who you are.'

She had gone white. 'I told you, I'm innocent,' she said in a terrified whisper.

'Tell me who you are,' he repeated. 'I shall count to five, and then I shall bind your wrists and take you to the castle. One. Two.'

As he said, 'Three,' she burst out: 'Batsheva. My name is Batsheva.'

'Good,' he said. 'And where do you come from?'

'How far back do you wish to go?' she muttered. Then, before he could answer, she said, 'Recently I have been living in Norwich, and before that, in London. But I was born in Rouen. I was an only child, and my mother died giving birth to me. My father and I were consequently close, and he was my teacher as well as my parent. He—' She stopped. It seemed to Jack that speaking of her father was painful. 'We came to England, Father and I, at the request – many would say the command – of Duke William of Normandy, or, rather King William, for that is what he had become by the time he required the presence of men like my father in his new kingdom.'

Jack already had an idea of who and what her father was, and what his value had been to the first King William. There were clues: her name, her olive complexion, her fine, bold features, the dark eyes and the black hair. And she had rejected his ham, which of course came from the pig. Moreover, he had heard tell of the first two Williams of England's need of such men. William the Conqueror had valued their business skills, the ease with which they developed a thriving merchant class, the fact that no religious ban existed on their lending money, their ability to advance credit. Wherever they went, commercial success soon followed, and there was little that a new king valued more than that. Jack had heard it said that small communities had been present wherever William I had put up a castle, for castles cost money.

And, in a newly subjected, resentful and impoverished land, who better to lend it to him than the Jews?

Yes, she'd probably been right when she suggested William had commanded their presence in England rather than inviting it.

She must have sensed his inattention, for she had stopped speaking. She was watching him, brows raised.

'Go on.'

'My father, as I imagine you have already guessed, was a Jewish merchant. That was how he began, at least, although his prosperity led to his being more of a funder of other men's enterprises than the controller of his own. He was well known in our community in Rouen, and we came to England in 1073 and settled in London. We were happy there, and there were enough of our own kind around us to make us feel that we were not alone. Most importantly, however, was the support of the king. We knew we looked different, ran our lives by different rules, and were allowed to do work not allowed to others. But as long as the king valued and needed us, we were safe.'

She paused. Watching her, he noticed that the heat from the fire had brought colour to her pale face. Now, as if she had just noticed too, she threw back the cloak that lay over her shoulders and drew the bodice of her gown away from the flesh of her throat and upper chest.

He saw then how beautiful she was.

Her face, of course, he had already registered. But now, afforded a glimpse of her body, he realized that she was a woman with a very strong sexual appeal. Her breasts were full, her waist narrow above the generous curve of her hips, and she held herself with an air that seemed to say, *I know you are looking at me. I know you admire what you see.*

He forced himself to concentrate on what she was saying.

'But then my father died.' She said the words starkly, and he knew she was suppressing her emotion. 'He had never been strong, and when the sickness struck he did not have the resources to throw it off. And so I was left alone, and I realized very swiftly that I was not the wealthy heiress I had believed myself to be. My father, you see, had been failing for some time, and the drive and the energy that he had once put into his work had been directed instead at trying to keep himself alive.'

'I am sorry that you lost him,' he said, his voice stiff and formal.

Although he had caught the glisten of tears in her eyes, still he saw her smile. 'Thank you,' she said, equally formally.

'And so you left London?' Deliberately he

222

moved her – and himself – away from the imminent emotion.

She didn't reply for a few moments. Then she said, 'I had lost my protector, but quite soon I found another one. He was a man of means, and he offered to care for me.'

There was no need for her to say what form that care took, nor what would have been required of her in return.

She said, 'No doubt you are thinking that in exchange for security, I bartered the only commodity I had.'

'Of course,' he replied. 'But I'm also thinking that you had little choice.'

'I had no choice,' she corrected him. 'I told you just now that although we lived among our own, we were in effect an isolated little community within a large one?'

He nodded.

'As such, we were, and shall always be, vulnerable. My misfortune was that, just at the time I lost my father, my people had to face one of those periods of resentment that occasionally crop up. It was not very serious – some daubings on the wall of the synagogue, fist fights between bands of Jew and gentile youths, an old and much respected rabbi beaten up. It was unpleasant while it lasted, however, and it made me the more willing to accept the offer that my new protector made. He suggested that I leave London, and that he would set me up in my own small house in Norwich, which, he told me, was considerably closer to where he resided.'

'And did you like your new home?'

She shrugged. 'It didn't matter if I did or I didn't. In fact, I did. Also—' She hesitated. He sensed there was something she wanted to say, but wasn't sure whether to reveal to him. She must have decided in his favour.

'It is not necessary for a woman in my position to like her benefactor,' she said calmly. 'There is little point in railing against it, for it is the way the world works and cannot be changed. Not until women have the right to work, earn and save their own money,' she added softly and with vehemence. 'Not until women are free of the patriarchal society that so favours the male and so undermines the female.' She shook her head, as if dismissing that thought. 'I should perhaps admit that not only did I like the man who stepped in when I lost my father and my security; I came also to—' She stopped. 'To have an affection for him.'

Jack was trying to weld her tale together. 'He lived here, in Cambridge?'

'He did.'

And he was young – perhaps considerably younger than you – and fair-haired, he thought. There didn't seem any need to say so aloud.

'And you came here to search for him,' he said slowly, 'only to find that he was dead.'

She nodded. 'Yes. I didn't— Nobody could tell me—' But she couldn't go on.

He watched as she lowered her head into her hands and wept.

Fourteen

I woke early after our first night in Mercure's house to find myself lying with Rollo spooned behind me, the curve of his body cradling mine, his arm around me clutching me to him. For a while I just lay very still and enjoyed the sensation of being held.

But that was all it was: a warm, comforting hug. Both of us had rolled up in our separate bedding when we settled down to sleep, and, this morning, we were still chastely wrapped up with several layers of clothing and blanket between us.

Presently he murmured sleepily, 'Is this all right?'

'Yes.'

He took a strand of my hair in his fingers. 'You were weeping. I wanted to comfort you.'

Weeping?

It came as an unwelcome surprise, for I hadn't been aware of it. I had been dreaming – I could remember that – and the dream had involved nursing the baby I'd just lost. In the dream I had seen Jack's face, and he had tears in his eyes.

No wonder I'd been weeping.

I wasn't ready to share any of that, even with Rollo. I lay for a few moments, enjoying the sensation of his smooth stroking of my hair, then said, 'It's time we were up.'

He sighed. 'Yes. I suppose so.'

As I wriggled out of my blankets, I met his eyes. There was a question in them, one which I still didn't know how to answer. But he was entitled to one: I said, 'I'm here with you, doing what you asked of me. I *want* to be here, but I . . .' I wasn't sure how to go on.

'You are still worrying about your Cambridge lawman,' he finished quietly for me. 'Yes, I can see that.'

I was angry suddenly. 'Rollo, when last we spoke of these matters, you reminded me just how long you've been away, and, as if I could have forgotten, that you sent me no word in all that time.'

'Yes, and I also said that you were perfectly free to—'

'When I couldn't sleep a night or two ago,' I went on, not letting him finish, 'I calculated just how much time you and I have spent together, and it's *days*! Well, it may add up to a few weeks, but no more than that.'

He said, 'I didn't think time was relevant.'

Slowly I shook my head. 'I didn't either.'

I turned away and went outside to the privy and the water trough. As I was washing my face and hands, my mind played an unkind trick. Out of the depths of memory, it presented me with another dream, or perhaps it had been a vision, I'd had long ago: of the child I had believed Rollo and I would one day have together.

I pushed both arms into the cold water, right up above the elbows, then plunged my face in too. The sudden chill gave me a brief stab of

226

pain in my forehead, but it drove away the old dream, so it was worth it.

As we ate the porridge Rollo had made while I concocted a hot drink, he told me, in a matter-of-fact tone that seemed to say we weren't going to talk about our emotions again, that he'd been working out how to put into action the plan to lure the man who was hunting us to the island.

'That's good,' I said, making my voice bright.

He shot me a glance. 'You may not agree when I tell you the details.'

'Well, tell me, then, and I'll see.'

He had finished the food, and now he placed the bowl on the floor and folded his arms. 'It's quite obvious that I am his target,' he said. 'So, reasoning that you'll be safe because he doesn't want or need to take your life too, acting as the lure and laying the trail that brings him here is your job.'

I wished he had put some expression into the words. Some sense that he was sorry it had to be this way; that he knew it might be dangerous but that there was no alternative.

I waited until I felt calm. Then I said steadily, 'So I'm to set out on a foraging expedition – fishing, perhaps – and wander around further and further from this little sanctuary until I'm quite sure he's seen me, whereupon I'll lead him back here so you can kill him.'

He had drawn a sharp breath as I spoke. Now he said, 'In essence, yes.'

After a moment I said, 'How do we know he's anywhere near? Isn't it more likely that he still believes we died in the monastery fire? You said you saw him standing by the ruins, so he'd surely have counted the bodies.'

'Yes, he did. But I've been thinking, Lassair. He also went to the stables – remember, I told you he set the other travellers' horses free?' I nodded. 'He's good, this man, He's very good, for we led him a roundabout trail and he followed it, apparently with ease. I am all but certain that, sooner or later, what he saw in the stables will have penetrated his urge to get away as fast as he could from the monastery, and forced him to go back and check.'

'What he saw in the stables?' I echoed. 'But what would he have seen? We – I – had packed up and taken the horses well away by the time he got there, and I'm certain I didn't leave anything behind!'

'No, I'm sure you didn't,' he said swiftly. 'Please, don't think I'm blaming you. We left no sign of our presence, but without a doubt our horses did. Fresh droppings, disturbed straw, partially emptied water buckets, for example.'

'But even if he did go back and found evidence that two more horses had recently been in the stables, he wouldn't know they were ours!'

'We could comfort ourselves with that thought, yes,' he said. 'Or we could imagine what would happen if this shadow who has attached himself to us – this very experienced, very skilled, very intuitive hunter of men – decided that the two dead travellers who burned to death in the monastery were not in fact you and me. That we'd taken the precaution of sleeping out in the stables with our horses, that we had managed to evade him and that we were still alive.'

'He would come after us,' I said dully.

'He would.' Rollo corrected himself. 'He will.'

I was frantically trying to think back to the details of our journey under the cover of darkness from the monastery to Mercure's island. 'But he won't be able to follow us!' I said. 'We travelled by night, we took the tracks and the byways, and we only emerged from cover and out onto the road when there was no choice! And as for the island, well, even I had to look very hard to find it, and I've been here before.'

He looked at me for some moments. Then he took both my hands in his. He was warm, and his touch put heart in me.

I needed it, for then he said, 'Which is, I'm afraid, why you're going to have to give him a bit of help.'

Although I was still distressed at *why* I was setting out into the fens, all the same I felt my spirits soar as I waded across the narrow causeway and onto the firm ground on the other side.

The sun was climbing the sky to the east, and, without thinking very much about which direction to go in, I found myself walking on the fen edge with it on my right. I was going roughly north. It didn't much matter where I went, I reasoned, for neither Rollo nor I had any idea where our pursuer was, and he could as easily be this way as any other.

I had my satchel with me, and as I went I kept an eye out for seasonal bounty. I found some mushrooms and some nuts. I shelled the nuts and ate most of them as I strode along. Discovering peace, solace and relief in my own company, I didn't really notice the hours passing.

I think I had put my mind into a detached state, for I don't remember consciously thinking about anything very much. I knew this area so well, and I knew the fens like I knew my own beloved family. I had lived here all my life, and I understood what it meant not only to survive but to prosper here.

I was aware of the natural world around me. There was quite a lot of birdsong, for the day was sunny and the thrushes, blackbirds, robins and wrens were no doubt enjoying the unseasonal warmth as much as I was. Such trees as there were on the fen margins had mostly lost their leaves now, but here and there an ancient oak still bore some brown, shrivelled remnants. The oak is slow to come into leaf, slow to lose its foliage, I thought.

Then, quite suddenly, I knew I was in the presence of power.

It wasn't evil power, and I didn't think for even a moment that our pursuer was close.

I stopped, made myself relax, and let each of my senses take in what I'd found.

I was on the edge of a small clearing, where the drying grass and the rust-coloured bracken had been neatly cleared. It was deep amid the carr, however, and under the branches of a couple of alders. It was so well concealed that I was surprised I had found it at all.

I crouched down, then, for the ground felt

reasonably dry, sat down. I crossed my legs and closed my eyes. At first I sensed nothing, but then an image flashed into my mind and, cursing myself for being so slow, I reached into my satchel, unwrapped the shining stone and laid it, on its wrappings, before me.

Sometimes it shows me nothing, and remains a mute, blank, inscrutable sphere of black glass shot through with green lights.

Sometimes it shows me images.

Sometimes it seems to put images inside my head.

I don't know how it works. A part of me wonders if it serves as a conduit, giving me the confidence to look deep inside myself and access what is already there.

I don't often think about the *how*. I am profoundly attached to the shining stone, and over the years of having it in my keeping – never, never would I allow myself to think of it as being in my possession, for nobody could use such a word in connection with such an ancient, impenetrable, mysterious, magical object – it has become a part of me. Or, perhaps, *I* a part of *it*.

Now, as I let myself descend into the light trance state where the seeing happens, if it's going to, I experienced the familiar sensation of the shining stone and I uniting.

The first thing I saw was more in the nature of a confirmation, for my deeper mind already knew who had sat here before me in this secret little clearing. I saw Hrype, cross-legged, eyes closed, with his pale green rune stones set out before him on the special piece of cloth in which he keeps them. Yes. Hrype was abroad, he had been here very recently, and there were questions to which he needed answers.

I set that thought aside. I didn't believe that even the shining stone could show me something that Hrype didn't want me to see. It wasn't that I doubted the stone's power, only my own ability to understand what it was revealing to me. Hrype is the second most powerful magician I know.

I let my mind grow quiet.

Nothing happened for some time.

Then I became aware that I was staring at something inside the stone. It had gone very dark, and I'd begin to wonder if its power had been withdrawn. But suddenly I was looking into a patch of brightness . . . It was golden, as if the sun shone down into a glade similar to the one I was sitting in. It wasn't this clearing. I was quite sure of that, for there were many more trees, and the underlying vegetation was different. It was nearby, though, for I recognized the fenland landscape.

In the patch of gold stood a figure. Although I had never seen him, I knew straight away who he was. I don't know *how* I knew; I just did.

He was of average height, slim-built, long-limbed. He was dressed for the wilds, in the sort of clothing that is durable, comfortable, that keeps you warm and reasonably dry and that, because of its nondescript, dark colour, lets you blend in with your surroundings. In short, he looked exactly as I'd have expected him to look.

He wore good boots, knee-length, made of

soft, supple leather. They were dirty, as if he'd been long on the road.

He stood absolutely still. Sometimes I thought I'd lost sight of him, but then I'd spot him again. Oh, he was good! I wondered, fear making my heart speed up, if he was about to approach the island; if, even as I sat there in the clearing, he was preparing to kill . . .

For the most striking thing about him was how well armed he was. A sword hung in a scabbard at his left side. He had a big knife stuck in a sheath attached to his belt, and two shorter blades hung low on his hips. One for each hand.

He had a tightly tied bundle of bolts slung across his back and in his hands he held a crossbow.

I loathe the crossbow. It's a foul instrument, for it sends its bolt with such force that men hit in the leg have been known to be pinned to their horses. My aunt Edild has been forced to extract crossbow bolts, arrows too, in her time, and once she instructed me in how to do it. She commanded my father to fire a bolt and an arrow into a haunch of pork, again and again, taking me through the extraction process until she was confident I could do it.

I stared at the crossbow that hung from the hunter's hands. The wood of the stock gleamed as if it had recently been polished, and the light glinted off the metal that strengthened the curved bow. It was primed: a bolt lay in its groove and the string was taut.

With a speed I wouldn't have believed possible, the hunter swung the weapon up to his shoulder and fired. There was a noise of crashing, of falling, and an animal cry of agony. The hunter ran, leaping over tussocks, splashing through shallow water, and then, crouching, drawing out one of the smaller knives, he ended the life of the young deer whose throat was transfixed with his bolt.

I closed my eyes.

When I opened them again, the shining stone was black and empty. I folded it in its soft, protective wool, put it away in its bag and stowed it in my satchel. When I stood up, my legs were shaking.

I made myself walk away. I had been steadily going northwards, but now I turned around. I'm not sure why: perhaps it was that my home lay in the direction I'd been following, and I didn't want a man like the hunter anywhere near my kin and my friends.

And anyway, I told myself, it was more likely that the hunter would approach in the same direction that Rollo and I had come from, which was from Cambridge, to the south-west. I set off, retracing my steps along the fen edge and, avoiding the island, headed back towards the familiar road between the town and Aelf Fen that I had trodden more times than I could recall.

I walked for a long time, almost as far as the spot where the well-concealed, winding path into the fens joins the road. Then I turned and went back again, on different tracks this time, criss-crossing my outward route. I knew the ground so well that had there been anything out of the ordinary, I thought I would have noticed. I saw nothing.

Finally, tired, very hungry, the softly falling darkness beginning to make me see odd-shaped shadows and strange shapes where in truth there were only the natural phenomena of shrubs and stunted trees, I reached the point where the neck of land leads across to Mercure's island. It was still submerged, but the water was a little less deep. I only got wet to my knees.

No light showed from the house. As I approached, I had the sudden, acute fear that Rollo had gone. But then the door opened the merest crack, an arm shot out and he pulled me inside.

'I hope I didn't hurt you,' he said, eyeing me anxiously as I rubbed my arm.

'No.'

'I had to get you inside before you opened the door too widely,' he went on. 'I haven't yet lit a lamp, but the glow from the fire will be visible from a long way off.'

I didn't agree with him, for the carr and the trees grew too thickly to allow good visibility. But I just said, 'I understand.'

He had food ready, and water steaming in a pot for making drinks. I took out some packets of herbs and made up a mixture.

'You saw no sign of him?' Rollo asked as I stirred.

'No.' I wasn't ready to tell him what I'd seen in the shining stone.

'I guessed as much,' he said. He looked at me, smiling. 'You'd have come racing in full of your news if you had.'

'So, what have you been doing?' I asked.

He made a soft exclamation. 'Ah, that reminds

me.' He got up and went outside, again opening the door the merest crack. He was quickly back. 'I've set the trip wire,' he explained as he sat down again. 'Obviously, I couldn't do so until you had returned. Now, though, it's in place. It works – I tested it – and if anyone tries to come across the causeway, we'll hear him.'

'Good.' That was reassuring news. I gave a shiver, thinking of that crossbow.

He noticed. 'What's wrong?'

'Nothing. I'm tired, and I'd got cold.' I smiled at him. 'Better now, and this food's wonderful.'

He was still watching me. 'The trip wire isn't the only defence,' he said quietly. He inclined his head towards the door. Peering into the shadows, I saw a small arsenal of weaponry. His sword, three knives, a heavy cudgel, an axe, a log splitter. 'And I thought that, after we'd eaten, we'd go through to the workroom so that you can select any materials belonging to your old wizard that could be used in our offensive.'

'But I don't—' I was going to say that I didn't know anything about that part of Mercure's and Gurdyman's work. Only then I remembered that maybe I did . . .

It had been magnificent.

More than that: but there were no words to describe it; no earthly experience with which to compare it. It had been like a vision of some far-distant star exploding into dazzling brilliance.

As that vast, expensive, luxurious house had caught fire, the night sky had lit up as if noon had arrived unexpectedly. The flames had soared up to the stars, and the showers of sparks had been like terrible rain. The heat had been so fierce that the red, orange, yellow and finally white fires seemed to outrun and consume the billowing smoke. It had been like a storm, and he could still hear the howl of the wind as it was sucked into the vortex.

The thrill had been sexual, and its intensity had demanded every particle of him. Afterwards, when he had staggered away and was safely in his hiding place, the sleep that ensued had been more like unconsciousness.

Now, waking soon after nightfall of the next day, he sent out sensors through his body. He was hungry and thirsty, but both needs could be readily satisfied. He was frugal in his habits, and content with bread, water and a little cheese.

He got up, rolling up his meagre bedding. He rarely felt the cold, and the single thin blanket was enough. Anything bulkier would have been less easily transportable: as always, convenience and efficiency went before comfort.

He ate his simple supper. Then, making absolutely sure that he had left no sign of his presence, he slipped out of his hiding place and jogged off to where he had left his horse. As the moon rose, he was heading out of town and towards the fens.

Fifteen

Some time around dawn, Jack woke from deep sleep, thrown into wakefulness. By a dream? He attempted to recover whatever it was that had alarmed him, trying to breathe calmly and still his racing heartbeat. Had it been some noise outside that had woken him? One within the house?

He listened. The deserted village was utterly silent, and even his ever-attentive geese were quiet. Nobody out there, then . . .

He raised himself up on one elbow and peered into the gloom of the rear room. He couldn't make out much more than the dark hump of a shape in the bed, but, listening, he heard her steady breathing. No disturbance in here, either.

Which meant that whatever had woken him so suddenly had emanated from inside his own head.

He turned onto his back, folding his hands behind his head. Stilling his mind, he tried to go back to whatever dreaming thought had woken him up.

And after a while, slowly at first but then rapidly gathering itself once again into the forceful nudge that had set his sleeping heart thumping, the same question came into his mind.

If Batsheva had come looking for whichever of the fair young men was her lover, or protector, or whatever it was that he had been to her, why had she been watching Gaspard Picot's house?

Slowly, steadily, he recalled several things.

He heard Ranald's voice; Ranald, who knew a bit about the Picots because he'd been sent to guard the great new house while it was being built. Whose cousin's wife's sister Maudie had been the lady Elwytha's maid. Ranald, who had first told Jack the lady's name. Who said she was a *short, skinny, white-faced, self-absorbed, nervy sort of a woman, with that pop-eyed, lash-less look that puts you in mind of a rabbit.* Who'd had narrow hips, a figure like an undeveloped girl, and, as Lard had crudely put it, no tits.

And he heard Ranald's voice again, speaking of his relation by marriage and saying that Maudie hadn't had to put up with the bad temper and the violent nature of Gaspard Picot because she'd been his wife's maid *and the lady had separate quarters*.

And then he thought about Batsheva. About her firm-featured, handsome face and her intensely dark eyes. About her strong shoulders and arms, her voluptuous body and the lush, pillowy comfort that a man would be afforded by her full, round breasts.

Very softly, the words almost mouthed rather than spoken, he said to himself, 'I believe that, wed to a woman of great wealth and position who possessed neither good looks nor the smallest hint of sexuality, Gaspard Picot took a mistress.' He paused, thinking carefully over what Batsheva had told him. 'He found her in London.' That, he thought, was quite likely, for

239

both the sheriff and his late nephew had been known to visit the capital regularly and, many years back, Gaspard Picot had spent several months there. Neither he nor the sheriff, Jack recalled now, had ever taken their wives with them. Gaspard would have been free to seduce, pay for and otherwise bed as many women as he wanted. 'And, meeting a young woman who he realized was in urgent need of a new protector, her father having died and left her destitute,' Jack finished, 'he removed her from her former home and set her up in Norwich. Which was,' he added, 'a great deal closer to home.'

He thought about that for some time.

It occurred to him that he should have asked himself why she was watching the Picot house much earlier. Last night, for example, when at last her fierce resistance collapsed and she began to tell him what he wanted to know.

Why hadn't he, when now it seemed so obvious?

Because she didn't let you, a soft voice said inside his head.

He jerked his head, as if he hoped to hear it speak again. It didn't.

Was that right? Was he only able to see the obvious *now* because he was out of the power of Batsheva's eyes? Was it true that, in her presence, with her watching him so intently that she could *hear* what he was thinking, he might have begun on that path but somehow she had diverted him?

But that would mean she possessed some sort of mind control; some sort of magic. He didn't want to believe that. He wasn't going to . . .

240

He lay still, and outside the first pearly grey crept up the eastern sky.

In the end, he had to accept the truth.

He was beginning to like Batsheva.

He was deeply suspicious of her, and it was still possible that she had committed murder and arson. He was forced to admit that this was actually more likely now, for if she did indeed have some sort of power – he was still fighting the idea – then it could even be she who had implanted in his mind this belief in her innocence.

All the same, there was something about her that he admired; or, perhaps more accurately, something that aroused his sympathy and his protectiveness. She'd been secure, living in her little Norwich house, her lover and her protector a regular visitor, until, one day, Gaspard Picot hadn't turned up when he was meant to. And he went on not turning up, until finally she was driven to come to Cambridge and find out what had happened to him.

He thought she was courageous to have come here. He imagined how she'd have felt when she learned Gaspard Picot was dead. He thought she was—

No. He wasn't going to allow himself any further down that seductive path.

But an unpleasant truth was nagging at him. If he was right and she had been Gaspard Picot's mistress – he was sure of it – then, before someone else did, he was going to have to tell her who was responsible for her lover's death.

Once more, Jack thought, she had been left entirely alone in a tough world. This time, it was because of him. He remembered how he'd felt guilty about leaving the lady Elwytha a widow. How much worse, he realized, feeling sick, did he feel about Batsheva.

It was still early. He wondered if he could sleep again, and he decided it was worth a try. He settled down on his side, made himself relax and quite soon felt himself drifting off.

In the sort of half-dream that flies through the mind as wakefulness battles with oncoming sleep, he saw an image of a baby, and wondered if Batsheva had borne Gaspard Picot any children. One of the two fair-haired men, perhaps? *Both* of them, and what's his name, Gurdyman's friend Hrype's son, attacked because they'd been mistaken for him? But why would anyone want the young man, or men, dead?

Were the ages right? Originally he'd thought Batsheva too young to be the mother, but he realized now that he had no accurate idea of the dead men's ages. Nor of hers, come to that. He wondered who would know about the young men, and remembered that Gurdyman had seen both bodies. He'd go and speak to him later today.

His mind veered away from the thought that the woman sleeping in the next room might just have lost both lover and sons.

Baby.

For just an instant, something flashed into his mind like a bright star glimpsed for the blink of an eye through a hole in a night cloud.

But then it was gone, its presence so brief that he forgot all about it.

* * *

242

I was awake before Rollo the next morning. Once again, I emerged from deep sleep to find that he was curved around me. Once again, I loved his closeness.

I got up and went through to Mercure's workroom, a lamp in my hand. I lit two more lamps. I needed plenty of light, because I was going to be searching through his supplies and it was very important that I didn't mistake something potentially harmful for something innocuous.

I had a memory of a lesson that Gurdyman had given me. I'd found him with a wooden bowl of fine black powder in his hands, and he'd told me with unusual urgency never to touch it. Since, naturally, that aroused intense curiosity, he told me what it was.

'I learned of it when I was a young man in Muslim Spain,' he began – I love his tales of his exotic youth – 'and it is a secret method brought by traders from the far side of the world. The man who showed it and its powers to me had in turn been instructed by a man with a yellow face, a long black pigtail and eyes set at a slant.' I could barely contain myself by then. 'In the way of so many procedures,' he went on, 'we mix three quite ordinary items together to produce the extraordinary; in this case, charcoal, yellow brimstone and saltpetre, which as you probably know is the exudation that comes from the old stones of dank, dark cellars.' As he so often did, he assumed knowledge I didn't in fact have. 'Now once these elements have been crushed – separately, mind – in the pestle and mortar, we combine them and we make the dark powder.' Slowly he turned the bowl in his graceful hands. 'And, if the separate ingredients are pure enough, and if we have the proportions exactly right, we have a substance which, treated in a certain way, will disappear with a crash like thunder and a flash brighter than lightning.'

I don't know if Gurdyman ever put theory to the test. If he did, it wasn't when I was close enough to witness or to hear.

Wandering round Mercure's workroom, I had found two of the three ingredients. There was a whole sack of finely powdered charcoal, and he had a jar containing lumps of brimstone.

I couldn't find any saltpetre, which was just as well. While the idea of rushing back to Rollo and announcing I had conjured up a barrel full of dark powder and knew exactly how we could use it to make our enemy disappear was very seductive, it was a totally impractical plan. For one thing, there was no saltpetre, and, even had there been a convenient stone-walled cellar where I might have found some, how on earth would I go about purifying it, and to what degree of purity? No. If I'd made the attempt, I'd probably have succeeded in blowing my hands off, to say the least.

We were left with Rollo's arsenal of weapons and our own wits.

That night as we settled for sleep, Rollo took me in his arms. Holding me close, my head on his shoulder, his hand stroking down the length of my hair, he said, 'Lassair, I'm sorry to have brought you into my troubles. When I asked you to come with me it was, as no doubt you fully understand, because I needed somebody to fool the man who has been hunting me all this time. It didn't fool him, and now here we are, on a lonely island, and I have managed to isolate you from your family, your work, the comfort and security of your home. And from those you love.' He spoke the last words in a barely audible whisper, but I knew what – who – he meant.

I thought for some moments before replying, for I wanted to be as honest as he had just been.

'I had my own reasons for agreeing to your proposal,' I said eventually. 'I'd already fled Cambridge but then, because of what happened when I got to my village, it wasn't really any better there.'

He made a soft sound of sympathy. 'I could tell, as soon as I saw you, that you'd recently suffered badly. You looked awful,' he added.

I grinned. 'Thank you.'

He laughed. 'It's not a criticism, Lassair. You always look beautiful to me, even when you're deep in pain and despair.'

I waited until I thought I could speak without a tremulous voice giving me away. 'So, you see, in a way the excitement of you turning up, and asking me to undertake a risky journey into the unknown with you, was just what I needed.'

'But in a way it wasn't,' he said, a harsh edge to his tone, 'because first you only just avoid getting burned alive, next, you're forced to bury yourself out here and ruthlessly commanded to lead a killer to our door.'

I barely heard the last words for suddenly I

245

knew that the moment for revelation was here. I paused, wondering if I really wanted to say what I was about to, and I realized I did.

I said, 'Rollo, I slept with Jack Chevestrier once, and I conceived a child. I didn't realize for some time – I was too busy looking after him – but, when I did, I had no idea what I was going to do.' He made a sound as if to speak, but I didn't let him. Having embarked, I wanted to finish. 'I didn't tell him. He's a good man and I know that he loves me. Knowing I carried his child, he'd have insisted on my marrying him, immediately, even if he was still so ill that his loyal followers would have had to carry him before the priest. So I ran away.' I paused. I could feel the tears already, but I fought them back. 'When I got to Aelf Fen, everything was different. My aunt Edild who I lived with had married Hrype, and Hrype and I don't really get on. Then my friend Sibert was attacked and needed someone to look after him, so I moved in with him and his mother. Soon after that, I lost the baby. Three days later, you arrived.'

I'd said *I lost the baby* so quickly that I wondered if he'd even heard. It had been deliberate; the only way I could get the words out was to say them almost in passing, as it were, in the hope that my heart wouldn't hear.

But my body betrayed me. My empty womb gave a profound sort of clench, as if it was belatedly trying to clutch on to what was no longer there. It had only been ten days; days in which I'd often been riding almost non-stop, worrying, frightened out of my wits, cold and hungry. It was as if, once I'd recognized that I had every right to be in pain, both bodily and emotionally, the barriers I'd put up all came crashing down.

I turned into Rollo's lean, muscly chest and wept.

He turned then from the detached, preoccupied king's spy into the man I remembered. The man I'd kept somewhere in my heart, during the months and years of his absence.

He just held me and let me cry.

When at last I stopped, he said, 'Thank you for telling me. I can see how hard it was. I understand, now.'

What did he understand? Why I hadn't wanted to make love, yes, of course, and I was glad that he now knew I'd had a reason and wasn't trying to pay him back for staying away so long with no word. But I suspected he also meant that he understood about the strange little triad we made: he, I and Jack.

Well, I thought with a small smile, *if he understands, I do wish he'd explain it to me.*

After a while he got up, made up the fire and said, 'Do you want me to put water on to heat?'

'Yes, do, if you want a drink,' I said, struggling up from the tangle of bedding.

He sighed and looked down at me. 'Dear Lassair, I was thinking of you. I've watched you come up with precisely the right remedy for a dozen needs, seen faces twisted in agony miraculously smooth out as the draughts go down. You are very obviously in pain, so I simply wondered if you might consider ministering with similar compassion to yourself.'

I'd badly wanted to, but I'd had my reasons for resisting. 'I can't,' I muttered.

'Why not?'

I hesitated, but it seemed honesty still prevailed. 'Because a mixture of the pain suppressant herbs that's strong enough for my needs will also make me sleep very deeply, and this is not the place or the time for that.'

He gave an exclamation of disgust, but I knew that it was with himself and not me. 'Let me see to our defence,' he said roughly. He put water in the pot and set it on its trivet over the fire. Then he pushed my satchel into my hands and said, 'Go on. Make it strong.'

It was very late in the afternoon that Jack finally managed to achieve his urgent wish to speak to Gurdyman. The day had been disturbed by a visit from Walter, who, hearing via the swift and ever reliable mechanism by which everyone in the castle soon knew about pretty much everything that had been going on there, had turned up to hear it straight from one of the protagonists.

'He's still puce in the face and spitting nails,' he said with a grin when Jack had finished his brief account, 'but our sheriff's not a man to take an attack without fighting back, and we're all paying the price by way of extra duties, tougher discipline and harsher punishments.'

'I'm sorry,' Jack said instantly. 'It wasn't my wish to inflict any of that on hard-working men.'

'We know,' Walter said. 'It'd be worth it, but in fact the harsher punishments are only a threat. So far,' he added. 'Look, chief,' he went on, clearly noticing Jack's worried expression, 'you only said what had to be said. Yes, Sheriff Picot will be like a cornered boar with a sore foot for a while, but there's nothing new about that. The important thing is that you've pointed out a few truths to him, such as he's lost that sod of a nephew and he may well find life a bit lonely from now on. Especially given that he can no longer ignore the popular voice, which speaks – shouts – for an honest man. You, that is.' He grinned.

Jack stared down into the fire, affected in many ways by what Walter had just said. *Honest*, he thought. *Yet here we sit, this good, loyal, brave man and I, and I'm hiding a secret.*

Making up his mind suddenly and very definitely, he turned towards the rear doorway and called out, 'Come in here, please.'

And, as Batsheva emerged from the dimness of the back room and advanced to sit between the two men, Jack explained to Walter who she was.

Knowing he had to go out to see Gurdyman later and not trusting Batsheva, Jack had asked Walter as he was leaving to send one of the lads – Henry or Iver – to come round at nightfall to guard her. It was Henry who arrived, his face eager and excited.

'Not much of a mission, Henry,' Jack said softly. 'There's a woman in there' – he jerked his head towards the rear room – 'and I want her to stay there.'

'Oh.' Henry's face fell.

'I don't expect to be out long,' Jack continued,

249

'and the fire's warm, there's stew in the pot and newish bread to go with it, and a flagon of ale standing by the door.'

'Oh!' Henry's smile returned. 'That's all right, chief, you be as long as you like!'

Gurdyman answered Jack's first soft tap on the door, as if he'd known his visitor was coming and was waiting in the dark hall.

'Do you mind coming down to the crypt?' he asked, already leading the way along the passage and down the steps. 'Only I'm right in the middle of something and, although it doesn't require any action for the time being, it does need careful watching.'

'Of course not.'

As he followed Gurdyman into the crypt, however, Jack was already regretting his willingness, for something was simmering in a small copper pot over a brilliant blue flame and sending out thin clouds of smoke, or possibly steam, that seemed to bite the throat.

'I should stand over there,' Gurdyman said hurriedly, pushing Jack towards the furthest corner of the crypt. 'If you put your head just there' – he demonstrated – 'there's a welcome little draught of fresh air.'

Jack breathed in gratefully. He wondered how Gurdyman stood it, for the old wizard was leaning over the little pot and apparently immune to the fumes.

'I'm used to it,' he said, in answer to Jack's unasked question. 'Now,' he turned to Jack, 'that can take care of itself for a time. I had the sense that I would see you tonight, and I've been wondering why.'

Putting aside the obvious question – *what on earth made you think I'd come?* – Jack gathered his thoughts and said, 'I believe you told me you saw both of the two young men who were killed, the one on the road to the fens and the other found in the river.'

'I did,' Gurdyman agreed. 'The sheriff sent for me to have a look at the first body, and I was also summoned for the one in the river.'

'And?'

Gurdyman made a brisk sound of impatience. 'And what? Be specific.'

'What did they look like, and how old do you think they were?'

'You know all this, Jack,' Gurdyman said reprovingly. 'Young, fair-haired, quite well dressed. As for age, the one found by the track was perhaps in the early or mid-twenties, perhaps a little younger, but the one from the river had been damaged by insertion in the water and also by some degree of depredation by river creatures. However, he was, I believe, about the same age. Both men were well muscled and reasonably well fed.' He went on speaking for a while but then, possibly sensing he had lost Jack's attention, stopped.

Early or mid-twenties, Jack was thinking. And Batsheva is perhaps fifteen years older? But I have not seen her in the bright daylight, and it may be that I underestimate.

'If you're not going to share your obviously compelling thoughts,' Gurdyman said caustically,

251

'I shall turn my back on you and return to my experiment.'

'I apologize,' Jack said. Briefly he told Gurdyman what was on his mind; how he'd come to the irresistible conclusion that the woman in his house had been Gaspard Picot's mistress, and that the two young men, similar in looks and, it now appeared, in other respects too, were her sons by him.

Slowly Gurdyman nodded. 'And do the ages tally?'

'I think so,' Jack said slowly. 'She is perhaps fifteen years older than the men, maybe more, so it is possible. I have not scrutinized her appearance sufficiently carefully to judge for sure.' Meeting Gurdyman's quizzical eyes, he said, 'I've only seen her in the dark, or in dim interior light.'

'And a beautiful woman cares enough about her appearance to enhance her good looks, and in so doing, prolong the illusion of youth,' Gurdyman observed.

'How do you know she's beautiful?'

Gurdyman smiled kindly. 'Oh, Jack, Jack. You gave away the fact that *you* think she is the very first time you spoke of her.'

Sixteen

Returning from his visit to Gurdyman, still disturbed by some of the old man's remarks – in particular the final one – Jack went into his house to find Batsheva and Henry sitting either side of the hearth. They appeared to have been deep in intimate conversation, and the furtive way in which Henry leapt up and, with a perfunctory farewell, immediately hurried off, seemed to support this.

Jack went after him. 'Everything all right?'

Henry turned and gave him a too-bright smile. 'Fine, chief.'

'I'll need you again tomorrow.'

Henry nodded. 'Yes, chief. I'll be here.'

Thoughtfully, Jack went back inside.

Batsheva looked up as he closed and fastened the door. 'Your young admirer has been telling me all about you,' she said. There was an edge to her voice, and he wasn't sure what it signified.

'Oh yes?'

'Oh, yes,' she echoed. 'He said what a fine man you are, and how he and all the others are hoping you'll soon be back to lead them. In particular, they need you to be a strong influence over your Sheriff Picot, because he's a bad man – well, that was not in fact what he called him, but I will leave you to fill in the more colourful word for yourself – who is greedy, cruel and corrupt, and who has always abused his power.' She paused, frowning slightly. 'He said that the moment was ripe because the sheriff has just lost the man who was his closest and most trustworthy supporter, in addition to being his nephew and a man who was as repellent as the sheriff, if not more so, as well as being a crook, a thief and a man of extreme violence, and that it was high time the town had an honest man in a position of power.' She paused, her head on one side. 'I believe that is a full summary of his observations.'

Jack said quietly, 'I'm sorry.'

Her dark eyes narrowed with suspicion. 'For what?' she asked guardedly.

'That you should hear such things of the man you loved.'

'But you cannot—' She stopped. For a while there was utter silence. Then she said very quietly, 'How did you know?'

He shrugged. 'I do not believe that you murdered the widow Elwytha, nor that you started the fire. The next logical question was to ask myself why else you were watching the house.'

'A leap, was it not, to decide that it was because my emotions were engaged with its late master?'

'You must have been aware that it was perilous for a stranger to be seen lurking outside the place where a woman had been murdered, yet you stayed. There had to be something more than prurient curiosity.'

'And you settled on love.' Her words were a mere breath.

254

'Yes.' *And if you say I'm wrong*, he added silently, *I won't believe you.*

Yet still he thought she was going to deny it. Then, lowering her head, she said softly, 'I believe I did love him, yes. For sure, I was grateful to him, for he was kind to me, in his way, and he rescued me when I was alone and afraid.'

'And did Henry also tell you how he died?'

She gave a deep sigh. 'Oh, yes.'

'I regret that he died at my hand,' Jack said. 'But, without the blind support for me and the drama that I'm quite sure Henry introduced into the account, the facts remain that I went to arrest Gaspard Picot for theft, I found him with the goods in his hands, and when I advanced towards him he leapt on me with a knife in his hand. I drew my own blade, and as he threw himself on me, he was fatally wounded.'

'Yes, that is basically what the lad told me.' She raised her head and her dark eyes met his. 'That he should be the first to draw a weapon does not surprise me, for he was a fighter and a man quick to temper and to violent action. Not with me,' she added swiftly, for Jack had made as if to speak. 'Never with me, for it seemed to me that he came to me as to a quiet, calm place where he could leave aside the man of action and, yes, of violence, that he was in the world.' She closed her eyes briefly. 'You will not believe me, I'm sure, but there was a better man inside him; a happier man, I think, for his life as trusted deputy to a narrow-minded, bigoted uncle and husband to a dissatisfied, irritable wife was not one he had chosen.'

'But he—'

She did not let him finish. 'That he should act impulsively and with such sudden violence, yes, that I understand, especially when he felt himself to be cornered,' she said. 'But that he should be a thief, that I do find hard to believe.'

'Nevertheless it is the truth.'

She nodded. 'Oh, I'm sure you're not lying.' She glanced at him again. 'You are, I sense, an honest man.'

It was strange, he thought, that her tone almost implied it was something shameful, or, at the least, naive.

Perhaps she was right.

He studied her. She made a graceful figure, sitting beside the fire, her skirts modestly arranged, her head bowed on the elegant neck. For some time he let her be, for he sensed she was deep in the past.

But there was another matter, and he could not let it rest.

'You had sons by Gaspard Picot,' he said.

Her head shot up. Her eyes were wide, her mouth slightly open. But she did not speak; he felt she was waiting for him to go on. To see if he would be so insensitive as to bring up the subject of her further loss and her grief when she had not?

But it was no time for fine manners and the observance of delicacy.

'Both are dead,' he said, 'for I assume them to be the two fair-haired young men of similar appearance who were killed here recently.'

She was studying him intently. 'And why should you assume that?'

Rapidly he summed up his thoughts. 'They were

killed shortly before the widow Elwytha, and the three deaths had certain similarities. It is not unreasonable to believe the same hand was responsible for all three deaths. As to why somebody wanted to take the lives of these victims, I cannot answer that. Yet,' he added firmly.

She was still staring at him. For some moments, he read absolutely nothing in her expression. He was just beginning to wonder if he'd been mistaken – for surely no mother could discuss with such equanimity the death of her own children – when she changed.

Lowering her head, she covered her face with her hands. Her body began to tremble, then to shake. After a moment, without a word she got up and went through to the rear room. She lay down on the bed, her face to the wall, and drew her heavy cloak up over herself, until she was covered from head to toe.

He deeply pitied her grief. Was this, he wondered, its first full outpouring? Had she been stopping herself from accepting what had happened, until, just now, he had forced her to?

But something was nagging and poking at him . . . something to do with reaction, and the unmistakable sights and sounds of a truly genuine emotion . . .

He realized after a while that he was only going to frustrate himself further if he went on trying to pin down what he sensed was amiss.

Instead he turned to the equally perplexing question of who wanted the sons – and the widow Picot – dead.

* * *

257

When Henry arrived early the next day, Jack left him to resume his guard duty and set off into the fine drizzle of the morning. He had worried at the problem of how to find the killer for much of the night. He had come up with nothing. He had decided, shortly before dawn, to find out more about Batsheva, and now he was on his way to the remains of the destroyed village beneath the Picot house, to see if he could locate her hiding place.

He reached it swiftly, and a part of his mind was pleased at how his strength and fitness were continuing to grow. He followed the ruined wall until he came to a gap. From its position relative to the Picot house, and to the bench where he had been accustomed to sit and watch, he guessed it was through here that he had chased Batsheva on the night of the fire.

The maze of narrow little alleys, broken walls, jumbled stones and the general detritus of destroyed homes struck him much harder now, in daylight. He stopped and simply stared. Fury rose in him: fierce and hot, at the casual cruelty of a man who broke up a poor and modest community simply because he wished to clear space for his own dwelling; simply because he was the man with the power and he *could*.

Since his conversation with Gurdyman the day after the widow Picot was killed, thinking about the death of Gaspard Picot and his own part in it no longer brought a stab of remorse. Now, standing where a cruel and greedy man had ruthlessly imposed his will and got his own way, Jack knew that the guilt had gone for good.

He wandered on through the ruins of what, not so long ago, had been people's homes.

He found nothing.

Returning to his house, he thought about calling in on Gurdyman. But, he thought morosely, to say what? He had spent much of the night turning everything over in his mind and got nowhere. It was a failure that he was reluctant to share with the old man.

He opened the door to see Henry fast asleep beside the dying fire.

Knowing already what he would find, he leapt across the floor, and Henry's sleeping body, and into the rear room.

It was empty.

Batsheva, her small pack, her heavy cloak, were gone.

He went back to the hearth, made up the fire and then began shaking Henry until, after a very long time, he woke.

He sat up, rubbing his eyes and looking round, his face dazed. He looked at Jack, then peered into the empty room. 'Oh, *no*,' he breathed.

Jack let him suffer for a few moments. Then, picking up the coarse pottery mug lying on its side beside the hearth, he said, 'She made you a drink.'

'Yes, she did,' Henry agreed. 'And very tasty and welcome it was, too, as I'd been coughing – it's these chilly, damp mornings – and she said she'd make something that'd help, and she put honey in it, and although I found it a bit bitter at first, I soon got used to it and she encouraged me to drink it all down.'

259

'I'm sure she did,' Jack said ironically.

He glanced up at the shelves where he stored his foodstuffs. Lassair had left him a supply of her draughts. Batsheva knew more than enough about them, he remembered, since she'd queried the one he'd given her.

Henry had worked it out for himself. 'She drugged me, didn't she, chief?' he muttered. His face was dark with anger. 'I thought she was just being kind and motherly!'

And what would you know about motherliness? Jack thought.

He knew some of Henry's story. He'd been found, abandoned, as a very small chid, almost dead from starvation, naked, foul with his own filth, covered in lice and open sores. The monks had taken him in and as soon as he could walk again, put him to work in the yard shovelling dung. Discovering he was intelligent, they had cleaned him up and taught him to read and write, although any hopes they might have entertained about him becoming one of their number were to be frustrated when he ran away.

Jack wondered fleetingly if Batsheva had picked up on Henry's deep and probably unacknowledged yearning for the mother he had never known. He surprised himself with the realization that he thought it was perfectly possible . . .

'Oh, dear, good Lord, I'm sorry, chief,' Henry was saying, scarlet with shame.

Jack reached out and slapped his shoulder. 'Not to worry, Henry,' he said. 'I'll admit I'm furious that she's gone, but I don't hold you entirely to blame. She's a clever and very determined woman and she'd have worked out in a matter of moments how to get round you.'

Amused, he watched several expressions cross Henry's pleasant open face. At first he looked relieved because he wasn't in the trouble he'd anticipated, and the relief turned to the beginnings of a swagger, as if he was thinking, *I got away with that one!* Finally, sliding a swift look at Jack, his grin faded as he understood that he'd just been dismissed as naive and easily fooled.

'Learn from this, Henry,' he urged the lad. 'People aren't always what you hope they are, and a prisoner under guard will try everything and anything they can to persuade you to like them and to be their friend. Without exception, it'll be to their advantage and never to yours.'

Henry nodded. 'I'll remember that, chief.' Then, a more honest smile returning now, he added, 'Thanks.'

Seventeen

I slept deeply and dreamlessly and then suddenly I was wide awake.

I knew that our enemy was close.

Trying not to wake Rollo, I slipped out from the bedding and over to the hearth. The fire was still glowing. Rollo must have banked it up well before sleeping. I added some small pieces of wood and poked up a bit of a blaze, then I got out the shining stone.

He was there again, just as I'd known he would be.

The dark figure with the crossbow was much clearer now, and I'd been right, he was nearby. Sometimes the shining stone is very easy to interpret: tiny, vague images mean that the person or the event is far away, in distance and on occasions also in time; and sharp, large images mean the warning concerns something imminent.

Then I heard again the sound that had probably woken me up.

It was a splash.

I crept over to the door and opened it a crack. I sniffed at the air. It was damp, with drops of moisture floating down. Not exactly rain, more like a tangible cloud. Everything was still. There didn't seem to be a whisper of breeze.

I waited. I stood there so long, face pressed

into the narrow gap between the door and its frame, until all my being seemed to have become focused in my eyes, nose and mouth – for I was trying to *taste* for danger as well as look and listen for it – while the rest of me went ignored, unnoticed. But then I tried to move and realized my feet and lower legs were numb.

I was also very cold. I warmed myself by the hearth, then crept in beside Rollo.

Had I really heard the man who hunted us, out there across the dark water? Or had it been no more than a night creature after its prey?

There was nothing more I could do now, for it was still night. In the morning I would tell Rollo of my suspicions, and together we would decide what to do.

But, just to be on the safe side, I would make quite sure I didn't sleep again.

Dawn brought the misty, damp day that the middle of the night had promised.

'He's close,' I said to Rollo as we ate our oat and water porridge.

'How do you know?'

It was gratifying that he didn't question whether I was right, only how I came by the knowledge.

But I'd never told him about the shining stone. I almost took it from my satchel there and then, but something stopped me. Perhaps it was my awareness that Rollo was not a man likely to put his faith in whatever world of spirits and arcane matters the shining stone's powers emanated from.

So I just said, 'I heard a noise in the night. It sounded as if somebody was throwing stones into the water.'

It was thin evidence, and I understood the dubious look he gave me. 'Is that all?'

'No, Rollo, it's not all,' I said impatiently. 'I know in ways that you wouldn't begin to understand, that you'd find highly questionable and that I can't really explain anyway. You'll just have to take my word for it.'

He nodded. 'Is it something akin to your ability to see the safe paths that, to everyone else's eyes, are invisible beneath the water?'

I didn't think it was, really, but both could roughly be ascribed to what people refer to as magic. 'Yes, in a way.'

'In that case' – he was smiling now – 'I don't need to ask anything more.'

I watched as excitement brightened his expression. He was eager, restless and twitchy, wanting to get going, to *do* something. I realized what the days of flight, of hiding, of trying to draw our enemy to us while still sensing ourselves to be at his mercy, and the unpleasant feeling that it was him who was in control, had cost him. He was a fighter. He liked to lead the assault.

And now he was going to.

Or, rather, I was.

'Now is the moment!' he said, picking up his sword and testing the edge. 'Our enemy wants to find us, and you tell me he's near, so go out and lead him to me.'

I was out on the fens for the greater part of the day. The mist cleared a little around midday, but there was barely a breath of wind to blow it right away. As daylight began to fade, it closed in again. Now it grew cold. I felt damp all over, and I couldn't stop shivering.

And I was frightened.

I'm used to the fens. I'm at home there, and it's rare for any of its natural phenomena to spook me. I know the sounds of the birds, and even the strange, eerie cries of bittern and nightjar I recognize for what they are. I've been jumping little streams and splashing through ones too wide to leap over since I could walk. I know how to keep myself safe when the thickest of mists descends and I can't see my hand in front of my face. I can find my way across the water, as Rollo had earlier reminded me.

But rarely had I gone out deliberately to attract an enemy with murder on his mind.

I kept hearing things. A soft rustle as almost-bare branches were pushed aside by a careful hand. The sharp crack of a breaking twig beneath a soft footfall. A tiny splash as a displaced pebble fell into the water. And then the unmistakable sound of quiet breathing, so close that my flesh cringed in anticipation of the touch of chilly fingers.

When I heard that, I resisted the urgent cry of my body to run, *run*, as fast as I could. Instead I forced myself to move slowly on.

Was I right? Had he been standing right behind me?

If so, I mustn't let him know I'd heard him. I must go on as I had been doing all day, wandering the fens as if collecting nuts and berries. Because if he believed I was deliberately trying to attract his attention and lead him where I wanted him to go, his suspicions would be instantly aroused and he'd be on his guard.

So I made my steps slow and dragging, as if, weary and cold, I was nearing exhaustion and finally, with the fading of daylight, giving up my foraging and going home.

I thought I heard him following along behind.

I froze.

I was nearing the little stretch of shore opposite the island. I couldn't move. I stood leaning against a young alder, panting for breath, my heart racing.

And out of nowhere a crossbow bolt flew right past my face and, with a loud thump, embedded itself in the trunk of the tree. Terrified, I wanted to run, to throw myself down in the bracken and the brambles, to hide where he'd never find me.

But I couldn't.

I said very softly, for my own ears only, 'Now.'

And I led him on towards Mercure's island.

He hated the fens.

Time seemed to pass at an unnatural, creeping pace out in this horrible, pestilential, secretive and accursed region that seemed to be both water and land and he had been on the point of giving up.

Would it matter? he wondered.

But he had set himself a task and he was not a man who stopped until he had achieved his end.

He had taken it upon himself to take the revenge that was due. Perhaps nobody would ever know, for he was a long way from home and sometimes he doubted whether he would make it back. But his heart was still full of the fire that had set him on this journey. Even if he didn't live to tell the tale, even if nobody ever knew what he had done and gave him the praise he would have earned, *he* would know.

And that might have to be enough.

But he was so cold.

And, although he didn't like to admit it, he was afraid.

At times it seemed that some of his skills had deserted him. He was disgusted at this failure, because he prided himself on being able to track his quarry in all types of terrain, relentlessly, infallibly. But this place was something different, and he'd never encountered its like before. He thought sometimes that maybe the gossip he had overheard in inns and on the road was right, and you have to be born in the fens to understand them.

He had spent his first night on top of a bank. It had been dry – the only relatively dry ground he could find – but being on even such a meagre height had meant his chilled body in its damp garments caught every breath of the wind out of the east. It wasn't even much of a wind, but in the cold, lonely watches of the long night, it had felt like a gale.

The whole of the next day had been fruitless.

He had slept briefly soon after sunset, then got up again long before dawn in the hope that those he sought were disguising their movements by travelling in the hours of darkness.

And then he had come across that weird little island.

He hadn't understood why, having found it, he couldn't tear himself away. They weren't there, and the fascination it held wasn't that he believed they were. For it was completely detached from the land, separated by a stretch of black, sinister and undoubtedly very deep water overhung with low-bending branches, the whole area dark and forbidding. And the island itself, with what appeared to be some sort of low, well-concealed building, gave off a sort of bristling hostility. He knew from the prickling sensation on the skin of his face and hands that there was peril there. Magic, perhaps. The island seemed to call out, *Keep away.*

Besides, there was no boat.

Nevertheless he had stood on the fen edge for some time staring out at the island. What small breeze there had been had ceased and all was utterly still. The black water at his feet was like a sheet of glass. Suddenly frightened – of what he had no idea – he picked up a piece of dead, densely tangled root and hurled it out into the water. It ought to have made a big, noisy splash, for it had been the size of his two clenched fists. But it didn't; it sank down into the water with barely a sound. After a time, confused, worried, he tried again. The splash was slightly louder this time, but still quite disproportionate to the size of the root.

It was as if some power beneath the surface,

not wanting to be disturbed, had halted it in its flight and gently drawn it in.

His terror burst out and, in a heartbeat, rose to screaming pitch. Before a sound could escape from him, he fled.

He was not a man who liked to admit to fear. In the morning, he planned to return and see how the island looked in daylight. He had little doubt that its strange power would have dissipated.

Or, at least, that was what he told himself.

But he didn't manage to put it to the test, because he couldn't find it.

His frustration turned to anger as the day went on.

He'd planned only to kill the man. Now, with the heat burning in his blood, he asked himself why the woman should be allowed to live. She was with the man; she'd chosen him. Why not kill her too?

And then, as the image of her he kept in his head steadily clarified with his resolve to take her life, all at once he saw her.

It was quite late in the day, the short autumn light beginning to fade.

He smiled to himself.

What was she doing? She seemed to be hunting for food. Probably she and the man had set out ill-equipped, and she was forced to find whatever she could to assuage their hunger.

He set himself on her trail. Sometimes he hung back. Then, as the mist thickened, he drew close. Taking advantage of a sudden white patch that

269

was all but impenetrable, he went right up to her and softly breathed out.

He could so easily have grabbed her.

But she was not his primary target. He slipped back and, as once more she set off, resumed his position a few paces behind.

Then she stopped.

Go on, he urged her silently. *Go on, back to wherever you and your man are hiding.*

She didn't move.

Fury surged up through him, burning away caution and sense. His mind filled with nothing more than the urge to make her do what he wanted, he raised his crossbow, drew back the string, placed a bolt and let fly.

Not to kill her, for even in his rage he remembered that before she died she must take him to the man. But to scare her; to make her run for safety.

Run to *him*.

He watched her. She froze, then she stared all around her and he could see the panic in her eyes. It made him smile.

Then she set off, plunging through the undergrowth, and he went after her.

I reached the shore opposite the island. I knew now where the safe way was and I leapt onto it with barely a pause. The causeway was well under the surface, however, and my need for haste was frustrated by water up to my thighs, sometimes to my waist. As I got to the far end and waded out onto dry land, I turned.

There was no sign of the hunter.

I didn't know what to do.

I'd thought he was right behind me. I'd imagined he'd see where and how I got across to the island and would follow. I was clenching my back muscles against the crossbow bolt.

I wanted more than anything to fling myself inside the house and bar the door.

But that wasn't the end that I'd gone into the fens today to bring about. If I obeyed my instinct and got under cover, he wouldn't know where I'd disappeared to, he wouldn't follow – wouldn't even hang around on the opposite shore searching for a way across to the island – and Rollo wouldn't be able to kill him.

And I'd have to do the same thing all over again tomorrow.

So I stayed were I was.

I heard him then. I heard the crashing of his body pushing swiftly through the carr. I heard him give a faint cry.

My eyes fixed on the shore, where any moment he would appear, I called out to Rollo.

I heard him fling open the door and then he was right beside me, sword in his hand, knife and dagger stuck in his belt.

I turned to look at him and saw his eyes widen in dread.

I spun round to see what he was seeing.

The hunter had his crossbow to his shoulder, and he was poised to loose the bolt straight towards us.

I screamed out to Rollo, '*Take cover!*'

He turned to me briefly, his face harsh with purpose. '*No!*' he shouted back. 'It's a long range

271

– he has one bolt and once it's loosed, he has to re-load.'

I didn't understand.

'That's when we charge!' he yelled. And he smiled.

But the hunter was standing there, so still, so sure. Yes, he was quite a way away, but the distance didn't seem to dismay him . . .

I turned back to Rollo and something in his face told me that confidence had changed to fear. He grabbed me and threw me behind him.

And, when the hunter let the bolt fly, Rollo was standing directly in front of me.

If the hunter had been aiming for the heart, his aim was off. But not by much. The terrible missile hit Rollo in the shoulder and he gave a sort of grunt.

I twisted round, terrified the hunter would try again. But he must have seen the great scarlet stain already spreading over Rollo's chest. He turned, headed back into the thick undergrowth and disappeared.

With my arm round Rollo's waist I supported him as best I could and helped him back inside the house. He was able to walk, but only just. Even in those few paces, I felt more and more of his weight on me.

I spread out blankets beside the hearth and poked up the fire, throwing on some of the dry wood that gave a quick, hot blaze. I put water on to boil. Then I unlaced Rollo's tunic and pulled his undershirt off his shoulder.

There was so much blood.

I raised him as gently as I could and inspected his back. It was as I'd thought. As I'd hoped.

I wrapped him in the thickest of the blankets, for already he was shivering with shock and his teeth were chattering. Staring down right into his eyes, I smiled and said, 'I can help you. I'm going to go through to Mercure's workroom, for there is something I need. Lie still.'

Through the increasing violence of his shuddering, he managed to say, 'I wasn't planning on doing anything else.'

It was brave, for I knew how much pain he was in.

I would do something about that, as soon as the water was hot enough.

I hurried out of the house and along under the covered way to the workroom. I strode along in front of the tightly packed shelves. I knew precisely what I was looking for and I was all but sure I would find it. Quite soon I did, and I sent up a prayer of thanks to Mercure, wherever his spirit was, for being so tidy and ordering his equipment so neatly and logically.

Then I went back to Rollo.

The water was already steaming; thankfully, it had been warm already. First I poured some into a bowl and put in the object I'd found in the workroom, for it had a sticky residue on it that I felt I should try to remove. Then I went through the packages in my satchel and put together a mixture that was probably the strongest treatment against pain that I'd ever made. As I added drops of the precious, perilous poppy, I hoped it wasn't *too* strong.

But Rollo was writhing now, his lower lip bleeding from where he was biting on it. I let the herbs steep, counting carefully. Then I added a little cold water and, supporting his head, gave him the draught.

It was swift-acting. Within quite a short time, he began to relax.

And I knew I couldn't wait any longer.

I lit all the lamps and candles I could find. I turned him onto his right side, his back towards the fire and the lights. I searched through my satchel and prepared several pads of soft, folded cloth. Then I took the object from the workroom out of the bowl, threw away the water and re-filled the bowl with fresh hot water and, with a soft piece of cloth, began to bathe Rollo's shoulder.

The bolt had hit him with such force that the tip had gone straight through him. I could both feel it and see its vicious iron point, sticking out of the back of his shoulder. *That's good*, I told myself. *It makes my job so much easier.*

As I've said, my aunt Edild had demonstrated how to remove arrows and crossbow bolts. Once the bolt fired by my father was sticking out of the shoulder of pork, she showed me what to do when the tip is hidden deep in the flesh. You have to make the track of the bolt wider, which is relatively easy when the flesh is that of a dead pig but, she warned me, much harder with a living body because as soon as the wound is received, the flesh begins to swell. By careful enlargement of the entry channel, however, she assured me that it was quite often possible to

274

insert the probing instruments down as far as the bolt head, surrounding it so that it is no longer held so tightly, and then, holding the entry channel open, ease the bolt out the way it went in.

What you must never do, she told me, is pull on the shaft, because if the point breaks off, you'll never get it out.

As I knelt over Rollo, I didn't recall Edild telling me what to do when the bolt had gone straight through. I thought I could probably work it out for myself.

The rear end of the bolt was sticking out of the front of Rollo's shoulder. The bolt was quite short, and a section of shaft only around the length of my hand was exposed, the flights sticking out on either side. I took a small, sharp-toothed saw and cut it off, as close to his skin as I could.

Then, returning my attention to his back, I took a deep breath and took Mercure's freshly cleansed, sharply pointed pincers in my right hand. With my left hand pressing down firmly on his back, holding the flesh as steady and taut as I could, I took a firm grip on the tip of the bolt and began to pull.

He screamed.

I went on pulling, for I had felt a tiny movement in the bolt. I increased the pressure, and the sounds he made all but undid me. But I didn't stop.

It seemed to take for ever,

But then with a sudden rush and a huge fountain of blood, the bolt was out.

I flung it aside and instantly pushed the pad of cloth I'd set ready against the hole it had left. I felt the cloth soak through with blood and exchanged it for another one.

I'd thought I was going to save him. The bolt had missed his heart, and I'd got it out.

But as his life's blood went on pumping out of him, I began to doubt myself. So much blood . . .

I didn't know where it was coming from. I'd hoped that steady pressure on the wound would make it stop. But something must have been torn or broken inside him.

I folded up the last of my cloths and pressed it against the back of his shoulder, wrapping the remains of his undershirt around it to hold it in place. Then I lay down beside him and took him in my arms.

He was so cold.

There was time for us to talk.

He said, 'I have gold. Some you already have, for you hid it for me.'

It took me a while to remember. Then I saw myself, crouched by Granny Cordeilla's grave. I wanted to say, *I don't want gold, I want you.*

But I didn't. He was doing what he could for me and I couldn't bear to make him think that his gold was as irrelevant as it was just then.

'There is more,' he said. His speech was slurred and it was difficult to make out the words. 'I made a list. Go and see Eleanor de Lacey. She lives by the river.' He paused, for quite a long time. I hugged him tighter. I could feel his heartbeat.

It was slow. 'Tell her who you are,' he managed. 'Tell her I said you're to have it all.'

I couldn't answer. My lips were on his face, and I kissed him. 'There was to be a house . . .' he murmured presently. 'A good house, set in wide green pastures with woods and a stream. A house – a *home* – for you and me.' He paused. His breathing was ragged now. 'I'd have stopped, in the end,' he whispered. 'Then it would have been you. Just you.'

I thought his strength had failed. I went on holding him.

Then, his voice barely more than a breath, he said, 'We should have stayed together.'

I kissed him again. His face was cold.

He died in my arms.

After a while I sat up.

I stayed were I was, on the floor, his head on my lap, for a long time.

I realized it was dark outside.

I heard a heavy thump. It was deafening in the silence. I jumped as if someone had stuck a needle in me.

Then I heard a sound like a distant chattering . . .

But then it wasn't a chattering sound any more. Even as I sat there trying to identify it, it turned into a crackle and then a howling roar.

My eyes didn't seem to be able to move from the door, for that was the focus of the noise. There was smoke coming in all round it, pushing its insistent way through the gaps between door and door frame.

And then the first greedy flame appeared,

licking along the top of the door and swiftly spreading upwards into the roof.

The house was on fire, and the flames had taken firm hold on the reed thatch.

Then I understood what the great thump had been: the hunter had loosed a flaming arrow, and it had found its target with devastating accuracy.

I had to move Rollo. I raised his head and shoulders and moved out from beneath him. I took hold of his shoulders – his blood was cold now against my skin – and pulled. I managed to get him a foot or so across the stone floor, but then I collapsed onto him.

I stared frantically towards the door. It was well alight now, as were the surrounding walls. The roof above was starting to drop big bunches of burning thatch into the house.

Not that way.

I looked over to the other, smaller door, that led to the covered way along to the workroom. The first faint hope stirred in me: *The hunter doesn't know there's another exit.*

If I could get Rollo's body out to the workroom, I could leave him safely there, make my escape and come back to him once the danger was past. Heartened, I leapt up and began to drag him.

I managed two or three paces, then, once again, my strength gave out. The air was filled with smoke and I didn't seem to be able to draw a proper breath.

I was seeing strange images in the smoke. I thought I saw my grandfather's silver hair and beard. I was drifting . . .

Then, quite clearly, Rollo said, *You have to go, Lassair. If you stay here you'll die.*

I threw myself onto him and cried, 'But I don't want to leave you!'

I know, he said, and his voice broke with love and regret. *But you can do no more for me. Go, get away, live. For me, for us both.*

I picked up my satchel, wrapped myself in my shawl, a fold covering my nose and mouth, and grabbed my cloak. I kissed his cold forehead, then I left him.

When I opened the low rear door, the flames already eating the room gave a great roar and doubled in size. The heat was terrible. I rushed out and slammed it shut. I flew along the covered way heading for the workroom, and—

The horses!

We had put them in a rickety old outhouse. Now as I stared across at it, I saw that one of its walls had been kicked out. The horses must have sensed the fire and, in terror, burst out of the outhouse. *Where were they?* They were stuck on an island with a burning building, how would they survive? But then reason said coolly, *Horses can swim. Do not worry about them, for they will save themselves.*

I raced on.

I don't know what made me do what I did. Perhaps it was the thought of Rollo's body, burning like a Viking on his funeral pyre; perhaps I wanted to make sure that the fire that sent my lost lover to whatever awaited him out there in the unknowable beyond was worthy of him. So I crashed into Mercure's workroom,

279

threw anything and everything made of wood into a pile in the middle of the floor, then emptied out every receptacle I could find on top. I struck a light, lit one of the small bunches of dry straw set ready beside the little hearth and threw it on the pile. Then I ran for my life.

The flames from the burning house were so dazzling now that I knew I had a small advantage. If I made sure to stay out of the light, I'd be able to see the hunter but he wouldn't see me. Keeping in the deep shadow of the overhanging trees, I crept towards the landward side of the island.

A slim, still figure was standing on the far shore at the landward end of the causeway. He still held his crossbow.

Well, I said to myself, trying to stay calm, *I can't go that way.*

I slipped back under the trees and made my way round behind the workroom – from which strange sounds and smells were already emanating, as well as the first thin spiral of smoke – and over to the far side of the island. I stepped down onto a narrow band of shingly earth, and, looking round, realized I was almost exactly opposite the causeway. And the safety of land.

I wondered if there really was a second way to cross the water. It was strange, but I seemed to be able to consider the question quite coolly and rationally. Would Mercure – or whoever it was who had first decided that a lonely, isolated little island made a good home for a solitary – have settled for just the one means of access? Yes, probably, I answered myself. For Mercure had no need of company and would have done nothing to make access easier.

Well, perhaps there was a way that nobody knew about.

I stood absolutely still. I tried to empty my mind, sending out a plea to the spirits of my ancestors. *You know I have this ability*, I reminded them. *Perhaps one of you did, too, and you bestowed it on me. Please, help me now. Give me the eyes to see what I must see.*

The house was alive with fire now. It was no longer possible to make out even the vague shape of walls and roof, for it was all one huge pyramid of flame, red, orange, yellow, white-hot.

And, closer to me – dangerously near – there were brilliant explosions like the simultaneous crack of thunder and flash of lightning. I felt the ground quake. Long trails of sparks were shooting up into the sky.

Mercure's workroom was burning.

I turned my back on it. I simply stood, staring out over the black water, waiting.

And then I could see the safe way.

Or I thought I could. The light was poor, for the night was overcast and the moon's bright light was diffused and soft. I could see only a few patches of clear sky. In one of these was the North Star. I thought absently, *There's more rain on the way.*

Sometimes I could make out the way, sometimes it seemed to vanish. I found it was easier to make out if I turned my head slightly to the side and looked at it askance. It began almost at my feet, then instantly snaked away to my left before turning back in a short dog's leg. Then it set off again, going due north for as far as I could see it.

North?

As far as I could judge from my mental image of the area, I needed to go east . . .

But I had asked my ancestors for help and it appeared they had provided it. I wasn't going to argue with them.

I stepped down into the water.

To begin with it was relatively easy. The water was quite shallow, and with my skirts tucked up I was only getting wet to the knees. It was cold, though. I didn't let myself think about that.

Then it got much harder.

There *was* a safe way here – I kept telling myself that – but it must have been very narrow. It was almost impossible to tell where solid ground gave way to quaking marsh and deep water, for the visibility was poor and, even looking sideways, sometimes the faint, luminous thread that I had to follow just wasn't there. Then I would have to advance in tiny steps, feeling for solid ground with the tips of my toes, testing it before putting my weight on it and moving forward. It wasn't too bad to begin with, but the problem was that slowly my feet were going numb.

I kept telling myself, *The hidden path is there. All you have to do is follow it, and it will lead you to safety.*

After a while I began saying the words aloud.

Then it began to rain. It was gentle at first – more a sort of exaggeration of the mist – but soon it became much harder.

I stopped.

I was in the middle of deep, black water, with the faintest, most tentative link to firm ground, and there was only me to find it. Only me to save my own life.

I turned and looked back towards Mercure's island, and I was amazed at how far I'd come. Either that, or darkness, rain and the disorienting brilliance of the fire that was still raging had distorted distance.

I felt so cold. So sad. So alone.

I pulled my cloak more tightly around me, fighting tears of fatigue, fear and self-pity.

It dawned on me that in my haste I had picked up the cloak Jack had given me. The costly, luxurious, fur-lined wool cloak that had been Rollo's gift was, along with Mercure's house and everything in it, by now burned to nothing. I felt a stab of sheer pain: the beginning, perhaps, of grief.

But then I realized that somehow I'd been guided in my choice, for Jack's cloak was lighter and it repelled the rain far more efficiently. The woollen cloak would by now have been soaked through, so heavy that it would have been more of a hindrance than a help. Jack's cloak was keeping me dry, and although my hands and feet were shrivelled with cold, my body was warm.

But it wouldn't stay that way if I didn't keep moving.

Heartened, although I didn't really understand why, I took a confident step, then another, and then another.

I was on my way.

Presently, as I'd known it must, the safe path turned east. I had no difficulty seeing it now, for the rain had stopped and the moon shone down, lighting the water to a sheen of silver. My confidence growing, I walked on.

I thought at first that the softly undulating black outline looming ahead was an illusion; the result of my need, making me see things that weren't there. But, although I blinked and rubbed my eyes so roughly that I briefly saw bright lights, the outline didn't alter. And, with joy and a great sense of achievement, I realized I was staring at the fen edge.

But I had one last challenge, for abruptly the water level rose. Alarmingly: one moment I was splashing along only wet to my ankles, or at worst my shins, then all at once I was up to my waist, then, terrifyingly, my neck. I could hear the sound of running water. This close to the shore, I could make out the noise of every stream and rivulet as it poured the run-off from all the rain out into the fen.

I went under once.

I thought I was going to die, but some sense of self-preservation made me spread my arms and my legs, and my face broke the surface again. I'd seen dogs swim, and I flapped my hands and arms in imitation. And my foot struck the fen bed.

But it wasn't the shore.

As I forced myself to climb up, I realized that I was on a small rise right out in the middle of the water. Somehow I'd found my way onto a little island; not much more than a hump of higher ground pushing up out of the dark water and perhaps thirty paces across.

As I stood there shaking with cold and shock, too frightened to feel much relief that I was still alive, I heard the sound I'd been dreading all along.

Splashing.

And I knew straight away it wasn't some water creature abroad on a night excursion.

It was him.

Somehow he'd managed to follow me. He'd found and braved the causeway onto Mercure's island, and he'd searched for me until he'd spotted me, making my escape across the water.

Why had he followed me? Why hadn't he gone back across the causeway?

The water level had risen. Had he not been able to find the causeway again?

In a moment of clarity, I understood that if he hadn't believed he could get off the island the same way he had gone onto it, if he didn't know his way across the fens and believed that I did, he must have realized that his only hope was to follow me.

But then I saw the crossbow. He had it in his right hand and even as I stared at him, he raised it to his shoulder.

He hadn't followed because I was his only means of reaching safety. He'd come after me to kill me.

Eighteen

I had to get out of his sight.

The island was tiny, but right in the centre a stand of low, straggly willows had managed to survive, surrounded by a tangled patch of carr and a lot of brambles. It was scant cover but it was all there was. I ducked right down, bending double, and went into it, instantly feeling the small pain of bramble prickles catching in my skin and tearing at me. I forced a way right through the undergrowth, under the willows and out again on the further side. Then I raised my head and looked out.

He was standing on the shore, staring at the willow trees. Then, seeing nothing, he began a frantic turning this way and that, searching for me. It would only be a matter of time until he realized where I'd gone.

Crawling now, I went down to the water's edge. I forced myself to put him out of my mind, for unless I found the safe way and immediately set off along it, he would spot me and kill me. Concentrating with all my force, I stared down at the water.

And there it was.

I thought at first that I must have made a mistake; that panic and terror were making my desperate eyes see something that wasn't there. For I could *see* the fen edge, perhaps thirty or forty paces away over to the *east*, exactly where I would have said it would be. Yet the safe path led off from the *north-west* of the little island.

Incredulously, I traced its progress with my eyes. It continued in the same direction for a while, then twisted and turned its way in a series of tight little bends until, finally, it turned for the final time for the short stretch to firm ground.

I could see it so clearly now that I knew I had made no mistake.

Just as the second path off Mercure's island had done, it appeared to set off in one direction, only to change its mind and take a different one . . .

But now wasn't the moment to dwell on the peculiarities of that.

I wriggled on my stomach down to the water's edge and, rising to a crouch, paddled out into the water and away from the shore.

He was still on the further side of the island and he hadn't seen me. It was raining again and that worked in my favour, making it harder for him to see. Praying my silent, fervent prayer of thanks, I stared intently down at the safe way and, slowly, so dreadfully slowly, the far shore came nearer.

He spotted me when I was scrambling through the shallows, with only twenty or thirty paces to go. There was a great cry of '*Stop!*'

I froze. Then, slowly, I turned round.

He was standing on the little stretch of shore that I had just left, on the near side of the island. In a straight line, he was only some fifteen paces away. He held the crossbow up to his shoulder. I couldn't be sure across the distance that separated us, but I thought there was a bolt pointed straight at me.

There was so much that I needed to know, so many questions I wanted to ask. I wanted to plead with him not to kill me. I wanted to demand how he'd managed to follow me.

But I screamed through the rain, '*Why did you have to kill him?*'

His voice came instantly back to me, his words seeming to bounce against my ears: '*Because he murdered my father!*'

My mind raced. His father?

I was in no doubt that Rollo had killed men, for he was a king's agent, and that was surely like being a soldier. Killing the king's enemies was his duty. But murder? And recent murder, for this dark young man to be so filled with grief, hate and the need for revenge.

I tried to work it out. It was so hard because this was Rollo we were speaking of, and Rollo was dead. I bit down hard on my grief and forced myself to think.

Perhaps Rollo had been forced to defend himself against Duke Robert's men as he fled the duke's castle, and, like this man, his father too had been one of them. 'And it happened in Normandy?' I shouted.

'In *Normandy*?' He sounded surprised.

'You're Duke Robert's man?'

'What? No!' He raised a hand to push his rain-soaked hair off his face. 'He killed my *father*! I told you, I just *told* you! I came here to find him, and they told me he had just died. He was *murdered*!' The word, emerging as a scream, seemed to bounce off the water in a series of echoes. 'There was a fight, and his enemy pulled a knife, and he – he died.'

Then I thought I knew the truth and, although I didn't understand, it was enough to send a deep shiver of abhorrence through me.

'And you – how did you get on our trail?'

'Ha! That was easy. People see, they hear, they are willing to tell you what they know if you pay them.' He was nearer now, for he had waded out into the water. The rain had eased, and there was no wind. He didn't seem to be speaking in much above an ordinary voice, but I heard him clearly. 'They told me, you see. They said that the man who murdered my father was the close friend of the healer girl. You're the healer girl. I *know* you are, I made sure of it, for I asked several people and they all confirmed that you were.'

The healer girl. Yes, a lot of people called me that.

'And then I *saw* you, I actually saw you!' he cried. 'I went to the house where you live on that very day, the day my father died, and I concealed myself at a safe distance. I saw you in his killer's arms with my own eyes, and I knew without a doubt. My prayers were answered, God was good and, although I was not actually shown the face of the man who had murdered my father because his back was turned to me, I saw enough of him to recognize him again.'

Amid my terror I felt a stab of pity for him.

'You're wrong,' I whispered. But the words were not for him. Aloud, calling across the water,

289

I said, 'Your father was killed in a fight, but it was him who struck first. He had broken the law, and—'

But he didn't want to hear it. With a huge cry of '*NO!*', he lunged straight towards me.

The strange inner eye that had allowed me to make out the safe way was still open. And I could see that the dark young man was heading straight into deep water, where the only narrow ribbons of firm ground beneath the feet were nothing but an illusion, for they were quicksand.

'*Not that way!*' I screamed.

He was still coming towards me. He was a third of the way across now, the water sometimes up to his waist, his bow held high above his head, his free hand scooping at the water in front of him. Sometimes I thought he was swimming, his legs kicking and splashing as they broke the surface.

Then suddenly he went down.

His head went under, and he simply wasn't there.

A moment later, he reappeared. He must have lowered his feet and found firm ground to stand on.

Or, at least, he thought he had.

He was soaked through now, and he had a leather bag over one shoulder. The combined weight of his waterlogged clothes and the bag was pulling him down.

Even as I watched, he began to sink.

His eyes were on mine. I saw a moment of panic, but then a harder, darker, lethal expression took over.

'Take off your clothes!' I yelled. 'Throw your

bag and your weapons to me!' I was poised on the very edge of the safe way straining towards him, water lapping round my legs, the sandy, muddy soil squidgy and trembling beneath me, my feet already making deep dents. 'You can do it, it's not too far! You must make yourself lighter, it's your only hope!' Still he stared at me. He still clutched his crossbow. If he freed both hands, might I be able to creep forward, slowly, slowly, testing the ground, and take them? I stared to move towards him. *'Throw me your bow!'* I screamed.

But he clutched onto it as if it were a strong rope. He shook his head, a manic gleam in his black eyes. 'Oh, no,' he said. 'You won't fool me that way, healer woman.'

He made a huge effort and threw himself forward.

I wasn't sure if he'd been afloat before, or if he'd been half-swimming and half-hopping along, one foot on the bottom.

If he'd been swimming, the skill seemed to have deserted him. If he'd been hopping, then the ground must have suddenly fallen right away.

And I watched, helpless, unable to reach him, as his head went under again.

This time, he didn't come up.

I went on.

I could see the safe way and now it seemed as if it shone faintly, and I had the strange notion that it was trying to help me by showing itself so clearly.

In the midst of horror, I clung to the thought.

The shore was close now. At first I went steadily,

careful step by careful step. But then I thought, my desperate eyes on the shore, that it wasn't getting any closer; or, anyway, not getting closer as quickly as I wanted. Then, panic flooding up, forgetting all about being steady and careful, I struck out towards that elusive black line, panting, sobbing, so desperate to be safe that I almost created my own undoing, for I missed my step and once more went right under. My strength had deserted me and for what seemed half my lifetime, I floundered beneath the water, desperate to breathe, cold water in my eyes, my ears, up my nose. But then I surfaced, spat out a mouthful of earthy, sandy water, and suddenly found myself on my hands and knees, crawling up onto the shore.

For what seemed a long time I just lay there, my eyes closed, breathing my thanks, trying to put from my mind those terrible moments when I was under the water.

Eventually I struggled to a sitting position and looked around me. I knew I ought to recognize the spot in which I found myself, for I knew the area so well, and I'd travelled along the fen edge in search of plants so many times. Quite often I'd walked along it on my way to and from Cambridge.

There wasn't one single landmark that I recognized.

The water level is quite a lot higher, I told myself. *Of course everything will look different. Don't worry.*

I rose unsteadily to my feet. I took off my cloak and gave it a good shake. A lot of water seemed to fly off. I was wet through, but somehow the cloak's waterproofing qualities kept in my body heat. Without a doubt, I felt warmer when I was wrapped in it than when not.

I looked up into the sky. The clouds were building once more, but for now visibility wasn't too bad. I could see the North Star and I knew – hoped I knew – which way to go. For some moments I stared up at it, and the presence of its guiding light was comforting.

Then I started walking.

I was trying to get home.

They say that wounded, frightened animals make instinctively for their holt, their burrow, their place of safety, and I was nothing more than an animal that night.

I wasn't wounded – not bodily – but I was certainly frightened. And I was in deep shock, for I had just seen two men die right before my eyes. One had drowned. I hadn't known him, and, given that he was trying to kill me, I should have felt more jubilant than I did that he was dead. Just then, I didn't feel jubilant at all.

The other had bled to death, lying in my arms. And it was only now, with his death, that I knew I'd loved him.

I put my grief for Rollo aside for now. I would think about it later, once I was home.

I knew had to get to warmth, to safety, for I was wet to my skin and could no longer control my violent trembling. My heart felt funny, its beat sometimes speeding up to such a rate that

I could scarcely breathe, and sometimes slowing right down.

But I didn't know where I was.

It was no good running up and down the fen edge in rising distress, trying to find a landmark that I knew and by which I could direct my steps to my village. So I stopped, waited until my breathing had steadied, and thought about it with as much common sense as I could muster.

I thought about the location of Mercure's island, which is to the north, or perhaps the north-east, of a long peninsula of land that snakes out from the higher ground surrounding the fens. I'd gone roughly north from there, for quite a long way, and, although the safe way had jigged about in almost every direction, overall I'd stayed on a northwards course. Then I'd turned east.

But it was foolishly optimistic to expect the safe way to lead me straight to my village, and, once I understood that, I knew what had happened. I realized, with a sinking sense of dread, that I'd made it to shore some unknowable distance north of where I'd been aiming for.

I struggled on for a time. My strength was almost spent. I carry my satchel with me all the time and I'd have said I was used to its weight, but now it was dragging at me, weighing on my shoulder, so that I was uncomfortably aware of it all the time.

With an exclamation of disgust at my dull wits, I realized what it was trying to tell me. I stopped, sat down on the soggy ground, crossed my legs and made an apron of my skirts, and drew the shining stone out of my satchel. The feel of it in my hands was a comfort. I made my mind go still and stared into it.

Its customary deep, dense black – I think of it as its resting colour – cleared very quickly. I saw the moon in its glossy shine, and it was as if that bright reflection cleared the dark shadows away. I saw a shimmering patch of green, a glittering ribbon of luminous gold, and then I was right down in the stone's depths.

I saw someone I recognized.

With a start of amazement, I raised my head and looked wildly around.

And I knew where I was.

I was at the end of the inlet where once someone I loved had moored a small boat, out of the way of the curious, for his mission was private.

With the higher water, it looked so different now that, without the stone's prompting, I wouldn't have known it.

And suddenly I heard my father's voice:

I'm to meet up with a new acquaintance soon . . .

He's a huge, white-haired old man they call the Silver Dragon, an Icelander, or so I'm told, and he used to frequent these parts when he was a young man . . . knew your grandmother Cordeilla, and wants to look up her kin.

I forced my aching legs and my burning lungs to make one last effort. If he wasn't there, I thought I would probably die.

The little waterway of my memory was full and flooded now. I kept to the bank on its right side, and at times I had to climb higher to get round some swollen stream splashing down to join it. I went on for perhaps forty or fifty paces. I didn't let myself even admit the possibility that I was mistaken, for the shining stone had led me here and the shining stone was my ally.

The inlet curved round in a gentle bend. And, ahead, I saw a small wooden boat tied up to the bank. Skins and lengths of oiled cloth had been rigged up over it, so that, inside, it would be like living in a low-roofed tent.

I broke into a run, my feet slipping and sliding in the mud. I called out, again and again.

Some sudden movement inside the craft set it rocking. Then soft light shone out as a gap was opened between two sections of the covering. A big, broad, very tall figure seemed to fly up the bank and I ran forward.

And my grandfather took me in his arms.

I think I must have been in a far worse state than I'd realized, for I have little memory of those first moments in Thorfinn's boat. I remember his distress, his shock as gently he touched my ice-cold hands and face, my soaked garments, my feet that I could no longer feel. I remember being told to strip off right down to my skin and the odd combination of his dictatorial voice and his compassion, for he understood my modesty and turned his back. I remember the rough way he rubbed me all over with a huge length of coarse fabric. I remember the agony as my numb extremities came back to life.

When I was as dry as he could make me, he wrapped me in layers: soft, fine woollen cloth next to my skin, several blankets, then, on the top, a luxurious fur. He took my clothes and disappeared out through the gap in the awning, and I heard him set about lighting a fire. He must have kept his wood dry, I reflected. Was he going to burn my clothes? Oh, but there was Jack's cloak, he mustn't burn that—

Then my wits returned from wherever they'd fled and I thought, *Idiot! He's not going to destroy your clothes, he's going to dry them.*

While he was gone I looked around the boat. I was seated on the bench that ran around its sides, and on an upturned chest in front of me were a pair of lamps. At the rear of the boat was Thorfinn's accustomed place, where there were a couple of lanterns and, beneath the bench, rolled-up blankets and what looked like spare clothing. In the bows there were chests of various sizes containing his supplies of food and drink and a small water barrel. As my eyes ran along the benches, I noticed that the seats were padded with well-stuffed sacks to keep out the cold.

Tentatively I flexed my toes. They were steadily getting warmer. I smiled. My grandfather was an Icelander. If anyone knew how to restore someone who had managed to immerse herself several times in dark fen water and who'd thought she was about to expire from the cold, it was him.

Presently he returned. He smiled at me. 'The rain will not return for some time, I'm thinking,' he said. 'I will go outside again now and then to turn your clothes, and I hope they will be dry by morning.'

I nodded. He didn't seem to expect an answer.

I watched his quick, economical movements as, humming to himself, he set about preparing food and drink. I hoped he wasn't expecting me to share his meal. I knew I wouldn't be able to eat a thing. I was doubting I'd ever be hungry again.

But then he reached outside and brought in a vessel of hot water, and he poured some of it into a coarse pottery mug. He added something from a small flask and thrust it at me.

'I can't,' I muttered.

'You can.' He took my hand and wrapped it round the mug.

Steam was rising from the mug, and it tickled and tantalized . . . against my instincts, I found myself taking a sip.

I tasted green herbs, honey, something very sharp, and, overriding everything else, strong alcohol.

I took another sip, and it felt as if this incredible liquid had flooded my body, warming me from my hair to my toenails. I sipped again, although in truth this was nothing so ladylike as a sip, more like a thirsty seaman's gulp.

And my grandfather, chuckling, said, 'Steady, now.'

While I was still reflecting in amazement over the miraculous drink, he was bending over the upturned chest, busy with something. Then he handed me a thick chunk of bread in which he'd cut a deep groove, now overflowing with a salty, savoury slice of bacon.

I felt my mouth water. *I'm not hungry, I can't eat*, my aching heart said. *I'm starving and this is irresistible*, replied my sensible head.

I gobbled down the bread and bacon. My grandfather prepared a second.

Then he made me another drink, although this one wasn't nearly as strong. He saw my disappointed expression as I tasted it, and grinned. 'You've had more than enough already,' he said. 'I doubt very much you're accustomed to strong alcohol.'

I wasn't accustomed to alcohol at all.

I drained my mug, then I was overcome by a huge yawn. Thorfinn fetched a pillow and helped me lie down along the bench. He tucked me up warmly, and for a moment I was confused, and I thought he was my father and that I was a small child again. 'My father—' I said muzzily. 'I love my father.'

'I know you do, child,' Thorfinn murmured. He smoothed his huge hand across my brow. 'Do not worry, all will be well.'

'It won't,' I said, but sleep was gaining on me. 'It won't because he's dead. Not my father – oh, no, no.' Thorfinn's expression had briefly changed, but my words seemed to reassure him.

'Someone else is dead, someone that you also love?' he prompted, when I didn't go on.

'Yes,' I whispered.

He took my hand. 'Loving hearts will always suffer,' he said softly, 'for they give without restraint and, when those they love die, as die we all must, the pain is indescribable.' His grip on my hand increased. 'But never permit yourself to accept that as a reason not to love, for without the strong ties and loyalties that love brings, the rewards that by far outweigh the pain, what point is there to being alive?'

Loving hearts will always suffer.

Something was niggling at me; something my aunt Edild had said, years ago, when she cast my natal chart. I was so tired, so warm, so comfortable, and I very much wanted to surrender and sleep. But, although I was too confused to work out quite why, I knew that this was important.

I closed my eyes.

Then, as if already I'd entered the dream world, I saw Edild, as clearly as if she'd been standing there before me. She was speaking. *You are essentially a private person, and your friends and your lovers will sense that they are never truly close to you. You must learn to distinguish between independence and its darker face, isolation.*

Her image seemed to shimmer, then it clarified again.

And she said, *You have a core that is private to yourself. Nobody breaches it, for it is yours alone.*

When she told me these things, I had thought – I still thought – that she meant I couldn't love; that I didn't know how to love.

And yet my grandfather Thorfinn seemed to be suggesting something quite different . . .

My eyes still closed – I didn't think I could open them – I whispered, 'Have I got a loving heart?'

He bent over me and kissed my forehead. His luxuriant beard and hair brushed against my skin. He said – and I was sure he was smiling – 'Yes, Lassair. Now, go to sleep.'

Nineteen

Jack was very tempted to set out after Batsheva straight away, but sense managed to make itself heard. It was now quite late in the day and already the light was fading. The mist was closing in again and it was raining. If he was to stand a chance of picking up her trail, it was surely better to wait until morning. But he was restless, and he couldn't do *nothing*. Although he had recently been searching the razed village, he returned to it and had one final look. If she had been there, she'd been very careful to remove any sign, and she certainly wasn't there now.

Trudging home again, he asked himself where she'd go. She'd lost her lover and her sons. He understood her need to get away from the place that had taken them from her. Would she return to the house in Norwich? His instincts told him not, for, with Gaspard Picot dead, what was the purpose in her living there? Furthermore, and far more relevant, if it had been him who paid the rent, she wouldn't be able to stay in the house anyway.

Angry, frustrated and in pain, Jack went back to his house, closed and barred the door and poured himself a large mug of ale.

He slept soundly and woke with a headache. He made himself eat and drink, then stowed some bread, cheese and a flask of water in a pack. Then he set out to the place just out of town where horses were stabled for the use of Cambridge lawmen. His favourite grey gelding, Pegasus, looked up with interest as he approached, and a short time afterwards the horse was tacked up and Jack was riding away. The gelding's long, silky mane and tail blew in the light breeze.

He didn't know where to start. He had no idea where she was. He was on the road to Ely and the fens, and eventually it met another road that veered north-east to Norwich. It seemed as good a place to begin as any.

It was late in the day when he found her.

She was sitting beside the road, and the hems of her skirts and cloak were wet and muddy. Her pack was on the ground beside her and, as he approached, she shoved a large and curiously shaped object out of sight beneath the folds of cloth.

He drew rein and stared down at her.

Her eyes, huge and very dark, met his. Hers were full of such grief that he sensed she was close to despair.

He slid off the grey gelding's back, tied the reins to a tree branch and went to her, sitting down beside her and putting his arm round her shoulders. For some time neither spoke.

Then she said, 'I was planning to go back to Norwich. Now, I'm not sure there is any point.'

He nodded. 'The house will no longer be available to you.'

She smiled very briefly. 'A tactful phrase, lawman, but correct.'

'Should you not return to collect your belongings?' For some reason it worried him to think that her former life could be so easily and totally abandoned.

She shrugged. 'Perhaps.' She turned to him, and he saw tears in her eyes. As if she'd read his mind, she said softly, 'But that life is gone, and I have no heart for the objects that pertained to it, Besides' – she sighed – 'it is a long way to Norwich.'

Silence fell again. Jack had no idea how to break it; how to begin to say all that was in his mind and his heart. His pity for her was almost overwhelming, but he couldn't think how to help her. She wasn't safe back in Cambridge, with Sheriff Picot still on the rampage for someone to punish for the widow Elwytha's death. And she'd just said she wasn't going back to Norwich . . . She was alone, all alone, in a hard world.

It didn't bear thinking about.

He tightened his grip on her and she leaned into him.

After a while she said, 'I had to get away from you to find him, to tell him he must let you stay alive because you are a good man who is very much needed in the life he lives and the town in which he resides.' She smiled. 'I'm not at all sure I'd have persuaded him, but you were kind to me and I had to try.'

He thought for a while, but even having done so, he had no idea what she was talking about.

In the end he said, 'Who are we talking about, and why would he want to kill me?'

She smiled again, and he even heard a soft laugh. 'My son,' she said. 'My boy Gideon, who I conceived by Gaspard Picot.'

Jack thought he understood.

'He sought vengeance,' he said quietly. 'He came to Cambridge to seek his father' – something must have prompted the young man, he thought, some sudden need to find the man who had, with his mother, brought him into being; perhaps, growing to manhood, he had come to resent the fact that this man kept his distance; that he was content to use his mistress for his own pleasure while his real life was elsewhere – 'only to find he was dead.'

Because I killed him, he thought.

'Yes, I believe that is how it was,' she said. 'He would have asked questions and discovered how Gaspard met his death.'

'He wouldn't have had to ask many questions,' Jack said bitterly. 'I imagine that everyone was talking about it.' He looked down at her. 'I am more sorry than I can say that he had to find out like that. He was alone, he had hoped to find his father and perhaps have some sort of reconciliation, some sort of recognition, but by the most awful stroke of fate, he arrived too late.'

But she shook her head. 'It is true that Gideon came to demand that Gaspard acknowledge him, for Gideon was so very angry.' She paused, eyes staring into the distance. 'He was . . . something had happened to him. As a child, as a boy, he had been happy with me in our little house, and I believed that what I could offer him was

304

sufficient. But then, he changed.' She glanced at Jack, a swift look, there and gone again. 'I believe something had entered his soul; something that was evil. Something that was very dangerous.' There was a brief silence and, just for an instant, Jack almost believed he felt the shadow of that danger, that evil, like a cold finger on the back of his neck.

Suddenly he remembered the lament he'd heard the night the widow Picot was murdered. He knew without asking that the terrible sounds of grief and regret had emanated from Batsheva, hidden away in the ruined village, huddled in shock and horror because she knew what her son had just done.

He gazed at her bent head, wondering how her mind managed to contain so much sorrow.

But then, her voice quite matter-of-fact, Batsheva spoke again. 'As for Gaspard acknowledging Gideon in any way, it would never have happened,' she said. 'Gaspard was a man of position and power; a man of wealth, or, at least, married to a wealthy wife, which amounts to the same thing. To accept a bastard son into his life, by even the tiniest deed or gesture, would have put everything he held dear at risk. Elwytha was a bitter, angry and very unhappy woman,' she added, and he detected sympathy in her voice. 'She couldn't bear him a child, and in the end his attempts to make her conceive became nothing but a burden and a humiliation to both of them, so they stopped.'

'But he had you,' Jack said.

She nodded. 'He had me,' she agreed. 'And

305

he also had Gideon, had he only been courageous enough to abandon the life he believed
he needed and come instead to the one that was
right for him.'

And that, Jack thought, he would never have
done.

'He would have killed you, you know,' Batsheva
said. 'I know my son so well. To arrive full of
hope, only to find his father had just been slain,
without a doubt would have driven him to take
revenge. He would see it as a matter of honour,
the son taking the life of the man who had taken
his father's.' Briefly she fell silent; perhaps, Jack
thought, in tribute to her son's stern and unshak-
able resolve. 'I knew what else he would do,'
she went on very quietly. 'Which was why I was
watching Gaspard's house, for all that it proved
quite useless.'

Jack recalled what had been done to Elwytha.
The bruising on the breasts and lower belly. He
tried to understand. He failed. He said, 'He'd
beaten her, on her – on the chest and stomach.'

Batsheva nodded. 'Yes.'

Jack waited but she made no further comment.
'Why did he do that?' he asked.

She turned to him. 'I imagine it was some sort
of recognition of the fact that she, Gaspard's
wife, kept in luxury and idleness, waited on at
every turn, was barren and useless, whereas the
secret mistress, always hidden away, unacknowledged, no part of any but the most private,
intimate part of his life, was the one who had
given him the longed-for son.'

I always knew there must have been a sexual

306

element in that murder, Jack thought. 'He must have hated her very much,' he said.

'Of course,' Batsheva replied. 'But then Gideon hated very many people.'

'And he burned down the house,' Jack said softly, speaking his thought aloud.

'He did.' She looked at him again. 'You very nearly caught him that night. He had only just fled when you came across me in the shadows of the old wall.' She lowered her eyes. 'I'd stayed to make sure everybody got out,' she muttered.

Because someone had to, and your son, who started the blaze, didn't care if innocent servants died, Jack thought.

He was going over the sequence of events in his mind. Many things had become clear, but some had not. 'But what of the two blond young men?' he asked her. 'Did he kill them too? If so, why?'

But she shrugged. 'I have no idea.'

And they sat on, beside the track, as the day wound down to evening.

After a time he said, 'It's getting late, and the temperature is falling. We should go.' He got up and held out his hand to her.

She too rose, and as she did so, the object she'd been concealing in her skirts fell free.

It was a crossbow.

Both of them stared down at it.

Then she said, 'It's his. Gideon's.' She gave a shaky sigh. 'It was his favourite weapon, and he was deadly accurate with it.'

'I see,' Jack said, although he wasn't at all sure he did.

307

'I was right over there' – she waved an arm towards the east – 'on the far side of the fen. It was washed up on a little beach, at my feet, as if he had sent it out onto the water in the hope that it would make its way to me.'

Then surely he is dead, Jack wanted to say, *for why else does a man abandon his favourite weapon?* But he held his silence.

She knew, thought, what he would have said.

'Yes, in all likelihood he is indeed dead.' She turned her face up to him and her eyes glittered with tears. 'But if I do not know for sure, then there is always hope.' She managed a smile. 'Always the consoling thought that perhaps he is alive somewhere, his demons vanquished, and happiness and contentment a possibility.'

But Jack, staring down into her eyes, knew she didn't really believe it.

'Where will you go?' he asked, his voice breaking so that he was barely able to speak.

She nodded, as if recognizing and accepting his compassion. 'I shall return to where I came from,' she said. 'To the place I was born, and where, until my father was commanded to uproot us both and come to England, I was happy.'

'Yes,' he said very quietly.

She reached down to pick up the crossbow. She had attached a length of fine rope to it and now, hitching up her cloak, she tied it to her belt, letting the cloak fall again to conceal it. 'I shall keep this in memory of my son, whom I have loved more dearly than anyone on this earth.' She stood quite still, staring up at him for a moment. Then she said, 'Farewell, lawman.'

'Farewell,' he echoed. 'God go with you.'

She turned and walked away, and he watched her go.

He untied his horse, mounted and rode on. He knew he should head for home – it was getting dark and he thought it was going to rain again – but something was drawing him on.

After a time, he realized what it was.

He was on the track that led to Aelf Fen.

He drew rein and for a long time simply sat there, the grey gelding restless beneath him.

The he turned the horse's head and set off back for Cambridge.

In the morning, my clothes were dry enough to put on. Thorfinn handed them to me, then stood tactfully outside while I dressed. I rummaged in my satchel and found a comb, and I felt considerably better once I'd got the tangles out of my hair, plaited it and wound it up under a fresh cap.

Thorfinn and I ate breakfast. He was watching me, and I knew he had something on his mind. I was pretty sure what it was.

After a while he said, 'Lassair, it's very clear that something very bad has happened to you. I won't press you to tell me until and if you want to,' he went on, for I had made as if to respond, 'but there is something I must say.' He paused, frowning. 'I have come to do what I should have done a long time ago, and reveal to my son – your father – the secret of his paternity. You, dear child, already know it, and I know that you have respected my request for confidentiality. In the past, indeed, you have quite rightly told me in no uncertain terms how unfair I am being to insist on a situation where you are forced to withhold the truth from your father, who I know you love profoundly.'

I could recall only too well the words I'd hurled at my grandfather that day. 'I shouldn't have spoken to you as I did,' I said. 'I'm sorry.'

But he shook his head. 'There is no need for *you* to apologize,' he said. 'You were right. I was being cowardly, and it is I who am ashamed. But I shall put it right. To do so, indeed, is why I am here.' He paused. 'What I need to know, Lassair, is whether whatever trouble you have encountered is of so grave a nature that it must take precedence over everything else. Over, for example, an old man finally finding the courage to reveal the truth to his son.'

He stopped speaking. For some time he sat still, looking at me. I tried to think how to answer him.

Finally I said, 'Grandfather, I have just witnessed the death of a man I loved. There is nothing I need to do, for his body burned on a pyre and now his spirit flies free. My grief is waiting for me, and I am not yet sure how I shall manage it.' I paused, for I'd felt my voice begin to shake. 'I do not wish you to change your plans. I haven't yet decided what to do next – I don't know when I'll be able to do that.' I paused again. 'So in the meantime, it will be my privilege to come to Aelf Fen with you, and to be as much or as little involved with you and my father as you dictate.'

310

I had watched his face as I spoke. His expression had changed as swiftly as light on water, and I could feel his love and his pity flowing from him to embrace me. I almost threw myself into his arms, and I knew he wouldn't have turned me away. But I was holding on to my resolve and my courage with my fingertips. Too much kindness just now would undo me.

I think he understood. He nodded once, curtly, and stood up, beginning to pile up our bowls and mugs. 'Very well. I shall ask you, then, to wash out these and store them while I prepare the boat. Then we shall set out.'

I did as he said. I also kicked out the small fire he'd made up on the bank, scattering the ashes.

The fens were still feeling the effects of all the rain, and the water level remained high. The best way to reach Aelf Fen was by boat.

I watched from beneath the ancient oak tree on the rise as my grandfather walked up to my parents' house. He was within only briefly before he and my father emerged. My father was smiling, but I could see from his face and from his demeanour that he was curious about this stranger; even, perhaps, a little anxious.

Thorfinn led the way back to his boat and they went aboard, the awnings falling closed behind them. I wondered if my father was surprised at this desire for concealment; for secrecy. If, somehow, he was already apprehensive about what was to come.

They talked for a long time. The temptation to let my steps casually approach the boat so

311

that I could hear what they said was all but overwhelming. I forced myself to resist. But I did leave the ·shelter of the oak tree; I just couldn't stop myself.

At one point I heard my father shouting.

I could barely imagine how he was feeling. I wanted more than anything to rush down to my grandfather's boat, push aside the awning and jump aboard; to go to my father, help him, comfort him. But I knew I couldn't. *He's strong*, I kept telling myself. *He will not bend or break under this.*

I wished I could be sure.

After what seemed an age, the awning parted again and my father emerged. His face was flushed and he looked furious. He glanced once back towards the house, then strode off in the opposite direction. Without a single thought, I set off after him.

My father is a big, tall man, and when he wants to he can walk as fast as I run. He wanted to now, and I couldn't catch him. I followed, panting, gasping, tripping and sometimes falling. He must have heard me but he didn't stop until he reached his destination.

He was standing on the shore immediately opposite the island where the ancestors are buried. As I panted my way to join him, he didn't look at me, simply went on staring out over the little island. Where, of course, his mother lay.

After a while, once I'd got my breath back, I said, 'Father, I'm so sorry.'

He didn't answer. I wondered in fact if he'd even heard.

Then, after quite a long time, he said, 'I didn't know you were back. You were here, staying with Froya and looking after Sibert after he'd been attacked, and we only knew you'd gone when Froya passed on your message.' The raw pain was evident in his voice, and although I knew that my sudden disappearance without a word to him wasn't really the cause – not the main one, anyway – still it stung.

'I had to leave, and in a hurry,' I said, trying not to let the emotion break through. 'Someone – a friend' – oh, Rollo, far more than that – 'a dear friend needed me, and I—'

'You set off on some new adventure with not one thought to those left behind who love you,' he finished for me harshly. 'It's always the same, isn't it, Lassair? You outgrew your home, your family and your village years ago, as soon as you'd discovered how much more lively and interesting life in the town could be!'

If only you knew, I thought, my heart aching with all sorts of different pains.

Tell him, a voice said. It sounded very like Granny Cordeilla's.

So I did.

'Life in Cambridge is lively and interesting, just as you say,' I said quietly. 'In addition, work is very hard, and I'm driven at a fast and relentless pace by my teacher. I'd be lying if I said I didn't like it, because I do, even though sometimes my head is aching with weariness by the time he releases me so I can go to bed. He doesn't really need sleep, you see, and he often forgets that other people do.' My father

313

began to speak but I didn't let him. 'In addition, I met a wonderful man who is good, honest and who got very badly wounded, and I nursed him, and before he was hurt we slept together and I was briefly pregnant, but I lost the baby, and then another man I loved before needed my help and so I went off with him, and someone wanted to kill him and they *did*, they shot him with a crossbow bolt, and although I got it out and I thought he was going to be all right, he wasn't and he died, and the man who had killed him set fire to the house where we were and I couldn't move the body, he was just too heavy, and so I added fuel to the fire and gave him a funeral like those of our ancestors, and then his killer came after me but he went the wrong way in the water and although I tried to save him he went under and he didn't come up again because he was in the quicksand, and then I was wet and so cold and I didn't know where I was, and – and—'

But my tears had begun when I spoke of Jack and the lost baby, and by the time I reached the bit about being wet and cold I was gasping and sobbing and my father had his strong arms tightly round me and was holding me against him, one hand smoothing my hair, dropping soft kisses on top of my head as he's done since I was a child and, all the time, muttering soft, nonsensical sounds that were as comforting as the sweetest, most tender music.

When he sensed I had gathered myself together – and *that* didn't happen very quickly – he pushed me away just far enough that he could look at me and said, 'Dearest child, I'm not sure how much of that you really meant to tell me, but I'm very glad you did and you have my word that I will share it with nobody.' *Not even your mother*, hung unspoken between us. 'And' – he was hugging me again – 'I am so very sorry for all your pain.'

His love and his kindness made me weep anew.

When I stopped, I said, 'I'm sorry too, Father, that I knew the secret you've just been told before you did. I swore not to tell you, because Thorfinn said it was something he must do himself. I told him it wasn't right for me to know when you didn't. I was actually a bit rude about that.'

'Yes, he told me,' my father said. I had the impression he was smiling, and when I looked up, he was in the very act of straightening his face.

I went on looking at him. 'What do you think?' I whispered. 'How do you feel?'

He frowned, and I guessed he was trying to think how to answer.

'I'm upset, of course,' he said eventually. 'I have to change the whole sense of myself. The gentle, unambitious man who I loved and believed to be my father wasn't, and now I have this large, silver-haired warrior of a man in his place . . .' He paused, and I saw something very painful cross his face. 'I also now know that my mother bore a child by another man, yet kept it not only from her husband but from everyone else as well.' He paused again, and now the intense distress was plain to see. 'I

315

thought she and I were close!' he whispered, his eyes filling with tears.

I was so horrified at the sight of my big, strong father in tears that I couldn't speak. But then, from somewhere very close, I heard a voice say urgently, *Help him, child! You know the truth of it, it's up to you!*

I looked out towards the island and replied, *Of course, Granny.*

'You *were* close, Father, and you know very well that you were,' I said firmly. 'It was you out of all her children that she chose to live with when she didn't want to be on her own any more, wasn't it? She loved you so much, and she knew how much you loved her.'

A silence fell, but it was a kind, soft sort of silence.

Presently I said, 'Will you tell the family?'

He met my eyes. 'Your mother, yes. This is not something I can keep from her.' He frowned. 'But as for everyone else . . .'

I waited, but he didn't go on.

'It depends, doesn't it,' I said, 'on whether Thorfinn plans to be a part of our life?'

My father raised his eyebrows. 'Does it?'

'Yes. Of course!' I was smiling, assuming he was joking.

But he looked perplexed and I realized he wasn't. I was going to have to explain.

'Father, who was at home just now when he came to call?'

'Just your mother.'

'Well, that's all right, since you've just said you're going to tell her anyway.'

316

'But I—'

'Father, if Thorfinn's going to stay around for a while you won't have to decide whether or not to explain who he is, since anyone with eyes will see for themselves.'

He still looked puzzled, so I took his hands in mine and said, 'He is an older version of you, and you could be nothing else but father and son.'

He went on staring at me and slowly he began to smile. Then he said, 'Better tell them, then, hadn't I?' and, still holding my hand, he led me back to the village.

Twenty

I knew that I must go back to Cambridge.

I went to Jack's house.

I didn't let myself dwell on his expression when he opened the door in answer to my soft tap. He stood back and I went in. I sat down on one of his tree-trunk stools and he stayed where he was, leaning against the closed door. I had the impression he was being very careful to keep his distance.

I said, 'Rollo is dead.' Before he could say a word – and I had no idea what that word might have been – I hurried on. 'I went away with him because he knew someone was after him. He was all but sure it was some agent of Duke Robert of Normandy, because he'd sold some information to the duke that he'd previously sold to the king. King William,' I added, as if there was another.

Jack's face was still. His eyes were fixed on mine. He said, 'Go on.'

'Rollo knew that the man on his trail was hunting for a man on his own. He suggested that I travel north with him – he was searching for the king – because the duke's man would over-look a richly dressed man and woman together. So we set out, but the duke's man managed to see through the ruse and he found us anyway. He burned down a small, desperately poor monastery because he thought Rollo and I were within. Five people died.'

I paused, for the telling of my tale was much harder than I'd anticipated. 'So I took Rollo out into the wilds of the fens, and we hid in the house that belonged to Gurdyman's friend Mercure. Then Rollo got tired of running away and he said we should lure the duke's man to us so that he – Rollo – could kill him. So I went out and sort of caught his attention, and led him back to where Rollo was waiting. The duke's man did exactly what Rollo said he would, but instead of Rollo killing him, he killed Rollo. With a crossbow. I got the bolt out and I thought he'd be all right, but he bled to death and there wasn't anything I could do.'

Jack made a very faint movement towards me. Then he stopped.

'The man sent a second bolt into the door of Mercure's house, and this one was on fire and soon the house was as well. I had to get out and I couldn't move Rollo so I left him there. Then I realized the man wanted to kill me too so I got away, along the hidden ways across the water, but he followed me. I asked him why he killed Rollo and he said, "Because he killed my father."'

Very slowly Jack nodded. 'His father was Gaspard Picot.'

I was astounded. 'How did you know?'

He shook his head. 'It doesn't matter. It was a guess, really, but I can tell from your reaction that it's right.'

There was silence for some moments. Then I

319

said, 'I didn't understand at first why the man believed Rollo had killed Gaspard Picot, but then I did.'

'Then tell me,' Jack said, irony sharpening his tone, 'because I have absolutely no idea.'

I paused, putting the words together in my mind. 'He came here to find his father. By the very worst of misfortunes, he arrived at exactly the time that Gaspard Picot died. He tried to find out what had happened, and he discovered that his father had died at the hands of the close friend of the healer girl. That's me,' I added.

Jack nodded.

'I worked out what must have happened. After you – after you were hurt, I went to Gurdyman's house.' Something horrible and terrifying had happened there, and I didn't want to think about it. I hurried on. 'And then Rollo came to the house to find me. I told him about you, how you'd been so badly wounded, how I feared you—' But I didn't want to think about that either and I was quite sure Jack didn't. 'Rollo saw how distressed I was and he was so good to me. He just put his arms round me in a close hug full of comfort and kindness, and I was so thankful for his presence, for his support, that I let myself collapse against him.'

And Rollo and I had still been entwined as close as the lovers we'd once been when we'd emerged out from Gurdyman's house into the little alley outside.

But I didn't think I could tell Jack that.

'He still had his arms round me when we came

320

out of the house. Gaspard's son must have found out that I lived and worked with Gurdyman, and he'd come looking for me. He must have seen Rollo and me together and jumped to the obvious conclusion that Rollo was the man the people meant when they referred to my close friend.'

There was a long silence. Then Jack said expressionlessly, 'So Gaspard Picot's son killed your lover because he thought he'd murdered his father. Before he did so, incidentally, it seems he attacked three other fair-haired young men, killing two of them, presumably in the mistaken belief that one of them was the man he sought. He beat and tortured them, you know, perhaps to make them suffer, perhaps to make them talk. And, all along, the man he sought to avenge had in fact died at my hands.' I went to speak but he shot out his hand, stopping me. 'There is some sort of irony there, isn't there?'

I said, the words tumbling out, 'But it's not your fault, Jack! You're no more responsible for Gaspard's son killing Rollo than for Gaspard himself dying because he threw himself on your blade!'

And he said with harsh bitterness, 'Oh, well, *that's* all right, then.'

I knew then that I had made a huge error in telling him. Oh, I'd have had to explain it all to him some time, but I should have waited until my own feelings were not quite so raw. Until time and distance from the event had enabled me to see it with some detachment. Until I'd come up with a way of telling him

321

that didn't appear to say, *Rollo died and it should have been you!*

I looked up at him.

And whatever else I knew in that moment, I knew I was glad he was alive.

I'd forgotten the essence of him. Studying him now, I saw he was still thinner than he should be, but that the muscles in his broad shoulders and strong arms were beginning to show again.

I said, for I couldn't stop myself, 'Are you all right? Is your wound healed?'

He gave a curt nod. 'I'm fine.'

After a while he straightened up from leaning against the door and poked up the fire. 'Do you want a drink? Something to eat?'

I shook my head.

He turned, looking at me. 'What are you going to do?'

I shrugged. 'I don't know.'

'Will you return to your village?'

'No!' The answer came out far too quickly and emphatically. 'I can't. It's different there now.' I didn't really want to explain. I love my family, I appreciate life in Aelf Fen for a few days or even a couple of weeks from time to time, but just now, when so much had just happened, I knew I'd have found its rural peace utterly stultifying. As my father had so accurately said, I had discovered how much more lively and interesting life in the town could be.

Jack was still looking at me. Then he said, quite gently, 'I'm afraid you can't come back here.'

'Back here? To your house?' Until he'd said

those words, I hadn't realized how much I'd been relying on doing exactly what he'd just said I couldn't.

'If you're going to suggest you come back to me, to live in my house as we did before, then I'm going to say no.' His face was bleak and expressionless but I saw the pain in his eyes.

In that moment, all I wanted was to be with him.

'But why can't I?' I whispered.

'Lassair, you have suffered a great loss. You're grieving, and you need somebody to comfort you, to look after you.' He stopped abruptly. I could almost hear the words he was holding back; sense the effort it was taking him not to say them. Then, his voice colder, he went on, 'I'm afraid that somebody won't be me.'

He straightened up. He crossed to the door, opened it. He said, 'I'm going out now. When I get back, I'd like you not to be here, please.'

Then he walked away. Instinctively I leapt up and ran after him . . . One pace, three, four. Then I stopped.

I watched as he reached the bend in the alley and disappeared from view. Then, moving far more slowly than he had done, I followed him.

I went back to Gurdyman.

Gurdyman gave me the comfort, the sympathy and perhaps the love that I'd gone to Jack for.

When I knocked on the door, he took me along to the little courtyard at the back of the house. I told him where I'd been and everything that had happened. He let me cry until I'd reduced myself to a hiccupping standstill.

323

Then he said, 'Hrype is here. He's down in the crypt. Come and talk to him.'

Hrype was the last person I wanted to see but I let Gurdyman take my hand, lead me along the passage and down the steps. He left me standing at the foot of the steps while he went across to Hrype, who was standing at the workbench, and muttered briefly in his ear. Hrype nodded. He beckoned me over.

'Sibert told me you'd gone off with your Norman,' he said. It was what he'd always called Rollo. 'Strange, the way it all worked out.'

Strange wasn't the word I'd have used. I just said dully, 'Yes, it was.'

There was a wry smile on Hrype's face. 'You do have a way of bringing danger to the men with whom you involve yourself, Lassair.' Gurdyman made a soft protest, but Hrype ignored it. 'So, bereft of the Norman, you've come back to the lawman?'

'He doesn't want me,' I muttered.

'Well, from what I hear, you abandoned him without a word once he was on the road to recovery.'

'I—' I began. But what could I say? It was harsh, but Hrype was quite right. It was exactly what I had done.

Hrype's silvery eyes were hard on mine. 'Does he know about the baby?'

I gasped. Had Froya broken her word? Had she *told* Hrype? But she'd promised!

And then I heard the echo of Hrype's words: *does* he know. Not *did* he know.

And in a flash of insight I knew that Froya

324

had kept her word and her silence. It hadn't been her who had told Hrype of my pregnancy, for if it had been she'd also have told him how it ended.

'How did you know?' I asked. I was pleased at how calm I sounded. But then this was Hrype. It didn't do to show weakness when talking to Hrype.

His brows went up briefly. He jerked his head towards Gurdyman. 'He and I both realized, the day Gaspard Picot died and Jack received his wound.'

'But you couldn't have done!' I wasn't calm now. I was yelling. 'I didn't know it myself then, and it was some time before I realized!'

Hrype gave a slow smile. 'In some circumstances, it's not difficult to spot.' He obviously wasn't going to say any more, and the last thing I wanted was to demean myself by begging him to.

I turned away from his scrutiny, for it was making me uncomfortable. 'Well, if you're as skilled and perceptive as you claim, I'm surprised you haven't also spotted that I am no longer pregnant. I lost it.'

Briefly, before he could control himself, I saw surprise in his eyes. Amid all the pain and distress, I felt a surge of triumph.

And then Gurdyman was beside me, taking my hands in his, murmuring to me with such kindness that my tears began all over again.

It was a great relief when Hrype took himself off. Gurdyman and I were back upstairs again

325

– it was gloomy down in the crypt, and he clearly felt it wasn't the right place for someone as woebegone and full of grief as me – and sitting in the little courtyard. The sun had come out; at long last it seemed to have stopped raining. Gurdyman went inside and prepared hot drinks. Mine was potent, sweet and I knew that, whatever was in it, he'd made it strong.

I said as I sipped at it, 'May I come back?'

He looked at me in surprise. 'Yes, of course. Your attic room awaits you. But—'

I didn't let him finish. 'Oh, no, please, *please* don't say I can't go on being here either! I can't bear it if you turn me away too!'

He frowned. Quickly he said, 'Lassair, child, I'm not turning you away. You have my word. When I said *but*, it wasn't the start of *but you can't stay*. There's an idea I've had, though, and I'll tell you about it presently. I'm very sorry that this someone else has turned you away. Jack Chevestrier is a good man.'

'Yes.' It was all I could manage, for the dismay and the pain were far too new.

Gurdyman sighed. 'I suspected that is what he would do,' he murmured. He glanced at me. 'I'm sorry, child, that it hurts so much.' He waited but I didn't speak. 'Do you understand why he can't have you back?'

I shook my head.

There was another silence. Then Gurdyman said, 'He believes, I would conjecture, that just at present you would be returning to him for the wrong reasons. You have lost Rollo, after what sounds like a very frightening and dreadful time.

326

Prior to that, you were carrying Jack's child, and you lost it, although I don't imagine you told him that.'

I shook my head. 'No,' I whispered.

'You are full of pain and grief, Lassair, and sorely in need of someone who loves you, who will hold you up until you can once more do it for yourself.' I must have made some small sound, for he put down his mug and took my hand again. 'You probably don't believe it now, but you *will* recover, Lassair.'

He said it with such certainty that I believed him.

'You have, then, very good reasons for wanting to go back to Jack,' he went on, 'but they are *your* reasons, and have little to do with him.' He paused. 'I would suggest that Jack's rejection of you is because he won't let himself be hurt again.'

He was right. Oh, he was right. I saw it so clearly, although it didn't make me feel any better.

I'd lost Jack.

I couldn't bear to think about it.

I had to distract myself.

I said, 'Why does Hrype hate me so much?'

Gurdyman's eyebrows shot up. '*Hate* you? Oh, I don't believe he hates you, child.'

'You must admit he doesn't much like me.'

'Yes, yes, I admit that is how it must appear.'

'But that's not right either?' I surprised myself by smiling slightly.

But Gurdyman was frowning. 'Lassair, child, I believe he is jealous of you.'

'*Jealous?*' Incredulity turned the word into a

shrill squeak. 'What in the dear Lord's name have I done to make Hrype *jealous*?'

'Oh, it's nothing you have done,' Gurdyman said, 'it's what you have. What you are,' he corrected himself.

'What am I?' I whispered.

He met my eyes. 'Powerful.'

I shook my head. 'I don't feel very powerful now. In fact, I've rarely felt so helpless.'

He nodded. 'Yes, I know. We all have our moments of weakness, but it will pass.'

'Powerful.' I was still wondering at the extraordinary word he'd used.

'Did you not ask yourself, down in the crypt just now, how Hrype and I had known you were carrying a child before even you did?'

'Yes.'

'Because of what you are. I do not know whence the power came to you, although I suspect it passed down to you through your father—'

'He's not in the least powerful!' I protested. 'Well, he is, of course he is, he's strong, and big, and brave, but he's not – well, *you* know.'

'Indeed I do.' Gurdyman was smiling. 'What I was about to say was that I suspect the power emanates from the extraordinary woman who was your grandmother.'

'Granny Cordeilla? But you never knew her.'

'No, quite right, but I have been told a very great deal about her.'

It was a moment for confidences, and I knew Gurdyman would never reveal what I was about to entrust to him. 'My father's just found out that Granny Cordeilla had a lover, and he's that man's son.'

Gurdyman nodded, apparently taking what to everyone else was a world-shattering piece of news entirely in his stride. 'Yes, it's possible that he too contributed.'

'What about my sisters and brothers?' I demanded. Goda, bossy, discontented, selfish housewife. Haward, working with quiet patience out on the fens catching eels with my father. Elfritha the nun. My younger brothers Squeak and little Leir. 'If I've got this power, why hasn't it gone to them too? They're just as much Granny Cordeilla's grandchildren as I am.'

But Gurdyman didn't answer, other than to say enigmatically, 'And how do you know it hasn't?'

But then I remembered what we'd been talking about. A cold little shock ran through me.

'Were you just about to tell me,' I said cautiously, 'that you knew I was pregnant because you felt – you sensed—' I had no idea how to phrase it.

'Because we felt the baby's power,' he finished for me. 'Yes, in general terms, that is what it amounted to, although the detection of a new source is extremely delicate and fine, and also very hard to explain.'

'I lost the baby,' I said dully.

He took my hand again.

I felt his pity wrap around me. It was almost too much. So I said, trying to sound matter-of-fact, 'So Hrype senses I've got this power, and he doesn't like to think there's someone else who will one day be able to do what he can do?' It

329

sounded so incredibly presumptuous even to say it. 'I'm sorry, Gurdyman, but I can't make myself believe you.'

He didn't say a word. He just smiled.

We sat on out there in the pale sunshine. I felt as if the great, unsettling, painful whirling of the world had slowed down, although I suspected this would only be temporary.

But I was back in Gurdyman's house. He'd said he wasn't going to turn me away. He'd said he had an idea, and he'd tell me about it soon. It clearly concerned me, and I guessed it was some new project he had in mind for his pupil.

If it was, I would welcome it.

I wanted to work, harder than I'd ever worked. I wanted to lose myself in whatever task Gurdyman had in mind. I wanted to go into it and give it all my energy, all my emotion, all there was of my skill. My *power*.

The word still caused a frisson of chilling excitement.

We would engage upon this work, Gurdyman and I, for however long it took. When I emerged once more, perhaps the world would seem a happier place. It might even be all right again.

I could only hope.